SIOBHAN CHASE

Cover by Deranged Doctor Design
Paperback ISBN: 978-0-692-96370-8
E-book ISBN: 978-0-692-96372-2
Summary: After being attacked by vampires, Urban Fantasy author Ashiya Bride finds herself a part of a supernatural world her husband made her forget.

For more information on the author visit:
www.lvlyvamp.tumblr.com/
behindthepgs.blogspot.com

To Gwen Green for introducing me to the world of words, and my Dad for instilling in me the will to bring them to reality.

Life is Death.

Love is Beauty.

You are my Life and I am your Beauty,

but here comes Death.

CHAPTER 1:
Perfect Stranger

Once again you may have seen me when you came out this weekend to The Avenue's Barnes and Noble to support Niani on her first ever manga project! The manga of *Evanescence* with bonus artwork and stories following all the characters you love! I want to thank you guys for your endless support and continuous fanhood. You seriously are the best fandom in the world. I love you guys and hope to see you soon, though you may not see me. ;P

Jaa,

Ashiya

I wake up lying on my back. My open laptop at my side my silent partner in bed. I turn over on my side shaking the mouse pad and the laptop blinks awake, last night's post on my blog still up. I smile proud looking at the picture of the dozens of fans I took crowded around Niani's table from yesterday's book signing, hanging above my post.

I was of course nowhere to be seen in the picture. Since I signed my contract for representation with my literary agent three years ago it was important that I keep my identity secret. There was a clause in my contract that I never show my face. Partially, for my own privacy and that of letting my work speak for itself. That type of exposure made me uncomfortable, letting people in and having to be a face to judge in the face of my work. When I first started this, Niani and I released a joint statement letting people know the state behind my decision. There were whispers among the fans that it was a great marketing ploy for selling my novels. The fact that I showed up at my own book signings and posted pictures while on the scene on my blog added to the mystery and always brought out droves of fans trying to figure out *who* "Ashiya Bride" is and what she looks like. My agent thought it was great.

I could sit back and watch the fanfare my work created. Watch Niani sign books for fans dressed in the likeness of our characters. It made me humble to see how the books we created affected others. Sometimes I would just roam the book aisles of bookstores and sit down with unbeknownst fans and talk books. It gave me the best insight into what my fans were looking for and in turn give them what we needed. I liked it that way. I liked being on the outside looking in.

Niani is the one that likes the crowds, the excitement I revered as I watch her smiling face smiling back at me in the picture. She was a troop for being the face of our novels, the ones that we created together. Otherwise, she was illustrator and graphic designer to her own projects.

Niani is not only my writing partner and my best friend, but also practically my big sister. We met in our freshmen year of high school like any two friends unknowingly heading into creating one of the biggest fantasy followings since *Harry Potter* with only a dream to share our imagination with the world. Our like minds make us close as yin and yang. By the second week into our budding friendship we were writing stories together; me, the Writer and Niani, the Illustrator. Four years later, we were publishing our first novel *Whisper* with Simon and Schuster, the first story we wrote together during our breaks on the school gym bleachers. I smile thinking back on how over the years things have changed giving us unforeseeable results. Flipping the covers back, I slip out of bed.

Our office was separate from my and Niani's own apartments near the heart of Atlanta. Hotlanta as many like to call it, as it were on this ninety-four degree afternoon. After a year and a half of stacking our checks from book sales Niani and I decided to rent a separate office instead of commuting to each other's apartments every day.

I walk in to the office apartment the smell of fresh brewed coffee strong in the air. Niani was a huge fan of coffee. She had about three cups a day. Four if she decided to pull an all nighter. I was a tea girl myself. As I walk pass the connecting kitchen into the open floor living room, I notice the heating teapot on the stove. I smile. *She knows me so well.*

I pass our ivory L-shaped sectional to the French double doors in the back. Pushing open the right side door, I let it swing inside giving me full view of Niani at her work desk hunched over a stack of drawing papers sketching with a steaming cup of creamy coffee off to her side. Her short curly sandy brown dreadlocks frame her face casting shadows over her butterscotch skin with each stroke of her pencil.

"I almost didn't hear you come in, you dang ghost," Niani jokes, cutting her eyes up at me from her paper, her mouth stretching with the amusement.

I smile softly at her joke.

Walking the rest of the way inside, I take my seat at my desk across from hers to her right. I open my laptop bag and pull the MacBook Pro from its depths placing it on my desk. Pulling the screen up, I swing the cursor over to the *Infinite Ways* document icon clicking twice and pull it back up. That pure thrill of excitement bubbles in my chest ready to get back to work. Time to get things started.

"How does this look?" Niani asks, as she picks up her laptop and brings it over to my desk.

She turns the laptop toward me and on the screen is a prototype site page for the new horror book I'm finishing up this week with fading indigo borders and haunting black filigree.

"I like it," I approve.

"Good," she croons brightly, "because this is going up as a teaser site." She quirks her eyebrows teasingly and I smile, as she whirls back around to her desk.

Suddenly, ringing cuts through the air and I turn to the flashing cordless phone on the corner of my desk. *William Potter* reads across the screen. I look over at Niani meeting her nervous stare. The phone rings again cutting through the silence and I jump taking it in to my hand and pick it up.

"Hello?" I greet William.

Niani swivels around in her chair, listening in.

"Yeah, I can meet you there at four."

I look up at the clock mounted above the door reading 2:46 PM.

"Alright, I'll meet you around then. See you." I hang up the phone and place it back on the base.

"He wants to meet to discuss the movie?" Niani questions.

"Yeah," I answer, turning back before my laptop.

"You want me to go with you?" she asks.

"No, I should be fine," I say.

Niani trains her stare on me a mixture of concern and protectiveness on her face. I give her a small smile of reassurance and turn back to my laptop. Finally giving in, she turns back to her laptop.

The sidewalk is busy, as I pass pedestrians around a corner and a block from the café. The late afternoon parking traffic too crowded to find a parking space near a meter. I wonder what William has to say about the movie. The last few weeks has been about doing revisions to the script and hopefully this meeting would be in reference to actually putting a date on this thing, but this was the movie business. One could hope, but one never knew. Focus Films already had dibs. Now it was just about making it happen.

Atlanta was slowly becoming the second Hollywood and I was happy to know that *Reign* would be filmed here. Permits to film movies and tv shows here were a lot cheaper for the backing we could be getting for the sound stages in LA. It was great I could bring more business to my home of the last seven years.

Suddenly, someone bumps my shoulder and I hear a bass male voice say, "Sorry." I barely catch a glance of his black jacket going by when this scent hits me like a defibrillator to the chest. It's not intoxicating, but alluring. The smell of vanilla musk, amber, black pepper, and wood send me on sensory overload. I need to smell it again.

I open my eyes surprised to see I'm turned around and standing in the middle of the sidewalk like a pebble in a stream. I look around myself never noticing I turned around. Suddenly, I start laughing at myself. *Oh my goodness.* For this, I must question my sanity. Luckily, the man is nowhere to be seen. Focusing back on the movie, I turn back around and continue my way to the cafe.

I step in to the cafe and hear my name called to the left. Four booths down I see William waving me over. *William Potter.* All tall, dark, and handsome with dark curly hair, striking blue eyes, tan skin, and the jaw line of a Greek god, as Niani puts it and the Producer of this movie.

As I approach the booth, William stands hugging me to him his cologne wrapping its way around me. It smells good, but it's nothing like the person's I passed. It's too sharp, too much like everything else on the market. William pulls away and cranes his neck to kiss me on my cheek. Politely, I duck my head out of the way and take the seat across from him. Ignoring my dismiss, he takes his seat across from me his eyes leveling with mine.

Since I was approached by him to write the screenplay based off my novel, *Reign*, he has endlessly flirted and made passes at me. At first I thought it was all a part of his natural charm, but he's only made it known increasingly in the past few weeks. I try not to let it bother me and steer the focus onto the movie, but his advances make me uncomfortable to the point of physical pain from the slightest touch from him. His hands on me are like a stronghold grip to the deepest muscle tissue to the area. I thought it was something deeply psychological, a defense mechanism to the advances that obviously make me uncomfortable, but now - it sounds weird, but it's as if his hands aren't supposed to touch me.

I look up at William meeting his stare. He leans across the table on his elbows toward me slowly clasping his hands together heightening the anticipation.

"The company loves the revisions and would like to head straight in to casting," he says finally, his face splitting with his smile.

I could cry, my eyes immediately welling up with my smile. I hold my arms up in victory like Rocky. Finally, this was getting ready to happen.

I bound up the front steps of the office apartment entrance two at a time too excited to tell Niani about the movie's developments that I don't notice the person coming out. Reaching for the door, I barely get a hand around the handle when the door is thrown my way. I jump back barely skirting the door nearly hitting me in my face.

"Oh, sorry." I hear a deep husky voice apologize.

Meeting the face to the voice, I look up in to the eyes of a gorgeous young Korean man holding open the door.

"It's okay," I reassure him.

Intense, expressive dark brown eyes contrast below creamy skin, as if carved by a Renaissance sculptor with sharp angular features and dark silky hair framing his ears. Grinning softly, he reveals cute deep dimples completely unexpected from such beautiful features.

"Ladies first," he says, gesturing inside.

A sharp wind picks up suddenly whipping my hair across my face and that alluring scent whisks across my nose once again. Smelling it again affects me the same as it did before, if not more. For a brief moment I close my eyes and savor it, before opening them again. I pull my hair back off of my face and look up at him. He's wearing a black jacket. It must be him from earlier. A slight frown settles on his face and that starts me out of my musing, *fast*. I may have made him feel uncomfortable staring.

"Thank you," I say, stepping up onto the landing and releasing myself from this embarrassment.

He smiles with a nod and lets me pass. I feel his eyes on me, as I walk inside. The crunch of his shoes against the cement signal his departure when they stop.

"I like your earring." I hear him say.

Surprised, I turn around to him still propping the door open facing me. He taps the outer cartilage of his right ear with a teasing smile. Slowly, I reach up to my ear where I feel the small cross with an inset ruby hanging from my cartilage piercing. A gift from my sister or someone, I don't remember who I just decided to wear it today.

"Thank you. I love your cologne," I reply with my own smile.

"Thank you," he replies, his smile spreading to show pearly white teeth. "I'll see you again, Ashiya."

I frown suddenly at the fact he knows my name, as he turns and walks down the steps. Following him with my eyes, I watch him turn down the sidewalk. He must have heard my name through the apartment building sometime. Somehow, this perfect stranger knowing my name doesn't send alarms off in my head.

CHAPTER 2:
Instinct

"I miss you," a voice like silk whispers in my ear.

I start awake, instinctively reaching out for the voice. Realizing I'm in my room I put my hand down. I sigh, turning over on my back. It was just a dream. A dream with no faces just moving shapes and a voice. A voice as smooth as silk and all male. Somehow, that voice leaves me feeling empty and full all at the same time. Whatever that means, I don't know.

Sitting up, I swing my feet over the edge of the bed and stand. Suddenly, ringing fills my ears as a floating sensation claims my brain, knotting pain collects in my stomach, bright colorful spots flash in front of my eyes, and my equilibrium throws off causing my knees to collapse from under me. I catch myself on the bed steadying myself. At least I had enough focus to do that or my face would have met the hard wood floor. My stomach rolls, as my skin breaks out in a cold sweat. I pant trying to keep my nausea down.

Exhale. Focus. *Vertigo.* You've experienced this before. Get somewhere cool, I instruct myself instead of focusing on the symptoms racking my body. My hand slides across the side of the mattress. It's cool enough. Pressing my forehead to the cool side of the mattress I wait as the temperature against my flushed skin takes effect. Soon enough it ebbs away and I'm able to think clearly. Turning around slowly, I sit there letting the trembling in my limbs sift away. It's been a long time since I experienced vertigo. Finally able to gain full movement, I stand gingerly and make my way to my bathroom to get ready to meet William.

Sitting in a fourth floor lobby waiting to meet with an actor's agent I watch William lean over the counter talking to the receptionist. More like charming her aimlessly for the fun of it, which she's eating up with bashful vibrato. Feeling eyes on me I look to my right coming face to face with a man at least in his thirties blatantly staring at me. His striking pale blue eyes pierce as if looking straight through my soul. I offer him a small smile and he openly grins at me. My smile falters, as I feel my skin crawl. That grin sets off an alarming spike in my chest. Something in this man's grin tells me he's found something he likes and he's not letting go of it until he gets it. I look away from him, as panic rises in my chest feeling his stare on the side of my face. I hope he's an actor, because he could play the mute psychopath downright perfectly.

"Ms. Bride. Mr. Potter. Eric will see you now," the receptionist calls, looking up at William with a flirtatious smile of farewell.

I cringe as she says my name and force myself not to look the man's way as I stand. William turns from the desk and smiles at me mischievously. As I make my way to William, I feel the man's stare follow my every move. William catches the man's stare over my shoulder and frowns. Covering my back, I press the arrow pointing to the top floors of the elevator and step inside, William right beside me. The discomfort doesn't leave me until the door closes between me and the man's prying eyes.

The encounter with that man is still on my mind, as William and I step out of our individual cars onto the sidewalk on the way to another meeting. He's rambling on about how the fans are going to react once they hear of the book being adapted into a film. I'm just praying that man isn't a stalker or a serial killer.

"The fans are going to flip their lid, when they hear about the book coming to the silver screen. I can already see the comments on the forums and blogs. You are going to be a rich woman Ashiya, you and Niani. I mean this could blow Midnight out of the water," William gabs, as we walk down the sidewalk. I look at him with an amused smile.

"You mean Twilight?" I ask.

William grins at me, sheepishly.

"You know what I mean."

Suddenly, something hard slams in to my pelvis nearly shocking the wind out of me. I look down and meet the big doe eyes of a small Indian girl about the age of six with a cute curled high ponytail holding on to my shirt.

"You're pretty. Princesses are very pretty," her small voice says.

Awww. She's totally adorable.

"Thank you," I reply, bending down to her level.

I look up for her parents, when she is suddenly pulled away from me by her mother.

"Lia, I told you not to run," the beautiful woman scolds her.

Lia's mother turns to me and apologizes, "Sorry about this."

"No, she's fine," I assure her.

Her eyes linger on me for a second then widen, as if she is seeing something for the first time. She smiles at me then and looks down at Lia.

"Come on, Lia," she says, pulling Lia along with one last glance at me.

Lia looks back as they walk away screaming repeatedly, "Mommy, she's pretty! She's pretty, Mommy!"

William stares after them just as confused as I feel. This is the second time today I have been on the receiving end of strange looks. I follow in the direction of Lia and her mother feeling William's curious stare on my back.

Tired from the day's run around, I walk up the entrance stairs to the office apartments careful to watch for the door this time and enter. I've had this dull pain in my head for the last fifteen minutes and my head is spinning badly. It must be an after effect from this morning's spell. I've had vertigo before, but it's never affected me hours afterwards.

As I step in to the small foyer I catch the young Korean man at his mailbox through the glass windows of the mailroom. My head stills in that second and out of pure impulse I walk over.

"Hi," I greet him leaving a pause in the air, because I still don't know his name, as I stand at the door.

He turns around and looks up from the stack of mail in his hand, a smile already on his face.

"Hello Ashiya," he greets me in return, as if he wants to remember my name on his tongue for years to come.

A smile appears on my face almost instantly. Something about this moment feels familiar, like deja vu. I can't understand why it would though. With blemish free hands he taps his mail in his hand and closes his mailbox turning to me.

"Are you okay? You look tired." He frowns, stepping up to me.

My heart trips over itself in how much care is in his voice.

"Yeah, I'm okay. With a spell of vertigo this morning and having a lot of meetings running from this morning into the afternoon, I'm a little tired."

I have no idea why I just explained all that to him.

He smiles with a small chuckle, as if hearing all this before and signals me first out the door and I step out with him right behind me. I follow him to the elevator and he presses the button for the top floors. The door opens for us immediately and we step inside. I lean over to press my floor button and ask for his, when he leans over and presses the fourth floor button before me. I look up at him surprised and he gives me a soft knowing smile leaning back. I stand up erect as the elevator lifts us up, throwing us in to an easy silence when -

"How is the new book coming along?"

I whirl around at that grilling him with a betrayed frown.

"I know Niani," he follows up unflinching. "She didn't have to say anything. I made my own assumptions - *and* she dropped her papers on the elevator one day." He chuckles.

I join him, imagining it. That sounded like her. My laughter subsides and I answer, "Almost done." I nod, smiling.

"Nothing else? I don't get special privileges?" he jokes.

"You know Niani, not me," I play along, as the elevator dings reaching our floor and I step out.

He walks with me to me and Niani's office apartment door and stops before me.

"Make sure you get some rest," he says, smiling softly.

I smile myself and nod turning to open my door. Suddenly, the doorknob becomes two as the dizziness returns. I stop and turn to him, as I finally get the door open as normally as possible and watch as he walks around me to the door next to us taking out his keys. He looks over at me, as he opens his door with a small smile, and signals for me to go inside with a playful grin.

I wave him a half-hearted goodbye and walk inside.

I hear the door to his apartment close through the wall, as the door to our apartment closes behind me. Then I hear the miniscule squeak of the office door swing open. I take a step and my eyesight fades around the edges. I try to shake it off thinking I'm more exhausted than I thought. My vision focuses back in to view. My body feels like lead and I know something isn't right. Niani comes around the corner from the living room, when everything turns drastically and goes black. The last thing I see is Niani running towards me with a look of horror.

The first thing my eyes see when I open them is flashes of blue. I blink again and realize I'm in the upstairs bedroom with - a worried Niani at my feet and the Korean man leaning against the door, watching me.

"Thank goodness, you're okay," Niani exclaims, bouncing over to me. "William called saying you seemed off today. Mr. Jong came over as soon as he heard me call you."

Niani was rambling. She rambles when she's nervous. I blink again feeling like the foyer floor used my body to break its fall and turn my eyes away from Niani until they fall upon *Mr. Jong*. He came as soon as he heard Niani call me. I would smile if I could, but my body is slow to catching up with my brain at the moment. William called… saying I didn't seem to be feeling well? I was fine earlier. It wasn't until I got here that I didn't feel well, unless everything from this morning's spell showed on my face. Speaking of, William comes rushing in to the room immediately asking if I'm okay.

I look at Niani pointedly. She returns it with a nervous shrug. *I was worried. What else was I supposed to do?* her voice fills my head.

My eyes fall onto Mr. Jong, as he cuts his eyes at William and pushes off the door replying, "She'll be fine. She just fainted from exhaustion." He then turns to me and looks at me pointedly, saying gently, "Make sure you get some rest. No writing whatsoever. Doctor's orders."

I smile and Mr. Jong returns it. William catches the exchange and jealousy is written across his face instantly.

"Come on, Ashiya. I'll take you home," William says, as Niani helps me sit up.

"Wait," Mr. Jong cuts in.

William, Niani, and I turn to him to William's annoyance. Mr. Jong looks at me.

"If you do not feel better by tomorrow I want you to go straight to your doctor, okay?" he demands gently.

"Okay," I accede. "Thank you."

Mr. Jong nods with a smile placated. After acknowledging everyone in the room with a very businesslike nod he takes his leave. As William helps me stand, I watch after him wishing he would stay.

By the time I get home, all I want to do is sleep and maybe even dream of that voice again. William helps me through my apartment and in to my bedroom. Sitting me on my bed, William kneels down pulling my left foot in to his hands and begins unzipping my boot.

"You don't have to do that William. I can do it. You can go on ahead," I try to coax William away from my foot, as I pull it back. He pulls my foot back to him smiling.

"It's okay. You're not feeling well. I want to," he says, as he pulls the boot from my foot.

Something's not right. This feels wrong. Every muscle in my body tenses with a dull pain. He's not supposed to be here. He's not supposed to be doing this. I need to get away from him. I reach down to my right foot and pull off my boot letting it fall to the floor with a bouncing thud. Confused, William looks up at me as I pull away and slip from around him standing up.

"Restroom," I tell him quietly, as I walk away to my bathroom.

Closing the bathroom door behind me I press myself against the door sliding to the floor, as the tears spring to my eyes. What is wrong with me? A sob escapes my lips at the aching pain gnawing a hole in my heart. I breathe trying to control the pain of this big empty hole in my chest. I've never felt this lonely before. Tears leak down my face, as I let my silent sobs wrack my body. I hear William's feet shuffle behind the door. He knocks and I wish he would just leave. My heart pounds with a painful warning throb. He's not supposed be here. *He's* not supposed to be doing this. That's what it tells me as much.

"Ashiya, you okay?" William asks through the door.

Wiping away my tears, I pull myself up from the floor and pull myself together enough before trying to answer.

"Yes, I'm fine. Thank you. Um. You can go on ahead. I'm going to take a shower and get ready for bed. Thank you for all your help," I yell through the door.

I feel his discomfort at the prospect of leaving me through the door, as he shifts onto his right foot.

"At least let me see you before I go," he answers.

I sigh inaudibly, rolling my eyes. I turn around and open the door without a glance to check my appearance in the mirror. I don't step out of the bathroom, but lean against the doorframe, a silent barrier between me and him. William looks me over concerned and I smell something sharp in the air for a millisecond before he speaks.

"Yeah, you do look tired. I'll leave you to get some rest. Call me if you need anything," he tells me, putting a hand on my arm.

I recoil at the dull pain coursing through my arm at his touch, but not enough for him to notice.

"I will. Thank you," I reply. "Good night."

"Good night," he replies, with a small smile and turns, walking out of my room.

I stay there until I hear my front door close. Placing my forehead against the doorframe, I sigh gratefully and turn back in to the bathroom closing the door behind me.

CHAPTER 3:
All Else Must Be Miracles

"I love you," that silky voice whispers through my dream again in my ear and I feel warm soft lips press against the side of my neck.

I open my eyes. Once again, I wake to my quiet room and dream man's voice again. This time it came with an intensely intimate kiss I can still feel against my neck. They say reoccurring dreams are a message from God or the subconscious mind telling you to change something. If these dreams are trying to get me to change something I don't know what that would be.

I shake my head at my next thought. What if it's the man in my dreams I need? What if he's the one to change my life? I scoff. This isn't one of my novels.

My room feels quiet, lonely, as I lay there for a moment. *All right, that's enough.* I sit up and the room spins in response. Yeah, I'm definitely going to get this checked out.

Great. I suck my teeth.

I forgot that my car is still at the studio. Luckily, it's not too long of a walk from here. I'll just make my way over after I get something in my stomach.

Sitting in my designated room with the yellow manilla walls bordered with wallpaper of crayon drawn children playing, it makes me wonder if the colors they choose for hospitals are supposed to make people feel better or less worried about their results. I feel frankly calm, but there is that little twinge of worry creeping in the corner. Dr. Patel didn't appear to be worried about anything being wrong regardless of the evidence of my fainting, waking up with dizzy spells, and vertigo. I trust the fact that I very well may be exhausted, as Mr. Jong put it. I ignore the smile that sneaks up onto my face at the thought of him. The door opens to the room and in steps Dr. Patel.

"I'm back," he says in a singsong voice, closing the door behind him.

His optimism always puts a smile on my face. Taking his seat at the counter he opens my file and smiles up at me, his freshly lined mustache stretching with it. I return the smile feeling the effect of that happy brilliance reaching his hazel eyes calm my nerves.

He looks back down at his notes and says, "Well, you're in great health. Your body is just tired from an irregular sleep pattern and from overworking it. It may be also the baby's way of telling mommy to slow down, too."

Dr. Patel looks up at me eyeing me with an enthusiastic smile. That last sentence catches up with me fast.

"I'm pregnant?" I ask surprised.

"Three weeks to be exact," he says way too happy, as if he's the one receiving the good news.

Nooo. Three weeks ago, I was - I frown, trying to remember three weeks ago. I can't. I can't remember *anything*. But -

"Are you sure? I've -"

"I ran your blood work twice. You are pregnant," Dr. Patel assures me.

WOow.

Dr. Patel sees my frown and asks, "Is everything okay?"

I shake my head smiling softly and stand to deter any more questions.

"That's all?" I ask, clearly in a state of navigable shock.

"That's it," Dr. Patel says, standing along with me.

Stepping around in front of me, he places a hand on my arm that doesn't hurt and looks down on me endearingly.

"I've known you since you walked in to my office at eight. You're like a daughter to me. Remember, I switched practices for you. Now, you make sure that young man of yours takes care of you. I want you to take all your vitamins and attend every appointment to look after this little one, okay?"

I can't help but feel despite my shock a swell of happiness at his words and smile. He reaches over onto the counter and pulls a prepared piece of paper from atop of my file passing it to me. I look down at it. It's a list of things to help my pregnancy along.

"Now, I want you to go home and rest. I'm giving you a four day vacation away from your work to rest your mind and your body. We don't want anything to happen to the baby now, do we?" he asks seriously.

No. I shake my head vigorously.

"Good," he says, as he steps around me and opens the office door for me.

I step out and turn to him saying, "Thank you."

A proud smile slips on his face and he says, "You're welcome," with a nod. That being the end of it, I walk to the receptionist desk.

I park my MINI Cooper way too far from the office apartment and just *walk*. I may regret it later, but I could really care less right now. Seeing the embryo that will soon become my baby seals the truth that I am indeed pregnant, but the baby isn't what bothers me. But the fact that I'm pregnant with no recollection of the partaking in the deed it took to get me to this moment. I'm twenty-five years old and despite the memory loss I *thought* I was still a virgin. The result begs to differ though, I think cynically. I wanted to get married and then start a family. I wanted my child to have their father, but he or she is here and mine nonetheless.

Goose flesh rises across my shoulders, as I feel the weight of eyes on me. They're knowing. They're curious and something about them draws me in like a hyper awareness to look. *No.* I almost stop walking. Quickening my stride, I hurry to lessen the distance between me and the office apartment building. I couldn't wait to be between the office apartment door and Niani. Maybe I've snapped from shock, but if I didn't know any better I would think I could hear the murmur of their voices in my head.

I couldn't even make it pass the door. As soon as I unlocked the door I was on the floor sobbing my eyes out. I claw at my chest letting my world crash around me. Why can't I remember? What happened to me? Was I raped, kidnapped, drugged? The ideas of trauma and selective amnesia fill my head. Niani nervously steps out around me in to the hall, kneeling down beside me. She hugs me to her until my heart wrenching sobs subside. When my tears are finally gone, she gently lifts my face and wipes away the rivulets left behind. I look in to her eyes and I can clearly see the tears in her eyes. I can feel the pain I caused her in seeing me breakdown and I want to cry all over again, except this time for her.

"What happened?" she asks delicately.

I close my eyes unable to get the words out, my lips trembling. Inhaling and exhaling deeply I open my eyes again and say, "I'm pregnant."

Niani stills in shock, but then finds herself.

"What? *Really?* How far along are you?"

"Three weeks," I answer. "Niani - I can't remember anything from the last three weeks. Nothing." I look up at her.

Niani frowns, then her face falls neutral.

"Come on."

She takes my hands and pulls me up guiding me inside the apartment and closes the door. Setting me down on the couch, she turns and walks away in to the kitchen.

"I'll make you some decaffeinated tea," I hear her say in business mode.

Sipping at her coffee on the couch beside me, Niani asks, "You can't just miss three weeks of your life. Did you at least tell your doctor?"

"No," I answer, shaking my head.

Niani looks at me as if I lost my mind.

"Don't ask me why I didn't, because I can't even tell you why. Just know the baby is healthy. My doctor didn't find any sexual abnormalities. I have a clean bill of health, but I'll keep an eye on it."

Niani sighs heavily obviously frustrated, more so than I am. I look over at her.

"Can you remember what I did three weeks ago?" I ask.

Niani grabs her phone from the table in front of us, goes to her calendar and scrolls three weeks back landing on the thirteenth of June.

"Oh yeah. You left early. *Couldn't* stop smiling," she answers, as if mockingly annoyed. "I remember I had to get those drafts in for the next manga. You came back in Monday morning fine and ready to go on with the twelfth chapter of *Infinite Ways.*"

Yeah, that sounded like me.

"Nothing seemed wrong?" I ask.

Niani shakes her head. "Nothing."

I rub my hand across my face. "Okay," I sigh.

"On a lighter note, Mr. Jong came by earlier to see if you were okay. I told him you went to your doctor's. He seemed worried. I think he likes you," Niani says, looking at me out of the corner of her eyes.

I say nothing and just shake my head, sympathetically.

I could never get involved with him with a baby on the way, as much as I find myself attracted to him. I look over at Niani and take another sip of my tea, a thought occurring to me. "Do you have work to do? I don't want to keep you from it."

"If you're off, I'm off. Anyway, you're more important." She looks at me, smiling softly.

I smile back grateful to have her in my life.

"Have you thought about what you want?" she asks, raising her eyebrows in interest.

"It doesn't matter." I shrug, smiling.

"Names?" she fires.

"You already know this. Honor, if it's a boy. Ro, if it's a girl. Short for Rose," I fire back.

"Well, you never know things could have changed," Niani jokes.

"You know I'm Godmother right?" She looks at me with a raised eyebrow daring me to say otherwise.

"*Of course,*" I say, as if it's a no brainer.

"This is so great. I'm going to be an Auntie!" she exclaims, kicking out her legs.

I giggle glad to find at least one more spark of happiness out of this. As they say trouble comes in threes, so all else must be miracles. I'll take what I can get.

I step out into the hallway and lock the door to the office apartment behind me. When I turn around I come face to face with Mr. Jong.

"You're here," he says surprised.

"Yeah, I came to talk to Niani after coming from my doctor's," I explain.

"What did your doctor say?" he asks concerned.

"The same thing you did. I've exhausted myself. He gave me four days to recuperate. So, Niani and I took the day off together." I smile.

He nods, understanding.

"Have you had dinner, yet?" he then asks.

I shake my head.

"Would you like to have dinner with me?"

Immediately, my heart screams, *Yes!*

"Yes," I answer.

The smile that lights up his face I'll never forget.

Mr. Jong and I sit across from each other in an upscale Italian restaurant at a table for two. A dance floor to our right lays in the middle of the restaurant for all the restaurant to see, where professional dancers ballroom dance as entertainment pulling and encouraging guests onto the dance floor with a live band playing in a corner.

"Is your Ravioli okay?" Mr. Jong asks, as I put another in my mouth.

My goodness, is it good.

"Very," I tell him smiling ear to ear, as I cover my mouth with a hand to keep from showing my food.

He chuckles at my delight. I look up at him swallowing what's in my mouth.

"I've known you for three days and I still don't know your name," I say.

Mr. Jong looks at me wiping his mouth with his napkin.

"It's Kai. Kai Jung. Not Jong like Niani has been saying," Kai answers, chuckling at the last part.

I giggle myself, nodding.

Niani is known for getting names wrong. Who knows how many times I've had to correct her on one of our own character's names? Our waitress comes by to check on us a moment, before leaving us to check on her other tables.

"So, you're a Doctor?" I ask, turning back to Kai.

"Certified, yes," he answers.

"You sound like that's not the only thing you want to do," I observe.

"There are other things I would like to dedicate my time to. Other passions." He smiles, appreciating my attention.

"What are your other passions?" I inquire, enjoying the attention I was able to give him.

"Playing the piano, writing lyrics, *you* name it," he breathes passionately, staring me in my eyes.

Bothered in the most intimate way, I advert my attention to the dance floor. Kai follows my eyes, as the Bossa Nova song playing around us comes to an end.

"Do you dance?" he asks, smiling knowingly, as I turn back to him.

He must take my smile for a yes, because in the next moment I'm being escorted to the middle of the dance floor. The dancers step off the floor giving us space, as a jazz infused tango song begins filling the room with a seductive energy. Kai holds my stare across from him and I'm taken. He pulls me flush against him and leads me without a hitch. It's slow and sensuous, as we let our bodies do the talking. I'm pressed up against him and I feel more than safe wrapped in his arms and his cologne. I've never put so much trust in anyone, as I have with him in this moment. Something about him makes me lose all guard and be.

Eyes on eyes, hand in hand, I spin my hips in his hands from left and right. We slide down in a slow lunge and come up together. Here on the dance floor, we know each other. Our minds. Our bodies. Our hearts. He spins me and I drop hard in to a low lung again and the hall erupts in applause. Kai snaps me back into his arms and the intensity I see in his eyes - I've seen it somewhere before. My heart palpitates in its beating. He distracts me from my thoughts by leading me across the floor.

The music comes to a slow end and the restaurant explodes in applause, as Kai and I end up in one another's tight embrace, my forehead against his, sharing breath, a leg kicked up high around his hip. *I - I -* I pant unable to decipher the feelings running through my body. I want him to hold me like this forever. I close my eyes and open them to him looking down, watching me.

I pull a hand up and run it down the side of his face. Smooth skin brushes against my fingertips. He's beautiful. He closes his eyes and lets me. I drop my hand knowing I shouldn't and he opens his eyes looking at me, as if he understands why. Gently, we unwrap ourselves from around each other coming back to a room of applause. In surprise we bow and escort ourselves from the dance floor.

After paying for the check, we leave for my apartment.

"Thank you for this evening," I say, as I walk Kai to my door.

"You're welcome. I wanted to do this for you." Kai smiles turning to me, as we reach the door.

I smile up at him, when the doorbell rings interrupting our moment.

Reaching over, I open the door to find William on the other side staring back at us just as shocked at seeing Kai and I together. The air quickly becomes thick with tension, as we stare at one another. Resilient, Kai says good night to me promising to see me later and excuses himself. Returning the sentiment, I let William in and close the door behind him.

"Doctor paying a house visit?" William asks interrogatively, rounding on me as I turn around to him.

"I can not and will not have this conversation with you," I say calmly, walking around him in to my living room.

"Why not? You're afraid you'll get worked up again and faint? Don't worry, I'll take care of you if that happens," William says predatory, following me in to the room.

"No, you won't, because I won't let you." I turn around, putting my guard up fast.

"What is wrong with you?! I've thrown every hint in the book to show you that I have feelings for you!" William snaps, throwing his arms out wildly.

"Why don't you get that I'm not interested? We work together. That's it!"

In a few quick strides, William is in my face.

"Is it him?" he asks threatening.

If he touches me I will snap.

"Leave him out of this."

"What? He flashed you a smile? You maybe talked a bit and now you're ready to hand your heart over to him?!" he rages.

Casting a leering glance at William I walk around him.

"You're jealous."

"Please." He scoffs, turning around to me.

That's it. I'm done.

"You can't stand the fact that I'll be with anyone, but you. Well get this! You can't change the fact that he has my heart and you can't change the fact that I'm having his child!" I snap.

As soon as the words leave my mouth I regret it. I look up at William's crestfallen face and I can literally feel his heart breaking.

I can't believe I just said that.

"I'm sorry. I shouldn't have said that. It's not true," I apologize.

William starts, as if coming back to life and looks at me. He walks over and looks upon me without a word. I avert my eyes from his not wanting to draw any more attention to myself. He then leans down and kisses me on my forehead. I want to push him away, but I'm too tired to fight. Anyway, there's nothing overly affectionate about the kiss. It feels apologetic.

"I'll see you later," he whispers and turns walking out the door.

I follow him and quickly lock it behind him. I stand there for a moment and shake my head. Things just keep getting complicated. His kiss feels like IcyHot on my forehead. Sighing heavily, I walk in to my bathroom, grab a clean rag, and wash the kiss away. I look at myself in the mirror seeing how tired and stressed I look. Turning away, I head in to my bedroom hitting the bathroom switch as I go and head for bed.

Something wakes me. Instantly, I feel more than one presence in my dark room. The baby is my only first thought. Feigning sleep, I slowly reach a hand under my pillow releasing my switchblade from its handle and reach with the other for the tassel on my lamp. Calculating every move, I pull my switchblade out from under the pillow and pull the light on.

I sit up, looking to my left and a man with purple eyes jumps on me pinning me down by my biceps on both sides of my head. Still having function of my wrists, I maneuver the switchblade in my hand and stab it through his arm. His wounded cry fills my ears. Letting go of me, he leans off and I swing back slicing him across the chest pushing him off of me. Suddenly, I'm pinned down again my head pushed to the side exposing the side of my neck. *The baby*, I repeat like a mantra in my head, as I struggle against my assaulter feeling hot breath against my neck. I grab my switchblade hard ready to stab again, when the person is snatched away from me and I hear the shattering of glass. Suddenly, silver eyes replace my vision staring me in my eyes, their body covering mine.

"Kai," I whisper.

He turns over off of me with inhuman speed bringing a thick intricately carved gold and bronze baton before the chest of a woman with bright yellow green eyes on the other side of my bed.

"*Try* and touch her and you die," Kai threatens her.

The woman takes no heed and lunges. I grab on to Kai's arm around me scared for him, as Kai slings a blade from the baton the color of pewter lined in a burnt orange steel stabbing the woman straight through the breastplate, right through the heart. Like acid burning flesh, her skin cracks and fizzles eating away filling the room with an acrid death like smell. I knew it enough visiting a coroner for research for *Infinite Ways*. Within seconds she is gone. The only thing that is left is the burnt residue of her skin littering my floor and bed. Kai turns and looks me over checking me for any injuries. Next, he looks over the bed beside me. I follow his gaze and find crumbled burnt flesh on the floor where I pushed the man off of me. Kai looks back at me with a surprised smile and says, "Good job."

He pushes himself up off the bed and stands up beside me.

"Come on," he says softly.

Bending down and picking me up bridal style, he carries me away from my apartment.

CHAPTER 4:
Eyes Wide Open

My mind jumps from one scenario to another thinking back to the whole ordeal back at my apartment. I can't pinpoint a question I want to ask, though I'm curious I surprisingly don't want to know. All that matters is Kai lying next to me in his bed under his soft silver satin sheets he covered me in, waiting for me to say something. Anything. His once silver eyes are now brown. I don't know when they turned back, but they appear to me as natural as seeing them silver. Knowing that, it finally feels like it's time for the questions to begin.

"Who are you?" I ask quietly.

Kai sits up averting his eyes from mine and says, "You know what to look for."

I sit up curiously looking over his face, his body, his hands, any form of sign that can tell me what he is. He looks at me, his eyes trained on mine and -

His pupils.

They aren't black, but a starlit night sky. I've written something like this in... *Reign*. I never let my eyes waver from his.

"Vampire," I say sure.

"If someone shows you who they are, believe them," he quotes.

Maya Angelou. He knows my favorite quote. I shouldn't ask him how he knows that, but more in order of what I am to him.

"What am I to you?" I ask.

"My wife," he answers, staring unwavering into my eyes.

Even if I couldn't gasp out loud due to shock, I'm pretty sure my soul did.

"Explain," I request softly.

"Seven months ago we met, dated, then eloped about a month ago," he explains.

"Eloped?" I question. "Why?"

"You fell in love with everything you write about. I fell in love with someone - open. To avoid exposure to our families and my clan, we eloped," he answers.

He slips out of the sheets and walks over to the dresser picking up a picture frame and brings it back to the bed. He hands me the frame and in it I see a picture of us on a beach of black sand with me in this beautiful twisted one shoulder strap A-line wedding gown and Kai in a white dress shirt tucked into white tuxedo pants under a matching vest perfectly tailored to his body, as we kiss. My dress is something completely unconventional. Delicate white satin fabric hugs my frame until it falls flowing loose in to a bellowing skirt. The thick braid twisted tight is taken across my chest, over my shoulder, and down my completely open back, where it stops low meeting the top of the skirt and unravels straight in to a train fading from white into a deep champagne.

Champagne and ivory, homage to my mom who couldn't be there. Pearls for my dad. It's something I would do in this situation. I stare at the picture of us. We look so happy. We look deeply in love.

32

"What happened to us? Why can't I remember this?" I ask.

"My clan leader made an attempt on your life," he answers darkly. "Against law to turn you into a vampire."

"Why?" I ask.

"Your novels," he answers. "You've made a few people angry revealing secrets to the world no one else should know about us, our world, particularly with *Reign*. They think you've either been talking to someone or you have a very good imagination. Either way that's why my clan rather change you. You're valuable."

"But I wrote *Reign* over two years ago. Why now?"

"You've had many books since then that have garnered you a lot of attention. With the movie coming out what better way to strike you down than with the whole world looking at you," Kai states.

"If this was going on why didn't you tell me?"

"Because you're not supposed to know I exist. I would have led them right to you and if you were caught with me your punishment would be far worse. Taking your memories away of me and protecting you from a distance was my best advantage."

"I've heard about spouses' jobs coming between their marriage, but never anything like this," I say sarcastically.

Kai chuckles.

I turn to him. "How long has it been since you left?"

"Three weeks."

Three weeks?

"I left the night we got married," he answers.

I let out a joyous sigh, a hand coming over my heart in anticipation.

"What's wrong?" Kai asks alarmed.

"Three weeks ago you left, right?" I ask cautiously, unable to look at him. What if I'm wrong? "Did we?"

"Yes," he answers, already knowing the answer to my question.

"Talk to me," he urges gently.

I turn and look at him the smile unable to come off my face.

"I'm pregnant," I tell him.

Kai stares at me unmoving for *seconds*, before swooping in and kissing me so deeply I feel heat literally in the pit of my stomach. Despite every moral doubt in my mind that I shouldn't kiss him back I find myself doing it anyway. The man who but three days ago was a stranger, who I find out now is my husband, a vampire, and the father of *our* baby. I gasp as his hand brushes my stomach taking with it my kiss, my body turning on to his touch. I push in to him, as his arm wound around my waist pulls me in closer. Everything within me tells me this is right. *He's right. He's* supposed to be here. *He's* supposed to be doing this.

Laying me back gently, Kai slides down my body smelling me down my neck, between my breast, down my clothed stomach and stops. I look down trying to catch my breath and catch silver eyes staring back. He pushes up my tank and I lose my will to breathe, as he kisses me across my stomach, sucking the skin between his lips, smelling me around my navel.

I moan, as images flood my brain. Sensations. Kai naked underneath me. Deep inside me. Him watching my every reaction. I'm full of him. His love. *Him.*

I whimper, as more images come. I feel the pressure, as Kai squeezes my hand with his release. The warmth of my body after our love making. The dull ache between my legs. The smell of roses. The sound of wind chimes in the air. The soft sheets against my back, as I watch Kai's sleeping face beside me. I see it, feel it all from the outside looking in.

Kai slides back up my body pulling me from my visions and I watch him look upon me reverently.

"I'm here," he whispers in that low silky voice I've heard so many times in my dreams. "I'm here now."

My head is spinning. I want to cry knowing that voice belongs to Kai, as I focus on those silver eyes connecting that voice and Kai as one in my mind. Knowing that Kai has been with me all along comforts me in knowing that I haven't been as alone as I have felt. I now feel safe and complete. Secure knowing that the baby and I are safe with their father. That enough sends me over the edge of unconsciousness.

By morning, last night is all I can think about. The vampire's attack. Fighting back. My adrenaline is still vibrating in my skin because of it. Finding out Kai is my husband and the father of our baby. That still brings a smile to my face and the *images*. I can still feel Kai within me, around me.

I look across the counter at him sitting on one of the barstools lining the other side of the kitchen counter messing with my switchblade. I have no memory of him, yet from the very beginning my body, those vague moments of déjà vu, even my heart has been pointing me towards him. I watch him even now feeling a magnetic pull to him. I want to remember us. I want to know what it felt like to be with him. In the midst all that I learned last night I forgot to ask how he took my memories away.

I take a sip of the freshly made carrot juice he made for me this morning. Obviously, he never forgot my favorite juice either. Just like he didn't forget my favorite quote. He must really love me, I think with a smile or vampires have really good memory. Okay, watching him examine my switchblade is starting to become comical.

"What is so intriguing about my switchblade?" I chuckle at his extreme concentration.

"It killed a vampire last night," Kai answers, flipping the blade over.

"You're a vampire. You shouldn't be touching it." I look at the blade to him ready to protect him from its fatal results.

"I'm different. It won't hurt me." He looks up meeting my eyes calmly.

"How are you different?" I ask.

"I'm the only vampire that can walk in the daylight. Therefore, I share none of the weaknesses of my brothers or sisters," he answers.

Then he frowns, as he notices something on my switchblade and drags his baton sword from the counter slinging the blade from its hold making me jump and places it back on the counter with a sharp metal clang. His eyes jump from my blade to his sword seeing some similarity.

"Weapons of Choice," he says quietly.

"What is Weapons of Choice?" I ask.

"It's a natural affinity for a weapon or weapons," Kai answers me. "Supernatural weapons made with only one wielder in mind. The weapon chooses the owner by design from conception. Only one family makes these."

"This," He places my switchblade in front of me, "was made for you."

"Why?" I ask hesitantly, looking up from the pink quartz handle with mother of pearl butterflies in it. "My mother bought this for me. If everything supernatural is kept under wraps, how did this get in her hands?"

"I don't know." Kai shakes his head walking around the counter to me. He stops before me and looks down at my stomach placing a hand over it. "But it helped save your life." He looks up meeting my eyes. "And I'm going to find out why."

The intensity I see in his eyes is so different from the look I saw last night on the dance floor. It tells me he will go through high hell and water to make sure the baby and I are safe. I'm distracted for a moment by him dropping to his knees and lifting up my tank. He stops and looks up at me.

"May I?"

I'm so moved by the gesture I just nod my head. He leans in close and I watch him circle my stomach in that slow, sensuous way of his.

"What do you smell when you do that?" I ask.

He leans back and smiles up at me. "A mixture of us, but a scent all its own," he answers.

I smile as well.

"Is it okay that I be totally cliché right now?" I ask.

"It's why I married you." Kai chuckles.

He stands, towering over me and raises his eyebrows with a smirk waiting for my all so cliché remark. I bust out laughing unable to get the words out and Kai laughs as well wrapping his arms around my waist.

"Goodness, I've missed this," he sighs, placing his forehead against mine.

"Believe it or not, I've missed this too," I reference to my recent bouts of loneliness.

I close my eyes and run my hands down the sides of his face. He exhales heavily, breathing me in.

"How did you take them away?" I ask quietly.

Kai pulls back and I look up at him. His eyes hold his regret that he had to do that to me.

"A friend gave me an elixir I administered into your wine that night. She explained that it would block your emotions and memories attached to me, but also leave you with a heavy loneliness and your body a warning beacon against anyone that touches you in a romantic interest that isn't me. Only your body remembers me," he explains. "The more you're near me, the more we experience together, the quicker your memories will come back."

"Like last night," I say more to myself.

Kai's face scrunches up in surprise. "A memory came back?"

I pull away from him. My body feeling all hot and bothered just thinking about it.

"Yeah. When we made love," I answer.

A lopsided, teasing smile slinks on to Kai's face.

"Don't do that," I warn him, feeling the dizzying sensation of déjà vu.

"Don't do what?" He steps toward me.

I feel the pull in my body like a magnet gravitating toward him. I try to stay rooted to where I stand, but I can't. He takes another step forward and I propel myself into his arms taking his face in my hands and kiss him greedily. My body wakes up to the memory and how his mischievous smirk always turned me on, as he kisses me back hungrily.

Kai pulls away reluctantly and pushes back giving me space.

"I don't want to do too much, too soon," he explains with a bittersweet smile.

"I know what you mean," I admit. "The elixir mixed with being pregnant, the side effects suck."

Kai frowns, as if realizing something. "That's why you fainted. You being pregnant must counteract with the elixir forcing your memories to come back faster." He turns to me. "You are amazing. I don't know why I didn't think about that."

"That's why you married me." I smile, stealing his line.

Kai smiles at me biting the side of his lip.

"Wait here," he says softly.

I watch him run out of the room and turn up the stairs taking two at a time.

As I wait for his return, I look around the apartment having been too preoccupied to do so earlier. Everything is modern with a dark sophisticated edge to it. The complete opposite in color to me and Niani's office apartment, which is contemporary with a base of ivory and bright accents, but the same floor plan with Kai's bedroom being where we placed our office.

A perfect balance of deep black, soft white, and cream with accents of sharp metal gray pieces makeup the living room. A black suede couch sits against the white wall to the stairs facing the three large arch windows opposite of two matching armchairs sitting across from it. A glass coffee table takes up the middle of the room, as tall twisted black and metal grey sculptures take up the corner walls beside the metal fireplace with candles aligned across the mantle. *I love it.* It looks as if a personal curator of an art gallery came in to oversee all that was being brought in, then an interior decorator came and put the final touches on it. Beautifully dark, but minimal and inviting. I'm comfortable here and if I could remember it I could probably remember if I've been here before.

Under my feet I feel Kai's footsteps vibrate through the plush white carpet, as he returns telling me with each step how close he is. I turn from looking at the assorted candles across the mantle and look down to Kai on bent knee with an open black velvet box in his hand revealing a slim white gold band completely encrusted with small diamonds and shades of rubies placed throughout it sporadically.

"One more thing," he says, his eyes unwavering from mine. "Ashiya Bride, will you be my wife again?"

In the back of my mind, a memory floats back to the surface. A similar moment like this, where Kai is down on bent knee in this very spot asking me to marry him in the candlelight and I tear up.

"Yes," I hear myself whisper just as I had before.

Smiling fully, Kai slips the ring on my finger and stands up. I throw my arms around him and hold him tight never wanting to let go.

"I remember before," I sob in to his shoulder.

The love. It burns through every part of my being filling me with a heat that I never want to let go. You can't forget a love like this. A love I would die an infinity and one deaths for Kai. Even without this memory, *this feeling* I don't think it ever left. Over my shoulder, I feel Kai smile as he tightens his hold on me. I don't think I've ever been this happy.

I wake up to Kai watching over me, as I sleep. Amused and embarrassed, I cover my face with a hand.

"I'm sorry, I fell asleep on you," I mumble in to the covers.

"It's okay. You need the rest," Kai soothes, smoothing down my hair. "This is your spot anyway. There were plenty of times when you would come over and sleep right here, because I didn't want to be alone."

I remove my hand and look up at him that admission striking a chord in me. It must be even lonelier with me without my memories.

"Without my memories am I different?" I ask.

"A little," Kai admits. "Gina said that might happen. You're nervous. Afraid to give in to the feelings your body is telling you. She said it'll be like that until your memories come back."

"How was it when we were together?"

"Fun." He smiles. "You used to walk around here naked."

My mouth drops open incredulously.

"I'm kidding." He laughs.

I slap his arm playfully. Suddenly, a burn ignites in my stomach and I bury my face in to the mattress to muffle the moan escaping my lips.

"What's wrong?!" Kai panics.

"A hunger pain, just harsher," I gasp, as another wave of pain hits me.

Noticing Kai went quiet I look up at him as the pain continues to carve in to my stomach. His face is set in a pensive frown, as he stares down at me.

"I'll be right back." He snaps out of it and slips from the bed leaving the room.

He comes back with a mug handing it to me, as I sit up in the bed.

"Drink it. It'll make you feel better," he says.

I look down in to the mug and see little drops of what looks like red ink swirling in the juice and I know it's

41

blood. It's nice that Kai tried to disguise it in case I wouldn't take it well. Meeting Kai's eyes, I bring the cup up to my lips and take a swallow. The juice wakes up my taste buds instantly, but the sweet and savory taste of blood takes over all together. It's like eating chocolate covered cherries with a pinch of salt to taste or maple flavored sausage. I knock the rest of the drink back without protest. Meeting Kai's stare as I bring the cup down I begin to feel like he's become my dealer fixing my addiction, my beginning addiction for blood. Every nerve ending in my body kicks in to a frenzy, shaking me. Kai fixes me with a knowing look. He takes the cup from my hands and sits it on the floor next to him, as he kneels down before me.

"You're okay. You're okay," he coaxes me, taking my hands.

"Why am I..." I ask, stopping mid-sentence and swallow.

"The baby and you are connected. The virus it takes to create a vampire must be seeping in to your bloodstream making you one," Kai explains, taking my face in his hands.

I breathe, as I try coming down from my high covering Kai's hands with my own. Kai takes our foreheads and places them together breathing with me. With each breath I take a jolt shakes me. My heart is beating so fast, I feel like I'm either in ecstasy or in hell. I can't choose. It only takes a moment for it to subside for what it seems could have gone on forever.

"I'm fine, now," I say, finally feeling better.

I take Kai's hands down from my face and hold them in my lap. Something out the corner of my eye catches my attention and I look up at a silver satin and lace babydoll dress hanging from a hanger on Kai's closet door. Kai follows my eyes and turns back to me.

"You wore that the night we got married," he says, as he runs his thumbs across the backs of my hands.

Kai's eyes. I smile at him understanding the sentiment behind it and stand. Letting go of his hands, I walk around him over to the closet stripping myself of my tank top as I go.

"How about we have a morning after?" I toss over my shoulder meeting Kai's wondering stare, as I grab the babydoll from the door and disappear into his closet.

CHAPTER 5:
The Fantasy

The next two days for us become the honeymoon we never got to have. We leave for Hilton Head Island the morning after choosing to get out of the state of our warrants and just enjoy ourselves. A small joy away from the supernatural matters, because I have a feeling all of that is about to change soon...

Kisses trail up my neck pulling me from sleep and I smile. I turn over and meet Kai's lips. Wrapping my arms around his neck, I deepen the kiss fervently feeling the passion of it run through my arms and up my neck. I turn us over and push Kai into the mattress with much more strength than I mean to. Kai looks at me shocked for a moment, before he's smiling and runs a hand up my right thigh slipping a hand under my satin pink shorts and palms my right glute.

"You are so sexy," he croons softly, looking up at me.

I feel pride strong and tight run through my body. I smile leaning down and pull his top lip between my own enjoying the feel of his lips against mine. Petal soft, warm, and perfect. Kai chuckles a whisper, his breath ghosting over my lips, as I pull back. Light catches across the diamonds and rubies in my wedding band and I turn looking at it. Happiness blooms in my heart looking down at the symbol of our union. Kai looks over as well and takes my hand bringing it to his lips and kisses the top of my ring.

Turning his head back to me, he asks, "So, what's on our agenda today?"

"I don't know. Staying with you in this bed all day sounds like a plan." I smile.

Kai smiles in return, a jolt of excitement shooting through him at the idea.

"That does sound like a plan, but we should go out. Do something memorable."

Memorable. It brings back the reality of my memories being gone. It has felt so natural between us that I completely forgot about that.

"Then we should go to the beach," I breathe as if thinking it over, running a finger up the middle of his chest.

Standing in the middle of our hotel room living room I wait, as Kai bends down grabbing his key card from the coffee table and slips it into his back pocket. He's wearing a white short sleeve V-neck and matching white swim trunks with his green BEATS hanging around his neck looking every bit of beach sexy casual. Blasting from his headphones I hear Don Diablo & Example's 'Hooligans'.

As if breaking through some sound proof barrier Example's voice blares in to my eardrums with the driving force of the beat startling the mess out of me, before abruptly dying out. I look at Kai's headphones, where the song is playing at the normal level I heard it on before. I figure it's a trick of my ears, until I hear Kai.

"You all right, babe?" he asks.

It's then that I notice my fingers are over my ears.

"Yeah," I say.

I pull my hands down from my ears.

We walk down to the beach out the back of the hotel the wind whipping against our clothing, as we get closer to the water. Kai drops our towels down on the sand and I slip my dress over my head unveiling my deep red bikini halter top and low rise bottom. I hear Kai's sharp intake of breath behind me. I turn to find him staring me up and down with suppressed desire.

"You want me?" I taunt him and his unfocused eyes find mine. "Come and get me." I take off for the water dropping my dress as I go. Kai growls playfully and rips his headphones from his neck kicking up sand and comes after me.

Climbing out of the water some time later, I trudge across the sand with Kai behind me his shirt gone and chest glistening with water droplets, panting. I collapse onto the sand not caring that sand is collecting under my bikini bottom a little. Kai falls into place beside me lying on his back with a heavy sigh and I laugh at him. I lay down laying my head on his chest and he puts an arm around me. I smile happy that I get to experience this with the person I'm falling in love with all over again. I open my eyes and look at the glittering sand beside us.

Suddenly, the sand magnifies and I'm looking at the sand in a crystalline state so that it looks like big chunks of sugar crystal half cloudy with quartz taking up my vision. I know what this is without having to ask. My vampire senses are coming in so much faster than I expected. I try and pull out of focus, but my eyes won't budge. I try again. Not even an inch. Panic starts to settle in my chest.

"Kai," I say, trying to keep my voice calm. "My senses are coming in. My eyes won't focus."

Kai pushes up with me against him.

"Close your eyes," he says softly, calm and in control.

I refuse to look anywhere else too afraid of what I might see. I close my eyes.

"Imagine you're reading a book and concentrate on the small print."

I imagine the small print from when I read *The Silver Kiss* and I see the burned image of a page against my eyelids. I feel my eyes adjust contracting as if a telescope. I open my eyes. The beach comes in to view, the sand wide and expanding, the ocean bright and shining in the sunlight.

"Better?" Kai asks, drawing my attention to his face.

"Better." I sigh.

"You ready for something to eat?"

That something turns out to be a picnic in a shady clearing in the park. Kai sets out a blanket on the grass and places a basket of food down on top.

"You had this all planned out didn't you?" I ask, smiling at the thought and care he put in to our last minute honeymoon.

"I had an idea," Kai answers, "and I know a few people," he adds, as he sits down on the blanket and pats the ground in front of him for me to come sit with him.

I walk over to him and he takes my hand guiding me down to sit in front of him, my back to his chest, as he wraps his arms around my waist.

"So, what's on the menu for today chef?" I ask, leaning back in to Kai's body, as Kai leans his head over my shoulder.

Kai reaches around me and unlatches the catch on the basket revealing containers of goodies, paper plates, and small plastic utensils.

"We have garbanzo bruschetta and crackers." Kai takes out two plastic boxes stacked on top of each other.

"Mmmm," I comment.

"Yummy yummy roll. Mild for baby here." Kai rubs my flat stomach affectionately.

"Strawberries and cherries dipped in red wine chocolate." I smell the sharp almost coppery scent of the red wine seeping through the top and my body reacts in a weird way. I feel something alive and beastly come to life within me and I want to tear in to the box, but I pull myself back frightening myself.

"Tempting, isn't it?" Kai jokes, placing the box down as well. He has no idea.

"And lastly, Arnold Palmer decaf." He pulls out a crystal plugged carafe and puts it down on the blanket as well. "What would you like to try first?" Kai leans in to the crook of my neck smelling my personal scent before he's leaning back over my shoulder again.

"I think I'll go with the garbanzo bruschetta and crackers."

"Good choice." Kai pops the top on the garbanzo bruschetta and crackers and builds a slide of bruschetta on top of a cracker for me and holds it toward my mouth. I lean up and take the appetizer in to my mouth. Building one for him, I turn and feed it to him. Lunch carries on this way, Kai feeding me, I feeding him, until the only thing left to stuff us are the strawberries and cherries. I reach over and pop a cherry into my mouth delightfully and sit back in Kai's arms. I'm in complete and utter content. Good food. Good man. I almost forget that we're in a park, when an older couple in their golden years passes by. The woman looks at me with a mutually happy smile, as her and her husband pass and I can't help but think how cute they look as he keeps his hand low on her hip lovingly. I think about how they grew old together and how Kai and

I never will. We will be forever young. Then I think, even I don't know that. I pull away from Kai sitting up and turn to him.

"Kai, how old are you?" I ask.

"Twenty-six," he answers.

"No, in vampire years," I clarify.

"Two years. I was changed year before last." He averts his eyes frowning, troubled by this information.

"What's wrong?" I ask.

He shakes head. "Nothing." He looks up at me all signs of trouble gone from his eyes. "Did you want to know something else?" he asks.

"You said I released secrets about *our* world in my books. How much of what I've written is true?"

"About 80% of every book. 20% is fiction."

"Wow." I nod. "That's a big percentage. No wonder they want to kill me." I look up at Kai again. "Can you tell me which parts are the real thing?"

"I can show you better than I can tell you," he says, "but right now let's wait on that. Let's enjoy our time now." He reaches a hand up and brushes my cheek. Automatically, I lean my face in to him and kiss his palm. He smiles glad to see my response becoming warmer towards him. I lift my eyes to him.

"Can you at least tell me one thing?" I ask.

Kai smiles and nods his head, allowing me this.

"Do we age?" I ask.

Kai's smile gets even bigger, as he breathes a laugh at my question.

"Yes," he says finally able to straighten his face and get the words out, "but very, very, *very* slowly."

"So, what I wrote was true. Only vampires of the moon stay frozen and vampires of the sun live on."

49

"Yup." Kai smiles, staring down at me proudly. "Now, I believe there was an Abalone necklace you had your eyes on further up the road at that gift shop with your name on it."

My eyes widen in surprise.

"You spoil me," I say, smiling ear to ear.

Kai leans in close to my face. "I believe it's the other way around. You keep giving me things far better than I think I deserve," he says, rubbing at my stomach.

I tilt my head, my eyes softening, as I stare up at him.

"Kai, do you really think this is a good idea? Yes, we've been out all day, but if your clan can find me in Atlanta, which I have to add I've made a few people angry. Don't you think they can find me here?" I ask, facing Kai, as I place an earring of a long dangling cross in my cartilage piercing.

Kai stands across the hotel room slipping a cuff link into his shirtsleeve. Hearing my concern, he pulls his arm sleeve down and walks over to me.

"I won't let *anyone* touch you. This is our honeymoon. We should be able to have this time. You're safe here. Atlanta is their territory," he says firmly, placing gentle hands on my arms.

"Then whose territory is this?" I ask.

"No one you need to worry about," he answers with a sure happy smile.

I smile softly and turn back to the mirror smoothing down the long lace black see through dress I'm wearing.

Yet, I still can't help but worry...

A hostess escorts us out to the tables outside on the restaurant terrace and as Kai and I step out onto the landing guests occupying some of the tables look our way.

Suddenly, I feel overdressed almost naked. As if feeling my discomfort, Kai leans in and says low with bold confidence dripping in his voice, "Don't hide."

As if that is enough to assure the beast within that feeling from the park comes back to life and I grin. We follow the hostess to our table and Kai pulls my chair out for me, scooting me under the table before taking his seat across from me. I look around at the women shooting us glances and the men trying to keep their eyes down. I laugh to myself at the irony, as I hear Taylor Swift's 'Trouble' playing low over the outdoor speakers.

Kai meets my eyes across the table with a wicked smile and I imagine how we must look to them. My long lace dress and Kai in his neatly creased white dress shirt with silver spiked buttons and his classy silver cufflinks and black slacks. One word to anyone looking at us spells 'T. R. O. U. B. L. E'. I watch Kai's fingers drum to the beat, his red abalone teardrop pinky ring shining in the tables candlelight matching the pink abalone teardrop resting just below my trachea. He looks so regal, I observe as I watch him. Soon our waiter comes by and takes our appetizer order, before going off to send it to the kitchen.

"So, Mrs. Jung," Kai begins, gaining my attention, "how does your first night on your honeymoon feel?"

I smile, feeling the heat of my happiness fill my chest.

"What her black men ain't good enough for her?"

"Better than I could imagine," I answer, ignoring the obvious African-American women's voice reaching my ears. Her use of grammar makes me cringe and shake my head internally.

"Seriously, what could he do for her? He won't be able to understand her struggle as a black woman."

It's the man across from her that speaks this time. My sensitive ears pinpoint them two tables across from us to my back. What do they know about what Kai can do for me or my struggle? I ignore them and focus on Kai.

"What about you? Has this been everything you wanted it to be? Because if memory serves me right you had a hand in everything involving our wedding," I ask, getting flashes of the planning in my head leading up to our elopement.

Kai smiles wide, elated that I remembered.

"This has been everything I wanted and more. I have you."

I melt a little inside. I reach over and take Kai's hand into mine and hold it.

"I don't get interracial couples. What do they see in each other?"

I look into Kai's eyes wondering if he hears them, but his eyes are focused only on me, which I should be focused on him. I look down at his wedding band, a masculine version of mine with shades of garnet and tiny beats of silver, fingering it within our enclosed hands. Kai stares at me and I stare at him. Smiling. Always smiling. We must look goofy and I laugh at the thought breaking the spell, when our waiter comes up with our appetizer.

"Seriously, what is she wearing? This isn't the red carpet."

For the first time I look around the terrace for the line of voices. Over my shoulder I see the African-American couple across the patio. The woman's eyes lock with mine and I smile at her and turn away. A table of five women catch my attention, as they sneak not so secret looks at me and I turn back to Kai. Their emotions are clear. They don't necessarily like me and they hate and yet love my dress. Kai smiles at me across the table.

"Unf. He is so sexy and look at that smile." I hear a woman from the table say lustfully, *"If he was mine -"*

I return Kai's smile and look out onto the beach in the distance.

"You want to - " I turn to Kai.

A high pitch cackle pierces my ears from inside the restaurant interrupting my question, the slide of a glass scraping across marble slice, the repeated slam of plate after plate crashes into my eardrums, as the chorus of voices around me climb to a deafening sound giving me a borderline headache.

I stand from the table gaining Kai's attention.

"I'll be right back," I tell him and bend down leaving him with a kiss.

The restroom is quiet and ultimately empty, as I let the silence alleviate the pressure in my head.

"You okay?"

I look up in to the mirror to see Kai behind me. Albeit, standing in the woman's restroom.

"How did you know?" I ask, turning around.

"I've been there. Remember?" He smiles empathically. "You're doing a good job of hiding it. It's hard to know when you're hiding something sometimes," he says, stepping up to me. "I smelled your anxiety."

His voice is comforting and like cool running water and I close my eyes. His hands slide low over my hips and I look up at him.

"You want to go?" he asks softly.

"No," I assure him.

His hand slips around to my stomach, when a group of women walk in to the bathroom. Three of them are from the women's table. They look at the two us acknowledging the serious atmosphere and see Kai's hand on my stomach.

"We'll be out of your way ladies. My wife wasn't feeling well," Kai says, turning back to me.

Four of the women turn in to the empty stalls, as the other two wait in line for their turn. I smile up at Kai and say, "Thank you."

With a small smile, Kai takes my hand and tows me out with him.

"*That was so cute. Can you believe he came in to check on her in the women's bathroom?*" One of the women's voice reach my ears, as we walk out of the restroom. "*I need a man like that in my life.*"

"*Yeah, one better than the consequential jerk you have at the house.*" I hear Kai whisper a chuckle, the volume amplified as if right in my ear. I can't help but break into a smile myself.

The night is quiet with no one else around as we walk across the wooden plank walkways with nothing but the sound of our feet and the waves coming off the beach. We stayed well until after closing and I now understand why Kai wanted to. It feels like we're the only two in the world. With no one else around, under the stars, and nothing but space and time stretching between us. It is perfect.

I stop and lean over the banister looking up at the stars. Kai steps up beside me, taking my hand with his and I look at him. He smiles at me and looks up at the stars. I do the same.

I can see everything. I can see the flares off the stars as they burn. Saturn light years away, hanging in the sky like a little sticker with rings. The moon. I breathe in awe. I can see every crater. I wish I could take a picture of this, but I have a lifetime ahead of me where I can see this any night

I wish. Every sound, every sight is enhanced and this is only the beginning. This is phenomenal.

"Ashiya run." I hear Kai say.

I turn to my left and see two dark figures standing in the shadows at the end of the wooden walkway. As soon as I see Kai pull out a long thin sword from the lining of his pants, I take off. I round on to the main street, cars barely driving by, our hotel six blocks down the road. I can see the lit sign of the Hilton from here. I open my ears listening out for anything - *anyone* in pursuit around and above me. Nothing. Just a few cars turning in the distance, a light changing, and a girl on her cellphone talking loudly inside her apartment overhead. It's hard to concentrate as other voices join in with hers. I shake my head to clear their voices from my head and pull back.

Adrenaline is pumping in my limbs, pushing me toward my destination. My body is screaming with the burn in my thighs and the hope that Kai is okay. God, please let him be okay. Please, if it is your will let him come back to us. I push harder knowing we only want to keep the baby safe. Four blocks. Three blocks away. That's the last thought in my head, when something hard collides into me and slams me up against a brick wall between two buildings away from the eyes of the main road by my neck. My heels connect with the brick wall as they dangle. My windpipe closed shut. I don't dare think this is my last moment as I stare in to the glowing caramel brown eyes of the male vampire in front of me.

I reach for my switchblade at the back of my dress and don't have the air to scream as the vampire grabs my wrist and snaps it. I clench my teeth together as the pain rips through my arm and I feel my wrist dangle at my side. Fresh tears flow down my face, as I pull my switchblade from the band of my dress with the other. I flip open the blade and at break neck speed slice open his skin at the wrist three times in a row, the bend in his elbow and across his neck severing his veins before he even knows it. I stumble as he drops me overcompensating on my heels and land hard on my broken wrist.

I look up from my crumpled position on the floor, as I watch him stumble back, shock in his eyes, a hand at his throat, his other arm limp and deteriorating from the bottom up, his skin littering the floor as it wilts away. I watch him, as he slowly becomes dust and debris in the wind.

As soon as I know he's gone I allow myself to finally breathe. My wrist is throbbing, on fire, but I don't allow myself to whimper or make a sound. A rush of heat flushes my body suddenly and everything goes quiet. I look up and around and I don't feel a thing as I see Kai come rushing in to the alleyway.

"Ashiya!" I hear him scream. He crouches down on the floor beside me and pulls me against him.

"Are you okay?!" he asks in a panic.

"I can't feel anything," I hear myself croak.

"What? What does that mean baby?" he asks, panicking even further. "Are you talking about the baby?"

I shake my head and watch as he sighs heavily in relief. His eyes search the alleyway floor catching the dead vampire's ashes and turns back to me. "Oh my God." He catches sight of my broken, swollen wrist.

"I can't feel it," I mumble trying to reassure him.

"Talk me through it, baby," he requests softly. "I can't move you unless I know something is wrong."

"Nothing's wrong. I was in pain then it stopped," I explain the simplest way I can.

Thinking it through instantly, I feel him run through a few causes of symptoms in his head, medical and vampire.

"The baby," he says partially to himself in a rush. "He or she cut off your nervous system. The part of your brain that feels pain. This sort of trauma isn't good for you or the embryo, so she or he took the discomfort away from you both."

"Come on. Let's get you back to the room," he says, picking me up the same way he did the other night I was attacked.

I come out of the bathroom dressed in my satin sleep romper after Kai washed the alleyway grime off of me, my injuries healed and long hair washed, damp, and cascading down my back. Kai looks up from his position at the end of the bed and he looks defeated. His shirt is undone, his sleeves rolled up from washing me in the tub, and his hair disheveled from running his hands through it too much. He's beating himself up over what happened.

"You okay?" he asks.

I nod my head. He nods his head in silent assurance and runs his hands through his hair for the umpteenth time I assume. I approach him and crouch down before him.

"Kai, I have vampires and who else knows what after me. You can't control what's going to happen and nor can we just *stop* living our lives. You took me out to celebrate our honeymoon and you're right we should be able to have this time. You didn't know this was going to happen. You didn't want it to and out of all the fifty states they're looking for an Ashiya Bride and they find us. It was bound to happen today, tomorrow, a month. It's okay, Kai."

His face scrunches up in rebuttal.

"I know. It's *not* okay," I respond. "A lot of things could have happened, but we're here. *We are here*."

Kai closes his eyes and exhales heavily.

"I want to kill every last one of them that are trying to hurt you or even *thinking* about hurting you. I only just got you back and now they're trying to take everything away from me," he says softly, trying to stay in control as he shakes, his eyes still closed.

"Kai, don't you think I feel the same way?" Kai opens his eyes and looks up at me in surprise, as I stand. "You told me I'd be nervous. Afraid to give in to the feelings my body is telling me. I may not remember a lot with us Kai, but I know I could have lost you tonight. I'm not afraid of what my body is telling me. I'm afraid of losing you and right now I need you."

The tears are swirling in my eyes, threatening to spill over and Kai pulls me to him straddling me onto his waist. He pulls my chin down to him kissing me with equal need and tenderness. My feelings for him burning inside my chest, I push his shirt from his shoulders and help him pull it off, throwing it on the floor. Eager to have me against him he takes the straps of my romper between his thumb and fore fingers and pull ripping my romper in half from my body.

I pull back with a smile and say, "This was my favorite."

"I know. That's why I have a second one at the apartment," he whispers against my lips, as I smile returning me back to his lips.

CHAPTER 6:
What Would Kwan-Min Do?

The crash of waves hitting the sand wakes me the next morning. I moan, turning over and grab Kai's BEATS from off my bedside table slipping them over my ears. I feel a familiar pool of warmth in my nose and jump out of bed rushing in to the bathroom. Kai rushes behind me and catches me push a wad of tissue under my nose to stop the bleeding.

He comes up to me pushing two fingers against the pulse in my neck and asks, "Can you feel this?"

I shake my head, 'No.'

"Your blood pressure is high," he says. "Keep your head level," and turns out of the bathroom.

"What are you doing?" I ask nasally, stepping out of the bathroom.

He grabs the phone from his side of the bed off his bedside table dialing a few choice numbers. "You need something to level you out. Your body is trying to adjust to the change and it's messing with your blood pressure."

I reach up to pull Kai's headphones off.

"No. Keep them on," Kai instructs. "Hi, I would like a bottle of your Big Red for room service. Yes, the Honeymoon Suite. Thank you," and Kai hangs up. He walks up to me and gently takes the tissue down from my nose inspecting if it's still leaking. Guessing it is, he walks around me into the bathroom and brings me back a fresh roll and replaces the sullied wad with it. He throws the used wad away and escorts me back to bed, slipping into bed with me.

"I'm sorry," I apologize.

"No need to apologize," Kai says, kissing the top of my head. "It's not your fault."

"Why did you order me wine?" I ask, starting to shake.

"Shhh," Kai hushes me. "Your body is in shock." And I curl myself in to Kai's body, as he wraps his arms tight around me.

Curled in to the passenger seat, as we drive back to Atlanta, I don't want to return from the ocean escape we called home for the brief weekend. But our home is in Atlanta and so is our lively hood, but then again so are *they*. Although we didn't get to cap off our Honeymoon, it turns out staying in bed all day was a good plan. I look over at Kai from my reclined position in my seat and take his hand resting between us on the center console, intertwining it in my own. Kai looks over at me from the road with a small smile and turns back.

In the short amount of time I've known him no amount of elixir or memory can tell me how I feel about him. I know. I *love* him. And the fact that we share some unknown past together makes it all the more exciting getting to know him all over again. It's a little scary our unknowns, but I wouldn't change it for the world. The not remembering could be the worst part, but it's not. It's not having control over your own body that is scary. I have to accommodate for this whole new being inside of me that isn't the baby. The vampire inside of me. The way I killed that vampire last night without blinking and without remorse. I can feel it getting stronger and stronger, closer every day to taking over and I like it. That's the scary part. Losing myself.

KAI

I walk in to the artillery shop jarring the bells hanging over the door. It's fairly brighter in here I notice without the crowd of buying bodies taking up the place. I let the door swing close behind me sounding the bells again casting the shop in its unusual darkness.

"Business a little slow, huh Kwan-Min?" I ask, approaching the man standing at the end of the glass display counter.

"I cleared it out just for you," Kwan-Min answers with a smile in his voice.

"Me?" I question. "What's the cause for occasion?"

I take notice of the place. Ashiya would like it here, a place come straight out of one of her novels. A warm coffee house vibe meeting the adrenaline jolting atmosphere of an underground arms ring. A conundrum at best with the swirling incense smoke in the air, the round tables in the back and endless assortment of guns in poly-glass cases. The swords, bows, staffs, and shields covering the dark marble sponge pressed walls with sharpeners, sheaths, knives, and daggers in glass display counters lining the front of the store - it wouldn't be hard to see why Ashiya would love this place.

"I believe a congratulation is in order with a pregnant wife at home," I hear Kwan-Min say, as I approach.

My body barely catches up with my mind, as I snatch a dagger up from the line of daggers across the counter he's stacking into a silver case and slam him against the countertop, pressing the dagger into his throat.

"How do you know about Ashiya?" I growl.

"Kai, you seem to forget my kind," Kwan-Min breathes. "We know many things."

"Your kind? I don't even know what you are. You just work for my clan," I say.

"Your ex-clan, you mean." Kwan-Min states.

"What. do you. know. about Ashiya?" I ask, digging the dagger in to his neck with each breath until I draw blood.

"That she is the future of the vampires and you're going to need my help if you want her and your children to survive!" Kwan-Min exclaims with a bark. "Now get this dagger out of my throat!"

I push off of him and wipe the knife against my pants and throw it back on the counter in line with the other daggers. Kwan-Min stands, straightening out his shirt with an angry tug, and turns back to the case going back to fitting the rest of the daggers in the case. We're both panting with concealed anger, but none more than me. I demand answers. I slam Ashiya's switchblade onto the counter beside him. I know he sees it, as I watch his jaw clench.

"This isn't your work. Who made this?"

Kwan-Min says nothing. I let him finish stacking the daggers into the briefcase. Closing the case shut and snapping the latches close, he turns to me holding it out to me.

"This is for Ashiya," he says.

With unhidden suspicion I take it from him.

He turns to Ashiya's switchblade on the counter and takes it in to his hands, opening it.

"This is my cousins work out of California," he says, studying the blade.

That's where Ashiya is from.

"The Blaizinium is hidden within the metal work purposely to create the illusion of a regular blade against any Hyper that may attack her."

"You and your family knew this was going to happen to her," I state matter of fact.

Kwan-Min looks at me. "Yes."

My eyes land on the blood stained around his neck. Then I realize he cleaned out his shop so that we could discuss Ashiya privately. I feel like an ass. I think back to how Kwan-Min used to look at me back when I was with my clan. He knew how things would end with them and then pick up with Ashiya. He and his family "*knew things*" and they protected Ashiya by giving her the switchblade. I roll my eyes to the ceiling knowing I was wrong and sigh heavily.

"I'm sorry about your neck, but I'm running out of people to trust."

"It's okay," Kwan-Min says, passing me back Ashiya's switchblade and I take it. "Your wife is a sensitive subject. I understand it all too well, especially given the circumstances."

I look at him, a moment of threadbare silence weighing between us.

"You've seen how important she is. What do I need to protect her?" I ask softly.

"You need Cassius and his team," Kwan-Min instructs. "They protected the Prince of the vampires -

"You know I hate that name."

Kwan-Min grins. "Well it's true, you were the Prince to the King of Darkness. It's only proper that protection be extended to the future Queen and your young."

"You make us sound like a wild animal observation off Animal Planet," I say, ignoring his statement.

"That's what we are, aren't we?" he asks, raising his eyebrows at me as if it's fact. "Wild animals in a racing underbelly only humans dream they could witness?"

I look away and roll my shoulders unwilling to answer that. Ashiya would understand that statement though. She was paying the price for it after all. I look back at Kwan-Min.

"Can I trust you?" I ask.

"This is what you ask me *after* I give you information to help you protect your wife?" Kwan-Min frowns with an astonished smile.

"A guy can never be too sure. After all, I still have a case of daggers in my hand."

"Your wife *is* a sensitive subject," Kwan-Min repeats monotonic. "I no longer work for the clan."

I observe his body language. Straightened shoulders, calm breaths, steady heartbeat. He's telling me the truth.

"I thought you and Marcus were besties."

Kwan-Min cut his eyes at me. "Don't ever say that," he quips with his characteristic clipped tongue. "We didn't see eye to eye."

"And that's all I need to know," I state, knowing his family's way with secrecy: meaning I'll never know why they didn't see eye to eye.

"Precisely," he states.

"Well, it's good I have you on my side."

"I always will be."

"Well, that wasn't cryptic." I smile. "Thanks, Kwan-Min." I turn for the door, heading out.

"Goodbye Kai, Prince of Vampires or shall I say *King*."

I sniff a laugh and turn around, as I walk backwards for the door.

"Shut up."

Kwan-Min smiles, as I push open the door and walk out.

ASHIYA

Lying across the plush white carpet of the living room, I wait for Kai to get home from the store. I'm glad Kai's apartment is the one place from my past and present I can come to and be "Ashiya" again. Where I can be as obscure and as invisible as I want to be, which is kind of ironic now that I'm becoming a vampire. Being obscure and invisible is all part of the package.

Thinking about what comes *with* that package resentment creeps into my heart gripping to the hilt of the vein. The gift that was supposed to make my life easier, worthwhile, has now put me in harm's way. All while I'm pregnant... with a man I barely remember, yet love. I couldn't be angry. Because as much as I wanted things to go back to the way they used to be, when I didn't have to worry about Supernaturals actually called *Hypernaturals* trying to kill me and nothing but deadlines, meetings, and events, I wouldn't change it. Not for knowing Kai, the baby we will have, and if I was listening to the little voice inside my soul: being a vampire. Even if I didn't see it now there was meaning to all of this.

Below me, the clear sounds of two teenage boys playing a fighting game two apartments below reach my ears. Closing my eyes, I listen closely.

"Yeees! Take it! Take it! Ken kicked your ass!" one exclaims.

"Whatever man! Do over!" the other retorts.

I chuckle at them and shake my head, as the crackle of ice dropping in the icebox from the freezer greets my ears.

65

I tilt my head towards the sound like collapsing bowling pins to my hypersensitive ears. I smile, taking in all the sounds around me, enjoying the power I have. Turning on my side, I look down the length of my outstretched arm and place a hand against my still flat stomach. Suddenly, the sound of footsteps coming down the hallway outside the apartment catch my attention and I sit up. Standing, I walk to the front door as the footsteps stop in front of it. I watch the doorknob, as I hear the slip of a key in the key slot and smile. The handle turns and the door slips open. Kai steps in and I launch myself into his waiting arms. Kai chuckles holding me up, a grocery bag in one hand, as I straddle his waist. I bend over and kiss him deeply, as he kicks the door closed behind us and makes his way into the kitchen. Placing the grocery bag down on the counter, he holds me up with both arms.

"I like this welcome," he teases, smiling up at me.

"You're getting ready to like it a little more," I entice him sultrily.

"You're insatiable," he states.

"I have three weeks to make up for," I say.

"So do I," he adds huskily. "Mianhe. I took a long time. I had to make a few stops along the way."

"It's alright," I return in Korean.

He places me down on the counter and takes my face into his hands, kissing me hungrily. Once again, just when it's getting good Kai pulls away. I sigh, as he pulls back and he smiles down at me reluctantly.

"I know." He sighs. "But I wanted to ask you something."

Sensing it's something important I sit up and listen.

He grins and says, "Move in with me."

"Yes," I say without hesitation, a smile covering my lips.

He chuckles, running a hand through his hair. "Good, cause no wasn't an option. I already have someone going over to fix your window I broke."

I sniff amused and roll my eyes, shaking my head at his assertiveness. Kai leans in close, as if to reward me with a continuation of that kiss, his breath warming my lips, when barely above a whisper he says, "You forgot your cellphone at your apartment."

He then reaches into his pocket and produces out my cellphone handing it over to me. Just as I'm about to place it down on the counter and continue where Kai was taking this, my cell decides to ring. Peering down at the display, I see 'Niani' flash across the screen. I look up at Kai and he presses a finger to his lips gesturing that he'll keep silent. I nod and answer my phone.

"Hey, I'm outside your apartment," Niani says over the line.

Kai's eyes lock with mine in alarm, obviously hearing her.

"Oh, I'm not home. I went out for a drive," I say, trying to keep the nerves out of my voice.

"Oh man! Boo! I came to visit you. Well, it's my fault. I should have called first." Niani sighs.

"I'm on the other side of town and I don't want you sitting there. Do you want to meet up somewhere?" I ask, meeting Kai's eyes for an okay.

Kai nods.

"Wow, that baby has you like the energizer bunny," Niani comments over the line.

Kai lifts his eyebrows at that and smirks.

"Yeah." I chuckle, playfully swatting a hand at him.

"But yeah, we can meet up somewhere. How about La Madeleine's?" Niani suggests.

"Yeah, that's fine," I agree.

"Alright," she says, finalizing our plan.

"Alright, I'll see you then," I reply.

I end the call meeting Kai with a smirk and he meets me with his own. Cupping his hands under my knees, he pulls me closer to him across the counter and takes the kiss he so previously wanted to give.

CHAPTER 7:
The Fairies Four

Thinking it's the moving men with my boxes, as I hear the doorbell echo through the apartment, I pull a shirt on over my head. The bedroom door swings open behind me and I look over my shoulder to Kai peeking his head in.

"Ashiya," he calls, nodding for me to follow him.

I follow him out of the bedroom to find four men with badges hanging from chains around their necks in civilian clothes standing in the middle of our living room. I look at them all the clean cut, intimidating sort of men you would expect involved in some highly classified, heavy stakes, off the government books agency. Kai comes around to me, placing a placating hand on my lower back sensing my nerves.

"Ashiya, this is Cassius, Z, Chief, and Tiberius," Kai introduces them to me in turn. "Agents a part of a private special forces unit under the Atlanta Police and Faeries or should I say Elementals," he says, giving the Faeries a look, "Faeries is more of an umbrella term," he adds.

I look at them. Cassius with his blue steel jawline and low cut blonde hair puts his right hand out for me to shake and I take it, shaking it gently. Z, next to him, with a buzz cut nods his head in gentlemanly fashion. Chief, big and brawny with dark warm brown hair spiked into a mohawk and a clean-cut beard with even warmer brown eyes steps forward and gives me a big bear hug. Then Tiberius, who appears to be about my age with short auburn hair pulled back into a low ponytail, he stares at me a moment before a small smile gives on to his face, but he otherwise says nothing.

Something sweet drifts into the room, cold like a winter's day and playful as a pixie dancing on the tip of my nose. I notice it's coming from Tiberius. I look at Kai and he looks at me already knowing. A mixture of scents join in with Tiberius' creating a powerhouse of confectionary coated aromas on my orifices senses. Honeysuckle, mocha, chai, juniper and it's coming from all of them.

I step back into Kai's side and I hear him say quietly into my ear, "I'll tell you later."

I tuck that in the back of my mind to hold him to and turn to the faeries four. "So, what do you guys specialize in?"

"Protection," Cassius answers, as if that was a given.
Of course.

"Don't mind him," Z states with a smile. "Think of us as your own personal secret service, Princess."

Kai jumps at that. "Let's not call her that."

That raises a few eyebrows. I look up at Kai and he refuses to meet my eyes. I step in front him forcing him to look at me and he finally meets my eyes.

"What don't I know?" I ask with a straight face.

"My moniker amongst my clan was 'Prince of the Vampires'. I was my leaders right hand man and protector, who was also known as the 'King of Darkness'. They - " He nods toward the Faeries Four, "were my protectors. *Faeries are all about formality.*" He cuts a look at the Faeries before him, at which he receives an inside grin from Chief.

"Therefore, I'm the Princess," I state.

"Yes." Kai nods.

Addressing the room again, Kai turns from me to the Faeries Four saying, "After the other night, we discussed you're not going out after nightfall," I nod, as he looks at me, "since that is when my clan does a lot of their Dealings. But we also talked about," He gestures to the Faeries Four, "the Hypers accessible to you during the day. And with me wanting to keep you safe, my patrolling, you working and I working, I'm not too proud to ask when I need some help," he says, directing to the faeries.

The faeries nod in agreement.

I nod understanding and turn to the Faeries Four. "Alright, you want to show the Princess what you can do?"

"I thought you'd never ask," Tiberius speaks up for the first time with a smug smile.

He reaches for a glass on the coffee table and turns to me.

"May I?" he asks.

"Go ahead," I permit.

He takes the glass in to his hand and holds it out in his palm. There is a stifling pause in the air as the glass suddenly collapses in on itself into a pile of sand, then builds itself bit by bit back in to the glass.

"I have control over earthly elements," Tiberius explains. "Using this I have the license to kill anyone who chooses to harm you."

His eyes hold a glint of pleasure at the thought. I have the horrible vision of an unfortunate vampire being disintegrated into dust just with the flick of Tiberius' wrist. I feel sorry for them, but then remorse runs cold in my heart for the unfortunate being. Their doing.

"Good," I say.

I have to account for that's the vampire speaking, because otherwise in my more compassionate mortal concern for life I wouldn't think, feel, or say that. *I'm never going to be the same again,* I think. Next, Cassius steps forward. He holds his palm forward hovering over my stomach. I step back in reaction.

"Careful Cassius," Kai warns.

I look up at Kai, as he stands calm watching Cassius. Cassius looks at Kai and pulls his hand back. As he does, I feel little sparks burst across the skin of my arms. He flips his hand out flat and I watch as electric blue currents jump from one finger to the next.

"Simply put, I can manipulate compression components in the air," he explains, as if it is meant to impress me.

"English Cassius," Chief quips behind him with a smirk.

"That sounded so much cooler." Cassius smiles at Chief over his shoulder. Chief smiles and Cassius turns back to me.

"I can produce and use electrical currents and shock waves from any conducting surface."

"Thunder and Lightning," I say, making it much more simpler.

"Right." Cassius smiles at me and steps back giving Chief the floor.

Chief lifts a thick muscular arm and a shiny cold metal substance coats his arm.

"Go ahead. Run a finger over it," he invites.

I run a finger over his metallic skin and feel a sharp knick cut my finger. I pull my hand back and watch as blood rolls down my middle finger. I look back down onto his arm and see even the hairs of his arm is coated with the metallic substance. I look up at Chief in awe.

"Metal." He smiles proudly. "I can be your human shield or most valuable weapon," he says in his southern drawl.

I smile. He can say anything and make it sound like southern charm. I turn to Z, as Chief backs up, curious of what he can do.

"Z's power is the most sensitive," Kai whispers in to my ear, backing us up cautiously.

A warning that his power can go dangerously and recklessly awry. Z lifts his hand tentatively, snapping his thumb and middle finger together and the stove pilots in the kitchen ignite without them being on. He snaps his fingers again and the fires grow taller reaching for the ceiling before dying out. In its wake is the smell of hot metal in the air.

"Now that is out of the way, Princess - ," Chief begins.

Before Kai can get a word out, Chief turns to him and states, "Shut up. I'm calling her that, so you can sail off with whoever else has a problem with it."

I laugh and Chief turns back to me. "How about we go grab your boxes downstairs and we get you settled in?"

"What?" I say dumbfounded. They had my boxes? But I thought Kai said he hired movers to get my things to slim the chances of me running in to Niani or any heavy lifting. *They* were the movers.

"The perks of being a Princess," he says with a wink and pats Tiberius on the shoulder for him to follow, as all the faeries file out to grab my belongings.

I sniff a laugh turning to Kai.

"I like them," I say.

Cassius and I step out into the hallway outside the apartment. Unable to stay in the apartment another hour unpacking my old life in to my new one I needed to get out. I volunteered to go get the guys some food and Cassius volunteered to come with me.

"Thank you again for your help," I thank Cassius, as I lock the door behind us. "I know moving my stuff isn't part of your job description."

"It's no problem at all. I'm willing to help anyway I can," Cassius says, as we turn down the hallway only to stop short seeing Niani standing midway down the hall staring at us. I wonder where she came from not hearing the ding of the elevator, when my eyes land on the emergency stair door swinging close around the corner from Niani's position. I was so caught up talking I didn't hear her walk up. What if we had said something she wasn't meant to hear?

She looks surprised as I approach her, Cassius right behind me and her eyes land on Cassius, the wheels in her head turning. Something pungently sweet permeates the air and I frown looking back over my shoulder at Cassius and see his eyes fixed on Niani. I look between the two of them, as they stare at each other. *Attraction,* I understand. Their scent, *arousal.* Go ahead, Niani. Caught you a nice one.

"Niani, this is Cassius. Mr. Jung's friend," I introduce them. "Cassius, this is my best friend and writing partner, Niani."

"Nice to meet you," Cassius smiles politely, holding out his hand to her.

She takes his hand delicately, as if she is afraid he's a mirage and shakes it.

"Nice to meet you," she says.

74

Cassius pulls his hand back and I watch Niani flinch just barely for it again.

"We better go, so we can get back," Cassius prompts, looking down at me.

I nod, agreeing.

"I'll see you later, Niani." I look at her following Cassius down the hall.

She doesn't say anything, as she watches us walk away, her eyes following us to the elevator.

"Can I ask you a personal question?" I turn to Cassius, as I close his truck door behind me.

"Yes, Princess," he permits, as he buckles himself in.

"Do you get to date that often in your line of work?"

He turns and looks at me. "Few and far in between," he answers honestly.

"I'm asking because I smelled you and Niani's attraction and - "

"Smelled us?" He chuckles in disbelief, covering a hand over his face.

"It's okay if you want to date her."

"You forget where I'm a Faerie agent and I create thunder and lightning for a living," he reminds me morose.

"It'll make the sex better." I shrug with a smile.

Cassius laughs and shakes his head, looking out his window. "Are you suggesting I tell your best friend what I do and what I am? Would you tell her what you've become?"

"If it came to that," I answer honestly.

"You might want to rethink that," Cassius warns, as he starts the engine. "The vampires have one rule and one rule only. If a human finds out about a vampire they have two choices: either they change or they're dead."

75

"And faeries don't have that rule?" I inquire.

"There is a lot more liability when it comes to a human knowing about a vampire. Other species don't have that issue."

"Blood lust," I answer my own question.

"Yup," Cassius pops his lips with the word.

"What other species are there besides us?"

"Draegos to the community also known as LongShen - dragon souls inhabiting a human body,"

I nod, remembering my research in to Chinese mythology for a previous novel.

"Phoenix, Cupids, Shatans - Shaman like Witches," he explains. "Anthrodynamai -"

"Humans with miraculous power?!" I ask, frowning.

"You know your Greek," Cassius says impressed. "They're the human basis of the Greek mythos."

"So, they're Greek g-"

"Yes, but don't call them gods. They don't like that. They have a long name so we just call them Greeks, and lastly we have Mermaids."

"What? No werewolves?" I ask.

"Fiction," Cassius answers in one word.

"So, what's our origin story? Where did we come from?"

"You've already written it." He looks at me from the road.

My mouth drops open.

"Vampires *actually* come from a resurrection spell gone wrong creating a living zombie able to drink blood *and* stay frozen at the age of death for eternity?" I ask in disbelief.

"Sounds far-fetched, but makes so much sense, huh?" he questions rhetorically.

"The same goes for what I wrote about Faeries?"

"Close enough. Instead of being created from the elements, we were created *with* the elements in order to protect the earth."

"It doesn't sound like there is much of a difference." I laugh.

"When you look at it *that* way. Yes." He chuckles, as we pull up in front of Thai Spice and park.

The restaurant looks packed from the outside with its Friday afternoon rush as Cassius and I approach the door.

"You're here for pick-up?" the hostess asks, as Cassius and I enter.

"Yes," Cassius answers. "Under Cassius."

"It'll be ten more minutes," she says, looking up from her notes.

"No problem." Cassius smiles. "Thank you."

The hostess smiles and we take a seat on the waiting booth by the door.

I watch Cassius' eyes trail over the restaurant looking for any sign of threat that bringing a question to my mind.

"What was Kai like in the clan?" I ask, as a server brings me the check. I place my card inside the booklet and he takes it away.

Cassius turns to me with a surprised frown on his face, as if to ask me why would I want to know that? I'm shocked by his sudden reaction. As if to check his expression, he looks down at his hands thinking back on it with a slight frown.

"He was hard before he met you. *Cold*," he answers, tapping his thumbs together.

I peer up at him sympathetically. He's wearing the same guarded expression Kai gets when he's talking about his clan. Whatever happened then must have been a really dark time for them. I feel sorry I brought it up.

"But that wasn't his fault," Cassius continues ominously, but more to himself. He looks up ahead of himself staring at a time far beyond us. I sit with him in silence wishing I could see what he's seeing.

"Did Kai tell you Z, Tiberius, Chief, and I are his God brothers?" he asks suddenly, changing the subject.

I whip my head around at that information. "No, he didn't tell me that!" I exclaim in surprise.

"Yeah," he answers. "We became like brothers inside the clan. So close, we made it official."

I smile at that knowledge. "You guys keep this protecting gig up and you'll end up Godfathers next."

Cassius smiles at me at that. I'm glad it can put a smile on his face, especially after the previous subject.

"Here we are," a voice rings out, as a server comes up carrying a large bag containing our food and my card and copy of receipt.

"Thank you," Cassius says, taking the bag from him, as I write the tip in on the server's copy of the receipt.

"Have a good day," the hostess and server call after us, as we head out the door.

"Thank you, you too." I smile back at them, as the door swings closed behind us.

As we climb back into the truck, Cassius buckles in and asks, "I know it's only been a week or so for you, but how are you doing with all this?"

I look over at him and I'm not sure how to answer that. The first thing I think about is that Kai should be asking me this. I scrunch up my face confused. It's a simple enough question, but the words don't come. How have I been doing since all of this? I've been taking everything in stride, one day at a time, trying not to be afraid to step outside my front door, focusing on my relationship with Kai, and my desire to protect the baby. After the other night, it let me know I am literally surrounded by Hypers. I've been adjusting...

I -

My chest tightens in frustration.

"Hey." Cassius looks down at me concerned. "What just happened here?"

"I'm sorry," I say, my voice coming out stronger than the tight coil in my chest should allow. "I just can't help but feel like I'm missing something here or out of my depth. I feel like I should know all *this* already."

"You may have technically wrote the book, but don't put all this in one basket. You'll get to know this world soon enough. Kai felt like this as well when he first joined his clan. The fact that you're being hunted is only making the feeling worse."

"That's what I'm worried about - *time*. I'm due in a week and 8 months and I would like this stopped before I bring my baby into this world with a noose around my neck."

Cassius stares at me sympathetically and stops the car.

"I'll make a promise to you." He turns to me. "We'll stop this before you bring this baby into the world. We have *a looot* of Hypers to get through." I chuckle. "All I ask for is your patience. Can you do that for me?" He takes my hand in his.

I smile. "Yes." I nod.

"Good. We'll take care of you Ashiya," he assures me.

"I know," I say, knowing in my heart that they would. All three of us.

CHAPTER 8:
Lie To Me

1848

"Papa no!" I screamed, grabbing for the rifle in his hand.

Indra stumbled back from his position at the bottom of the porch, his hands held up in mercy.

"Get in the house Amita!" Father bucked me off of him. "Stay away from my daughter creature!" he yelled at Indra.

Indra stayed, his grey blue eyes strong staring down my father, his hands raised in defiance.

Suddenly, my father took the shot catching Indra in the shoulder. I screamed, as Indra fell to the sand floor holding his shoulder, blood bleeding into the fabric of his cotton shirt. I ran to him, but my father caught me around the waist dragging me back in to the house.

"Indra!" I screamed, my fingers scraping against the doorframe, as I fought against my father's grasp.

I startle myself awake and turn looking over my shoulder at Kai lying next to me asleep. He has an arm tucked underneath his head and the other reached out towards me once draped over my hip. I feel relief flood me knowing the dream isn't real, but yet felt real. I can still hear the sound of the bullet as it drove through the barrel and ripped through Indra's flesh.

In the dream Kai was Indra. I could see the distinct back and forth flip of ethnicities in my head, as if my mind was trying to make an emotional connection. Indra's curly silky hair switched for Kai's short thick curtain of satin. Indra's golden copper skin for Kai's soft warm tan and I, Amita. Her slightly olive skin, long ebony hair, and rich blue eyes. I remember Indra's/Kai's eyes. Their burning desire to prove to Amita's father that he won't easily walk away from her. Amita's fight to get to the man she loves.

The effects of my own reality bleeding into my dreams. Me not wanting to lose Kai and not wanting him to lose me. It was hopeless, I think, as I look down at Kai. My dreams were a constant source of my fears and desires to spur on change in reality. But now I guess I can blame my pregnancy. It was common knowledge that women often have strange, vivid dreams while pregnant. I just hope in the case of the last week it has nothing to do with us.

"So, what brought you over to Mr. Jong's yesterday?" Niani asks, as she comes into the office balancing a plate with a peanut butter and jelly sandwich in one hand and a full mug of creamy coffee in the other. Not an appetizing combination I note, as she takes a seat carefully behind her desk.

"I was coming to the office, when we ran into each other and he asked me in for tea," I lie.

"Is he the baby's father?" she asks suddenly.

I balk at her question and turn looking at her incredulously. "Mr. Jung?!"

"No. Cassius," she clarifies.

Wooh, I sigh mentally in relief.

"It's just that I overheard your conversation yesterday and it had me thinking maybe - "

"No." I scoff, as if it is the craziest question in the world. "He was helping me move some stuff since Mr. Jung had to run to the hospital."

I look at her face and see the relief mixed with a soft smile. I quirk a smile at her obvious crush on the faerie agent. "I told him it was okay if he wanted to date you."

"Thanks, Ashiya. Just what I needed my best friend giving the man I'm interested in permission to date me," she says sarcastically.

"Well, it was more of a push. He was sort of reluctant giving to the fact that his best friend is interested in me and he's interested in you... You can see where this gets complicated?" I point out.

"Naturally," she says derisively with a shrug, as she takes a bite out of her sandwich in between both hands.

I smile. You can see why we're best friends.

"So, after this coming from the best friend you're still not willing to give Dr. Hottie a chance?" she then asks slyly.

A cut her a look. "This is not about me, so shove it," I bite softly.

"I'm just trying to push you through the right door. Don't kick me for it," she quips.

I smile and gather the casting files on my desk. As I tap them into a neat stack, I confess, "He knows about the baby and he understands why I choose to keep my distance. For now, we agreed to be friends." I slide a bit of my own truth in there. If ever she found out what I am, we would stay friends and she would understand I kept it from her to protect her.

"Oh?" she sighs softly, her shoulders sagging in sympathy and disappointment. "I'm sorry."

"Don't be," I reassure her. "Anyway, I get to live vicariously through you. You're going on a date with Cassius when he asks," I order.

"You mean *if* he asks," she corrects me, pointing her half eaten sandwich at me.

"He will." I smile, turning to my bookshelf.

On each shelf was a single signed edition of one of my novels along with every book that I have ever got an idea from or was inspired by for a story. I could see colorful post it notes peeking out from between the pages with my frantic scribbles written across the leaflets. Seeing it always makes me smile. The work that went in to creating these works and the admiration I hold for the authors that inspire me.

The last book on the shelf, the one most recently added to the library was a book on Asian mythology. Somehow, all of these books have led me right to this moment. A daylight vampire with some miraculous knowledge of this underworld I never touched until eight months ago. Placing myself in the very shoes of the characters I write about. I wonder what makes me so special to know about any of this at all? I turn away from the shelf before I can start to go in to theories. That wouldn't bode well with the pressure of my already dire situation.

Cobalt Blue.

Pale Blue.

The melding colors suddenly flash in front of my eyes. An aura signature. Another one of my vampire abilities, Kai explained called, *Auricpathy*, the ability to see and sense aura signatures. A light prickle pinches in my chest and before my body can fully catch up my eyes fly to the doorway. Niani follows my eyes questioning, just as the doorbell rings. Looking back at me, Niani and I both get up and walk to the door to answer.

Niani opens the door to reveal Kai on the other side holding grilled sandwiches neatly wrapped in wax paper. Too fast for Niani's human eyes to see Kai's eyes flick to mine with a wink, before falling back on Niani.

"Mr. Jong! Hey!" Niani exclaims.

"Hey. I made Paninis for lunch and thought I'd bring some over for you both," Kai explains.

"He cooks," Niani says, sending me a sideward glance with a suggestive smile.

I ignore her, throwing Kai a polite smile and step aside, letting him in.

"Couldn't stay away?" I ask with a smile, throwing away the wrappers from our sandwiches in the trash in the kitchen.

"I came to see my wife at work," Kai says simply, closing the refrigerator door behind him with the jug of apple juice in his hand.

I look over at Niani not so secretly watching us from the living room. I turn and grab a glass out of the cabinet holding it out to him.

"Just admit it. You missed me," I say quietly, my mouth barely moving to Niani's human eyes, but clearly enough for Kai to hear me.

Kai looks from the glass to me with an appreciative smile and takes it pouring some juice up to half glass and places the top back on the jug. I take the jug and place it back on the refrigerator shelf, as the doorbell rings and watch Niani out of the corner of my eye get up and answer it. As soon as I close the refrigerator door, I'm pushed up against it and kissed without an ounce of sense. I can taste the apple juice on Kai's tongue and that serves as the best aphrodisiac, as Kai's fingers touch the bare skin of my stomach under my rising shirt.

"I missed you both," he whispers against my lips, as he pulls away. "I -"

"Three weeks to make up for. I know. Just kiss me," I whisper back bossily and that's all that is needed for Kai to comply.

My senses are on overdrive. The taste of apples burst on my tongue. The electrical currents through the wires in the walls buzz in my ears. The hairs on my arms stand on end. My skin on fire. The scent of Kai's arousal. It's enough to make me go crazy. Literally. I feel the vampire awaken, her need to get closer to Kai. *Intimately* closer. My K9's elongate on their own accord. The rush of the first taste of his blood pulses in my gums. I snake my way to the spot between his neck and shoulder and - *bite*. The weight of Kai's body pins me to the fridge, as he moans with the pleasure my bite gives him. In the back of my mind Niani walking in on us is a distant concern.

I can feel his body awaken with every spasm of pleasure coursing through him. His thumb presses into the pulse in my wrist, as his fingers wrap around my wrist in a loving grip. The contrast of the cold fridge against my hot skin is ecstasy. Yes, I want him to take me right here. Right now, fangs and all. I push away from him feeling high, my head lying back against the fridge, as I lick his blood from my lips. Kai leans off of me, our pants intermingling as we stare at one another. This is what being drunk in love feels like.

"The baby likes us like this," I say, feeling that heat in my stomach again.

Kai smiles, getting down on both knees before my stomach and lifts my shirt up a little saying, "Well baby, I like us like this too," running his fingertips tenderly over my skin and kisses my stomach.

"I love you," I say, looking down at him.

Kai looks up at me from his position on the floor, all his love written in his eyes.

"Are you serious?!" We hear Niani exclaim from the front entrance.

Kai and I look at each other and rush into the foyer front. I should have known. His sharp cologne is the first thing I smell. Niani and William turn around, facing us, as we enter the foyer.

Niani bounces over, grabbing me by my arms and gushes, "Fame Squared wants me to work with them on the idea of *Reign* becoming a video game!"

I look over at William to see if this is true, only to catch him staring stone livid at Kai behind me. Kai lifts a hand to the small of my back, fingers running over my bare skin releasing protection and claim into his touch. I smile at Kai's quiet promise and turn my attention to Niani. Over my head, I feel the non-verbal dispute going on between Kai and William.

"They really want to turn Reign into a video game?" I ask William, turning him away from his silent argument with Kai.

William turns to me immediately.

"All they need is both of your say so. Since Niani is the Illustrator for the books and site, and they know she has a game design background they wanted to work with her closely," William explains.

I look at Niani's excited face. It's been her dream to work with Fame Squared since high school. I can't say no.

Anyway, it would be amazing to see *Reign* as a game. If it's anything like God of War, that is.

"Let's do it," I say sure.

Niani jumps up and down like an over excited child.

"Do you have a card or something, so we can get in contact with them?" I turn to William.

William draws a card out from the front pocket of his suit jacket and hands it to me sliding his fingers under mine seductively, as he pulls away. I pull away with a painful jerk, as a sharp pain rips through my fingers to my forearm and look at William as if I could punch him on reflex. Behind me, I feel Kai start angry going for William. I grab his hand at my back, holding him there. Cutting a look at William, I see him taunting Kai with his eyes as if to ask, "*What are you going to do about it?*"

My vampire scratches under my skin like an itch. *Retribution,* she screams. It's etched into my skin. I look down at the card and hand it to Niani all without looking at her, my eyes on William. It's only been a day and I'm already tired of hiding Kai and I's marriage.

"How about you call them and set up a meeting?" I suggest.

Seemingly unaware of the ensuing fight in front of her, Niani bounces on her heels excusing herself from the foyer. I can feel the blood pressure in the room rise as Niani exits. I still haven't let go of Kai's hand at my back and I can feel his anger feeding through me like hot tar through a funnel. The air is too tight, too quiet and I want it to end. Kai and I move as if on one accord. I step back and he steps forward, bumping into each other. I turn apologizing and Kai catches me at the forearm.

"Didn't you say you had to get back to the hospital?" I ask, acting as if it's suddenly important.

Catching on, Kai looks down at his watch as if pressed for time.

"Ah, you're right. I have to get back," he says, looking back up at me from his watch.

"I'll walk you out," I say and turn around to William. "I'll be right back to discuss the casting."

William nods, though he's not okay with it. I watch his eyes land on Kai's hand still wrapped around my forearm then lift to my eyes. If I could make it any clearer that I belonged to Kai right there, I couldn't. I turn my eyes from him and turn for the door, Kai in tow.

We couldn't risk it as much as we both wanted to throttle him. The less he and Niani know about Kai and I the better for both their lives. Today is a test to what I'm going to do about them and how I'm going to handle this situation with them. Either of them being remotely involved with me could get them hurt and I can't think of anything else to do *except* lie to them. It's not going to be easy, but it can be as long as I act like nothing has changed for them, like me telling Niani I wanted to wait until my second trimester before telling my family about my pregnancy. I didn't need her asking questions about whether or not I told them or accidentally blurting it out. The same goes for my family. What they don't suspect, I won't have to explain away. It would break me if anything happened to them. I can't bring this in to their lives.

Stepping through the glass door out in to the parking garage, Kai turns to me with cool angry steel grey eyes.

"If he touches you one more time, I'm breaking his hands," he threatens.

"Don't worry. I might beat you to it," I reassure him.

Kai checks his watch again.

"Alright, I really have to get going now." He sighs, looking back up at me. "Tell Niani, I'm sorry. I didn't get to say good-bye. I had to get back to the hospital and - I love you." Leaning down, he kisses me sweetly.

"I love you, too," I tell him, as he backs up and lifts his head with a nod to something over my shoulder.

I turn around and see Cassius leaning against the doorframe to the garage. So, Cassius is on duty today. He smiles at me. I smile at him and look over my shoulder at Kai, as he climbs in to his BMW i8 with a grin and soon pulls off.

I make it back to the office apartment, barely getting the door closed behind me, when a knock sounds at the door. I pull the door back open to find Cassius on the other side.

"Cassius?" I question. I thought he was going to stay in Kai and I's apartment?

He steps inside and I close the door behind him. As if his name was enough to conjure her presence Niani pops in to the foyer.

"Cassius?" she calls.

Cassius' eyes travel from their distrusting glare on William as he walks into the foyer from the living room to Niani with softness. My eyes roam back to William glaring at Cassius as if he's another rival vying for my heart. I hurriedly push Cassius aside and ask softly, "Cassius, what are you doing here?"

"I have to check out everyone that's in your life," he answers looking over my shoulder at William, "and I don't like the way he looks at you," he says haughtily.

"He has a crush on me," I say exasperatedly.

"You want me to do something about it?" he asks too excitedly, his green eyes brightening with the question.

"No, you can't strike him with lightning," I order, though the thought is amusing.

Cassius looks at me weird, as I say that. "I wasn't thinking about it, but okay...," he says slowly with a frown.

"Well, I won't stop you. Do your duty," I concede, stepping aside.

Cassius looks up at William and approaches him.

"I'm Cassius. You must be William. Ashiya told me about you," Cassius says, holding out his hand.

I look over at Niani who's eyeing me with closeted hurt and suspicion in her eyes at seeing how close Cassius and I are. She thinks I may have lied to her or Cassius likes me. *No.* I try to tell her with my eyes, but I have a feeling Cassius and William's next words may clarify that.

"And how do you know Ashiya?" Williams asks interrogatively, taking Cassius' hand and shaking it.

"I'm her protection detail until filming is over," Cassius states with authority.

"And when did the studio assign you?" William asks, that statement obviously striking a chord.

"Oh no, I was assigned by someone much higher to watch over Ashiya," Cassius answers curtly.

Niani frowns curious and looks over at me, I most likely wearing the same expression. He even makes me believe he was hired by someone much higher. I frown myself and look at the two as Cass and William stand hands gripped at a stalemate. There is a pause in the air as I feel the air change, warming - then William snatches his hand out of Cassius' as if - *struck by lightning.* I roll my eyes in exasperation. Cassius backs away and turns to me with a smile and winks. I act like I didn't see that and turn to William.

"William, you wanted to go over the casting?" I ask, pulling my attention away from Cassius.

"Yes," William says, sending a hard glance back at Cassius. "It was nice meeting you Katni- Cassius. I'll be seeing you around."

"See you around," Cassius replies, way too cheerful for my liking.

William follows me into the living room and I act like I don't notice Niani stays back in the foyer with Cass.

CHAPTER 9:
Cognitive

Once again, I had writer's block for the third day in a row. This isn't something an agent wants to hear, when it comes to business and deadlines. But no matter what when I sit in front of my computer to type nothing comes forward like all the words are compressed in my head, but can't be released. Walking up to the door of Barnes & Nobles I grab the door handle and pull the door open almost crashing into a young Korean man walking out, as I walk in. Handsome is the first adjective that comes to mind when I see his face. He peers down at me equally and says, "Sorry," simultaneously with me. He bares a charming grin and walks around me without another word. I look back at him, as he walks down the sidewalk toward the parking lot and I step inside an idea for my book already forming inside my mind.

Walking into Starbucks, I get into the line forming its way through the tables and corrugate displays. I reach down in to my purse and pull out my wallet seeing the sun's rays blaring through the window out of my left eye. Squinting, I look up at the window, my eyes quickly catching on to the occupied table sitting in front of it. The young man sitting there flips a page of the magazine he's reading and brings it down just enough for me to see the person behind it. It's the Korean guy. *He looks up at me from over the magazine and closes the magazine in one hand keeping his place, saluting me with that charming smile. I smile in return and step up in line, eyeing the menu behind the counter to keep from looking back at him, attraction strong in my chest.*

I grab my purse from the passenger seat and climb out of the car. I lock the car behind me and make my way toward the parking garage door, when I notice someone in the garage with me. Coming to a stop, surprised, I look into the face of the young Korean man walking away from his car. Once again, he smiles and this time walks toward me.

"Alright destiny, I give in," he says aloud jokingly, waving his hands in the air as if telling the world to bring it on, as he approaches me.

I giggle at his words, when he stops in front of me.

"Hi, I'm Kai," he introduces himself, putting a strong hand out.

"I'm Ashiya," I reply, placing my hand in his.

"Well Ashiya, can I take you to lunch?" Kai asks me.

It was an unusual request then, usually some said dinner, but lunch sounded good.

"Yes," I answer, giving him my number to call me on and there we were. That started it all.

Out the window, I watch the Atlanta traffic inch its way through the morning fog. Glad I'm not out there right now.

"You okay?"

Kai comes up behind me, sliding his hands over my bare stomach, his cheek resting against my temple. Folding my hands over his, I lean back in to the warmth of his body. Our bodies are still moist with sweat from exercising. A practice I gained from my father, but still continue with Kai. I love the fact that we share a love for keeping in shape. A ranking master in many martial arts, one such as Kuk Sool Won, Kai can't let his body go even for a minute. It's too engrained in his mind and trust me I don't mind. His body is phenomenal.

93

For me, something I've been doing since I was sixteen, belly dance and yoga is a big part of my life. Both centering and evocative, it's less vigorous and low impactive on my now pregnant form, yet beautiful on my body. Kai kisses me on my neck bringing me back to his arms. Turning around in them, I hook my thumbs into the low waistband of his drawstring pants tugging them a little lower.

"I'm okay. I was just remembering how we met for the very *first* time." I smile.

"But that's not all is it?" Kai asks, knowing.

"No," I answer, "I'm concerned about Niani and William.

"They're here. They're in my life and no one I know is safe, as long as these Hypernatural clans want me dead or undead. They will use them to get to me and I can't have that."

Kai takes my face in his hands and raises it from level with his bare chest in to his eyes. He sighs heavily.

"Baby, I can't promise you that they won't. But what I will tell you is if you want me to I will extend Cassius' team to watch over them. Your family -" He looks troubled looking for ways to keep everyone in my life safe, but with no one in our corner to do so.

I pull his hands down from my face. "It's okay. My family will be fine. You're not the only one with a few guardians around." I smile trying to be optimistic.

Kai smiles knowing what I'm getting at in the terms of faith and pulls me in holding my head to his chest.

"If my clan wants you they won't use anybody to get to you. They'll do it on their own terms," Kai explains.

"And what are their terms?" I ask softly.

"They do it alone."

I turn my head pressing my face into his chest not caring that he is still sweaty. So, in the case that the other clans follow the same set of rules my friends and family may be safe for now. But it's a maybe I can't afford. What if they get impatient? I don't see them waiting forever to have me dead. I turn back around in Kai's arms facing the window.

"Okay," I sigh, trying to let go of what I obviously couldn't control.

After a moment of silence, I ask, "Do you think I'll develop a stronger thirst for blood with me being pregnant?"

Kai lifts his head from my shoulder, but doesn't move away from me.

"No. Only night vampires have a stronger need for blood. I'm sure you would have exhibited it by now if you did. Night vampires have a different digestion system from us. They can't eat regular food and must drink blood on a regular basis, whereas you've seen we don't have to," Kai explains.

Pulling out of Kai's arms, I turn around to him.

"We're really that different?" I ask compassionately.

"Yes," Kai answers distantly.

But just as quick, he pulls himself out of his thought and looks at me. I don't even think he was talking to me anymore.

"How different are we?" I ask, pulling up to him.

I want to know everything there is to know about what I'm dealing with. If I'm ever in a position where I have to protect myself and my unborn child knowing what sets me and my enemies apart is what I will need. Kai looks down at me about to speak, when he suddenly ducks around me looking up out the window and I follow his eyes to the sun above us. Kai pulls back around before me and takes my arms into his hands.

"Can I tell you about it later? My lunch break?" he asks in a rush.

"Yeah," I answer, knowing he has to get to the hospital. Then it dawns on me that he was checking the sun for the time. Just as I'm about to ask him about it, my cell phone rings and I rush over to the couch grabbing it from the arm. I look over at Kai as I answer it and he nods to our bedroom letting me know he's going to go get ready. I nod in return listening to my agent talk.

"Hello?"

"Hey," I say, loud enough for Niani to hear me through the speakerphone, as I drive. "I'm just calling to let you know I'm not coming in to the studio today."

"Where are you?"

"On the way to see our agent. I have a translation assignment. As soon as I pick up the manuscript I'm going to start on it, so I'll be out of the studio," I answer.

"Okay," Niani says. "I'll see you tomorrow then."

I can hear the hesitation in her voice. The worry. This is the second day in a matter of three I've made an excuse not to come in to the office.

"Alright, I'll see you tomorrow," I say, adding extra liveliness in to my voice to pacify her concern.

"Alright," Niani says, then dead air fills the car.

Coming to a stop at a red light, I press the call off. It's true. I have a translation job to do and I've already been by to see our agent, the manuscript laying here by me in the passenger seat, but after that memory this morning I want to explore what other memories I can bring up. Most of

Kai and I's romance started here in Atlanta, so something here must drag up.

Gold plated words forming 'Noni's Bar & Deli' catch my attention and its recognition makes me keep on the break, as the car at the light before me goes. An almost hidden brick building attached to a brick alleyway connected to another aligns the road with other establishments shining like a beacon telling me, 'You Are Here'. Immediately, I pull over and get out of the car. Tiberius pulls over himself a couple of cars down and gets out.

"What's going on, Princess?" he asks concernedly, looking around the vicinity, as he makes his way over to me.

"Nothing. Just a memory," I answer.

The sight of the building sends my mind reeling to another time.

"Hey, you're on your way?" I ask in to my cell phone, standing outside what I dub 'Club Noni' on a Saturday night.

"Meet me on the floor," Kai says over the line, his voice huskier than ever.

In the next few minutes, I find myself easing through the sea of bodies toward the middle of the dance floor.

Music taking over me, I move to the music my arms raised above me hips swaying to the music. Hands slip over my middle seductively until strong arms wrap around me completely. On time with the bass, Kai spins me around to him. Green laser lights dance over us, as we lose ourselves to the track and in each other.

I come back to myself. The sweat and vibrations from that night still cling to me like a second skin. So much that I run a hand up my arm just to feel if it's there. The skin is still warm and dry in the low sunlight. The memory doesn't surprise me as much as I think it should. The me I've seen over the week is so different from who I used to be.

I used to be so caught up in my work. No time for dating or the rare case of going out, which was always on the whim of Niani. No time for fun, when you're making a living. Not until Kai walked into my life. It was something about him that inspired me to get out of the box that was myself.

Growing up my mom and I never had the best relationship. We were too completely different people. Where I was the dreamer, she was the realist. The way I thought, the way I did things were too different from her. One could guess if she and I even stayed in the same house.

Even when she was there, she wasn't. If I was in one room, she was in the next. Anything was a cause for argument. It was like she would bring things up just so she could drive me down a few pegs or make it known I was wrong or make me feel naive. She found joy in it. I was her nerve, her scorn, and her punching bag.

I remember when I was fifteen, she brought up if I had forgiven my uncle some time after he had cheated on my aunt and I said "yes". I didn't see the need to keep punishing him to go along with my family, who were still band against him. Yes, I was hurt by what he did, but he was family. I was close to both him and my aunt and I hurt for my aunt, but I couldn't keep going on something I had already forgiven and forgotten. They were separating and if they could find ways to move on, so could I. My mom said I deserved – no she *hoped* – to have a man do that to me, so I would know how it feels and have a friend continue to converse with the person who hurt me.

It's no secret to anyone that I'm more like my father, a free spirit and an optimist. I was in high school when my parents separated and it only strained my mother and I's relationship further. I reminded her too much of him and therefore took a lot of her frustrations. My dreams and wants for myself were shut down and criticized like I was incapable or it wasn't good enough. Everything I wore was me trying to be someone else or some*thing* and I never understood her animosity towards me. She made me feel like there was something wrong with me. So after a while I gave up. I became the person she could be proud of. I became her. Gone was the girl who streaked her hair the colors of the rainbow and dressed eclectically, but only keeping a piece of myself that made me, *me*. My writing.

By the time my parents got back together I was an empty shell of my former self. It was only when I left for college and returned to visit did me and my mom's relationship become somewhat cordial, but I found myself again. Then when I met Kai, he became the reason to put this rekindled spirit into him. I remember when I told him about my mother and me - and the thought startles me. Another memory. I pull out my cellphone, glancing at the time, and hit Kai's number on speed dial. After a couple of rings he picks up.

"Hey. Guess where I'm at?" I say.

"I don't know. You tell me," he says across the line playfully, sounding like he's getting in his car.

"Noni..." I reply.

"I'm just getting off. On my way," he says huskily, his voice reminiscent of that night.

"Alright. See you soon," I say and hang up.

Soon enough – a five minute or so drive from Grady - Kai is getting out of his car releasing Tiberius with a nod and standing next to me. We look at Noni, the memory of that night passing between us. Then I recall that Kai has an hour break for lunch. We need to get going. I slip my hand into his and squeeze. He looks down between us and smiles up at me.

"Let's get you some lunch," I say.

"Okay," Kai says, as he pulls up to me, taking the back of my head and leans down kissing me on my forehead.

Jumping in my car, I watch in my rearview mirror Kai get into his car before starting my engine.

Walking in to Cafe Intermezzo, Kai and I pass a party of four college students sitting at a corner table scouring over textbooks, notes, and open laptops scattering the table. As we pass, I feel their eyes lift up to us. I don't hear them say anything, as we take a seat at a table for two by the window, but I feel their eyes turn to each other confirming some uncertain knowledge.

Already knowing what we're going to order when our waitress comes over to take our drink order, I chance a glance over my shoulder at them checking to see if they're still looking. They're locked in their books. I turn back to our waitress giving her my full order and then she's off again to greet another table just seated in her section. My eyes fall back on the table once again, before I turn back to Kai. I'm not being paranoid. They may be just students, but I feel something about them. My senses tell me as much. I may not have Kai's clan after me in the daytime, but I still have the others and those stares mean something.

"So, back to our conversation this morning. How different are we?" I ask, getting back to business.

Kai looks at me and says, "It's not a question of how different are we, but how different we are from them." I frown, wondering what that means. "Have you ever noticed how our skin has a glow to it compared to those who attacked you that night?"

"Yeah." I nod, glancing down at the golden glow underneath the skin of my arm only Kai and I seem to notice. "Their skin had a darker glow. A bluer tone."

"Exactly. It's almost as you wrote. Think of our skin as having more melanin. We can go all day in the sun without it bothering us. Where if my clan went in to the sun, their skin would boil and blister until they burn alive."

"What a beautiful image," I snark.

Kai quirks his eyebrows curtly in agreement.

"This morning were you checking the sun for the time?" I ask.

Kai's smirk stretches into a smile.

"Yeah. That's another thing we are able to do. We have a built-in clock, where we are able to look at the sun or moon and be able to tell what time it is. It's weird. I can't explain it." Kai shrugs his shoulders.

I breathe a laugh.

"Only night vampires can tell by the moon, as you may have guessed."

I nod.

"The Blaizinium daggers I brought you from Kwan-Min," he goes on. I nod. "In the world of Supernatural lore we're all allergic to some metal, like faeries iron, werewolves silver, but luckily on equal playing field in our world we're all allergic to one metal, Blaizinium. That is except for me and now you." He nods his head, gesturing to my stomach. "The worse the wound, the quicker the death. A Hyper can stave off the effects of Blaizinium by flushing it out of their system, but only if the wound is benign enough."

I lean across the table, curiously.

"But how do you control something like that? If every Hyper is in the danger of being killed by Blaizinium how doesn't every clan have their hands on it?" I ask.

"Because like guns, it is a controlled substance if not *more*. That's why there is only one family that deals in it."

There is something in his words that gives me a foreboding feeling, as if this information is going to play a factor in something in the future.

I nod taking it all in, as our waitress brings up our entrees and places them down before us. All conversation is cut as we start in on our plates. Every now and again, I catch one of the students at the table look over at us, as we eat. I don't know whether they're looking at me or Kai now that I get a good look at them. They lean in to each other whispering every so often shooting us glances. As an author no one knows my face, but do they know Kai's?

"Kai."

Kai turns to me from looking out the window.

"I'm not trying to alarm you, but those kids have been watching us since we walked through the door."

Kai covertly looks at their table and turns back to me.

"Don't worry about them," he says, as he goes back to his plate. "I know them. They're okay."

That calms my nerves.

I smell something strong and rich and look over my shoulder to a woman sitting alone with a glass of red wine. I find myself sighing involuntarily. The vampire within me is loving the scent of it, but not wanting any. I turn back to Kai.

"Kai, do you ever find yourself craving things that's not blood, but reminds you of it?" I ask, stabbing some salad onto my fork.

"All the time," he answers, looking up from his plate. "My clan leader called it, the *Tempting*, because I was the only one that experienced it. I gathered that because we're able to walk in the sunlight and still eat food we're still attached to our human side and with that we crave things to substitute our want for blood."

That makes sense.

"I'm guessing yours is wine?" Kai smirks, his eyes skipping to the woman behind me and back.

"So observant." I smirk myself. "And what would yours be?" I challenge, sitting back in my chair.

"Anything tomatoes," he replies, matching my move with a smirk.

I laugh, sitting up and go back to my salad.

After our lunch is cleared away, Kai leans his head out in to the aisle checking out the cake display at the front end of the cafe and I catch the boy with dark hair at the college table look our way.

"I'll be right back," Kai says, getting up from the table.

As soon as Kai leaves the table the young man gets up from his table, checks to see if Kai is looking over, and swiftly takes Kai's unoccupied chair.

"Hi," the boy says.

"Hi," I reply politely, wondering what he wants.

"You must be the beautiful woman my dad keeps talking about," he says.

"Your dad?" I question.

"You seem to carry the world on your shoulders," he says, ignoring my question.

"No more than usual." I shrug unsure of where he's getting at.

"That's life, huh?" He says sagely with a nonplus shrug.

"Justin."

Justin turns around in the chair to Kai staring down at him sternly. He looks back at me with a smirk and turns back to Kai.

"Hi, Uncle Kai."

"Hi, Justin. What are you doing?"

Justin looks over his shoulder at me.

"Talking to your - ?" he turns back to Kai, as if he wants Kai to clarify it.

"Justin go study and stop pestering my -." Kai mimics him, flashing his silver eyes warningly.

Justin turns around to me whispering, "It was nice meeting you," before he's ducking back to his table.

"Oh, and Justin?"

Justin stops midway to his table and turns back to Kai.

"This never happened."

"Yes, Uncle Kai," Justin says with a smirk.

Kai reclaims his seat before me and places two bundled boxes of cake on the table before him.

"Uncle Kai?" I smile.

"Yes, Uncle Kai," Kai answers me smiling. "Justin is Chief's son."

"What?!" I ask, taken by surprise. I look across the room at Justin. I can see the family resemblance. He has Chief's smile and his same warm brown hair.

"Inquisitive kid," Kai says affectionately. "He gets that from his dad. His curiosity gets him in more trouble than he cares for. Always wanting to get to the bottom of something."

I smile. I can see that.

"Ready?" Kai asks.

"Yeah," I reply, grabbing my purse.

Kai pulls the top box of cake out of its tie and hands it to me, as we stand in front of his car in the parking garage.

"I know Niani likes Cinnamon Apple Butter Muffins, so I got her a few and I put something special in there for you."

I smile immediately and pull the box up to my face to smell for it, when Kai pulls it away laughing.

"No, it's supposed to be a surprise. You'll get it when you see it."

In happy resignation, I pull the box back towards me and hold it in my arms. Kai chuckles and bends down kissing me. He pulls away and something heavy burns in my chest and I'm suddenly aware of a very strong presence in the garage sneaking towards us. Kai stops and looks over his shoulder fast.

"Get inside, now. One four three," he grounds out softly.

I love you.

"One four three, three," I whisper, quickly backing up towards the door opening it from behind and step inside. I ascend the stairs slowly listening for any sign of a fight, but I hear nothing. Nothing, but the sound of Kai's careful footsteps on the concrete. The presence retreats and everything returns calm, the weight lifting off my chest. Soon, I hear Kai bursting through the garage door.

"Ashiya!" he yells.

Relieved, I sigh becoming aware that I had stopped on the stairwell and am tightly holding my switchblade out. Open. I close it and run down the stairs quickly running in to Kai on the second flight. Immediately, he engulfs me in his arms and I take him in. He pulls away and takes my face into his hands.

"I want you to go upstairs and stay in our apartment. Don't come out."

I nod vigorously, knowing the severity of our situation.

"They won't be able to sense you. And keep your switchblade close. I'm going to go track whoever this was down. They can't be far."

"Okay and put your phone on vibrate," I tell him, nodding again. "Tiberius is on his way back."

"I love you," Kai says with so much sincerity.

"I love you, too," I return and too swiftly is Kai kissing my lips, then my stomach that before I can blink he's gone.

Nothing solidified more than then, that at any moment the love of my life can be gone.

CHAPTER 10:
The Blood Bar

Niani never asked me why I needed a bodyguard. I guess Cassius did damage control knowing that him bringing up his protection did raise a few questions. Besides, she's been a little distracted lately. They have been spending a lot of time together. Makes me glad she has her own love life to worry about instead of mine per usual. Plus, she's been working with Fame Squared on *Reign* as a video game. So, in consequence, we haven't seen each other like today.

"*Princess...*" I hear whispered and swiftly look around the empty hallway.

Locking up the office apartment immediately, I swing a dagger into my palm out of the hidden compartment in the stitching of my slacks pulling the key out of the door.

"*This way...*" It's Tiberius' voice I recognize and follow it to the emergency staircase.

"Up here." His voice bounces off the stairwell walls and I know something's up. I smell it permeating the staircase, cling to the metal railings like sweat, vibrating through every surface. They're planning something. I step out onto the roof and immediately my arms are locked down from behind. Instantly, I pivot my hips around my attackers, kick my leg out behind his and allow gravity to take us both down. As soon as my assailant's back connects with the gravel, I spin off and raise my dagger coming face to face with Tiberius. Fear and surprise shroud his eyes, as I come down nearly stabbing him in the neck. My vampire realizing who he is I quickly back off, standing up.

Clapping fills the air, as Cassius and Chief come around the ventilation box.

"Good job, Princess," Chief praises.

I bend down and reach a hand out pulling Tiberius up. Another training exercise.

"I don't know what you're clapping for. She could have killed me." Tiberius cuts his eyes at Chief and Cassius.

I know I very well *would* have and could have if I chose not to turn around. It's hard for me to feel bad anymore knowing what I'm up against. It's been weeks now and Chief and Cassius made sure of that day one. I - *we* - my vampire and I are finding it harder to distinguish between who is friend and who is enemy. I like it that way. Every possible threat is a threat.

"Oh, stop it. You're alive. Stop complaining," Chief says, cutting in to my thoughts.

Tiberius gives him a none too happy look. On the other hand, Cassius' voice brings me back to why we're on the roof.

"We wanted to wait until Kai gets here, but -"

"He's here," Kai's voice cuts through the air.

I turn around, my heart stuttering in my chest at the sight of him. My own version of a sexy supernatural soldier in a tight navy blue zip-up with matching built-in metal arm guards, black pants under black mid-calf boots, and black gloves with black metal knuckle plates. The toned down version of what he would wear in his clan.

108

Mmph. All that is missing is his baton sword strapped to his back. Kai smiles, seeing right through me and steps forward taking me in to his arms, kissing me on the top of my forehead.

Man, this man is my sanctuary.

He pulls away slowly peering down at me and whispers, "Hi."

"Hi," I whisper in return, a cheesy smile breaking over my face.

"Shall we get started?" he asks enticingly.

"Mmhmm." I nod vigorously, my vampire and I anxious to get started.

I watch Kai pull away and fall in to place beside Chief, Cassius, and Tiberius behind us.

"I called you up here, because Cassius thought it was time we pass off your training today and start with *Levels,*" Kai explains. "Vampire transition comes in five stages: The Power, the Children, the Blood, and Them. I'll get to the fifth one in a minute. Your power is the first to manifest in order to help you defend yourself through the change. You won't notice it due to it being an enhanced version of the God given gifts you are already born with. Our power can be physical, mental, or both. The only time we ever tell another Hypernatural our ability is when we are going in to battle together. Which in our case, technically we are." He points to the faeries on either side of him.

"No power is the same. Your power is part of your identity. You learn it, you accept it, you claim it, because in the end it is one of the only things that is going to save you when no one else will."

His voice carries a vulnerable truth to it telling me he's experienced this lesson first hand and he doesn't want me to go through the same fate. His message sets into my heart as warning, take heed and I'll be able to live another day.

"Children," he goes on, "see what we are before we even realize what we are." That makes me think of Lia. "Though there are a select few adults who can, too." Her mom.

"Going by your face looks like you've been through this already," Tiberius says curtly with a matter of fact tone.

I cut my eyes at him.

"Yes, I have," I snap, becoming impatient with his attitude. I look back on Kai.

"And you've already had Blood. Vampirism is a lot like a transmitted disease. It takes time for it to show up in the system. For you it appears since you found out you were pregnant to be happening a lot faster."

"And *Them?*" I ask.

"Is the final divide between you and humans," he answers delicately, standing up a little straighter. "Your friends, your family, people you see on the street will sense what you are. They won't know what you are, but they will sense it and they won't like it. Everyone acts differently, some will leave you alone, some may start a fight, and some won't know how to act around you." Kai approaches me, placing his hands on my arms comfortingly. "But you will be okay with it."

I stare at him for a moment and nod finding comfort in his words. Somehow, I know they are right and I'm already okay with it. I know what it's like to feel different and ostracized for it.

"And the fifth thing?" I ask.

Kai lets go of me suddenly and walks back to his place beside Chief.

"The final stage ends with your death," he says, giving it to me straight. "Your heart will stop, your life will cease as a human, and the vampire will finally take over. You won't know when it comes. It will just take you."

"And the baby?" I ask, scared of the answer.

"The baby was conceived vampire. All that is left is for you to transition," he assures me. "The baby will be fine."

I am going to die. I tremble thinking about it. I mean I knew I was transitioning and we are the undead, but to die? What did I think, I was going to magically wake up one day and be a vampire? This was the process and that's how it's going to be. I will die and my child will be a vampire and so will I. It is my time.

"Okay." I exhale.

"Okay," Kai repeats, sighing as well. He wanted to be sure I would take this well. "Cassius."

Cassius steps forward.

"Now, none of your training will amount to anything unless you can recognize what you're dealing with. Follow me."

He walks over to the building ledge and looks over the edge with Chief and Tiberius. Taking my hand, Kai pulls me over to the ledge along with them. I look down on the street below seeing pedestrians walk by, rushing to their cars or driving by. The height makes me nervous sending my head spiraling, especially when the wind blows. I tighten my hold on Kai in an effort to stay upright and he wraps a comforting arm around my waist holding me to his chest knowing I don't like heights.

"Kai," Cassius says, as if handing me off to him.

Kai pulls me back from the ledge and turns me to him.

"Heights make you nervous, I know, but a big part of being a vampire and learning your instincts is becoming

111

comfortable with heights. There are going to be times when you're going to need to watch your enemies from a high vantage point. You as a *Limba* now are going to need to become accustomed to that."

Limba - transitioning human from tangic form to soul form of magical emission: Vampire.

I nod and step to the ledge by myself looking over the edge again.

"Okay, so what's first?" I ask, trying to brave my discomfort.

"Identification," Kai says, bending down to the ledge beside me and I follow his lead.

"Okay, you see that woman three floors down from the top, six windows from the left? The woman holding the baby?" I nod, seeing her. "She is a Shatan. When sensing another Supernatural you have to lead with your heart and not your mind. Focus on your heartbeat. Feel it with each breath you take and let your soul reach out to her."

I quiet my breathing focusing on my heartbeat. I feel a thrum vibrating through my body, then myself expanding - separating into silence and sound. I almost pull back scared of the sensation I feel, but I keep going knowing I have to get this right. I focus on the woman and feel the tether in the void reach out to her - then I see it. A ball of molten lava bubbling, but not enough to be threatening, then a small ember next to it burning, gaining strength. *Her baby.* I feel them both. I see their power. *It's beautiful.* I gasp and feel my heartbeat strong against my breastplate as I sever the line and come back to myself. I smile, tearing up.

"Beautiful, isn't it?" Kai smiles, watching my face.

I breathe a laugh and look down onto the street.

"Ready?" Kai asks, looking down as well.

I nod.

"See him?" He points to a man walking across the street. "He's a mermaid. Do the same thing you did with the Shatan and tell me what you feel."

I do it again focusing on the man, as he crosses the street. As the tether locks onto him I feel a tug in my veins and feel like I'm drowning, breathless. I suck in a breath and pull away from him. I turn to Kai meeting his knowing stare and say, "Cold. As if I've just jumped in a ice cold pool and I can't swim."

"Good. Now try it again, but remember to breathe with your heart. Don't get too excited where you forget to breathe. Sensing mermaids can be very tricky messing with your mind - make you feel like your drowning."

I latch on to the man, as he passes underneath us and this time I can breathe, but I see blue veins popping along his arms and neck. Alarmed, I pull back and ask, "What did I just do?"

"Sometimes when another Hypernatural is around and like you were sensing him out, similarly like the pull of the moon mermaids will show signs of their lineage with blue veins."

"Like the core of hot lava in Shatan," I state.

"Right," Kai says. "Every Hypernatural's physical sense characteristic will be different. Longshens, your skin will feel silky, almost like spiraling smoke. Faeries, you'll smell their natural scent. Phoenix, hot. Greeks, black grapes and olive oil. Cupids, light, sweet, and airy, which is literally where we get the quote, 'Love is in the air.'

I smile at that one softly.

"Now, you want to get to the fun part?" Kai asks, as he stands and moves to the side of the building away from the street.

I follow him to the ledge and look down onto the empty space of alleyway between this building and the next.

"The fun part?" I look up at him.

"Yeah, where you fly," he says, as if it is the easiest thing in the world.

"Where we fly?" I repeat. "We can fly?" I look over at Cassius, Chief, and Tiberius for confirmation. I've never written anything like this in my books before. Not until this new book. They look at me, as if I should let Kai explain.

"As vampires, our bodies are no longer tied to gravity. When we're turned we become more spirit. We can fly or basically *float*. Even without your complete transformation you can still tap into this, just like everything else. This was one of the first things I learned as a vampire and remains to be my favorite."

It does my heart good to learn he had at least one joy from his past. He steps back on the ledge and my heart spikes in reaction. He takes another step back, then another and he's standing on air. He brings his arms out wide and lets himself fall back and he easily floats to the ground. I look down at him standing unscathed on the ground below smiling up at me. Just as he was standing on the ground, he's standing in front of me again. I look back down at the ground. He leaped up here. *We can fly.*

"Your turn," Kai says and I look back at him in shock. "There is no wrong way to do this. Just imagine the air carrying you. There is no way you will hurt the baby. I'll catch you," he adds.

I look at the ledge and shakily take a step up. Kai takes a few steps back and hunches down in preparation to run. Nervously, I turn around slowly and spread my arms out wide following Kai. I close my eyes and let a breath go. Opening my eyes, I look up at the sky. I think about being weightless, the wind carrying me wherever I may go - safely to the ground - and I let go. I feel the vibrations on the air, as Kai runs and kicks off the building ledge and dives, as I fall. My body floats fast through air rushing to meet me, my hair a curtain of tendrils around my face, by the time I open my eyes and look up I'm in Kai's arms hovering at his fingertips on the ground, as Tiberius, Chief, and Cassius look down at us from above. Kai smiles proudly over me and removes his fingers from where they are pressed into my back. My body floats of its own fruition, hovering feet from the ground. I look around the empty space surrounding me, my hair fanning around my face in slow moving curls. As if by instinct, I turn my face back up and close my eyes.

Up, I think and as if being pushed I'm propelled back onto the roof and land standing in Kai's arms. I stare up at him astonished and I could kiss him for introducing me to something so exhilarating. This might have just become my new favorite thing in lieu of my fear of heights.

"Yeeaaah," Chief jeers approaching me proudly. He grabs me up into his arms around the middle taking me away from Kai and spins me around.

Setting me back down on the ground, he turns to the guys and asks, "What do you think guys? She ready for a little field work?"

I look around at the guys around me, all of their faces contort in a mix of reservation and uncertainty. Kai's silver eyes flare and darken, as they stare at me. I close my eyes suddenly feeling the sweet caress of hands not there snaking its way up my neck to my face, the darkest temptation coursing its way into my limbs. It feels good, but something that feels this good can only be so bad. I feel trapped in my own private hell, purgatory, and heaven. *Bliss on earth.* Then suddenly in stretched out procession I'm flooded with memories:

I'm trekking down a long dim hallway run with cranberry damask wallpaper lit by a single lamp at the end of the hall atop of a long mahogany table. The sour smell of hallucinogens and opiates sit on the smoke-filled air and I'm feeling the effects. I know it's going to be a hazy night as I look down over the banister on the dancing bodies below of the nightclub.

As I follow the men out back of the nightclub into the middle of the road wet from the earlier rain, I hear a melodic giggle like bells to my drug hazed ears and stop looking at two women laughing on the sidewalk in front of a red Nissan car. One has dreads, then she moves aside showing off her friend - and I see myself.

These aren't my memories I realize looking at myself through Kai's eyes. My long hair pulled back in loose curls at my back laughing with Niani on the street in front of her car. I remember this night. It was our "Girls date night". Dinner, drinks, and a movie, but we skipped the movie and went dancing instead. It's enough to know that's when Kai first laid eyes on me, when he fell in love with me and I didn't know it.

I open my eyes and look at Kai. He stares down at me and I at him and we both say, "Yes."

KAI

"You okay?" Tiberius asks, stepping up beside me, as we walk up the sidewalk to the club. "You haven't been back here since you left."

"I know," I say, looking up at the club ahead, the red awning sticking out over the black railing staircase leading up to the door.

I look over my shoulder at Ashiya behind me flanked by Chief and Z on either side of her with Cassius at her back. This is a bad idea. I wanted her to learn about this underworld not become involved in it, but I let my old memories, my old temptations drag her and me back in. The power. The beast my clan was so fond of. My own private hell, purgatory, and heaven. I never wanted this life for her, but here I am agreeing to it. God help us.

Behind me, I hear Chief explaining to Ashiya, "To know we even *exist* humans would have to know what to look for. Faeries, mostly work in public safety occupations, such as the police force, the military, the courts setting the laws for what's allowed for all Hypernaturals and human alike, but not all Hypers like this. They think it's impeding on their personal clan laws. Shatans on the other hand rather live on the side of the humans, since they are the most human like out of all of us. They are our chefs, forest preservationists, museum curators. They prefer only to associate with other Hypernaturals when it deems them necessary, otherwise we don't exist to them. So, don't be surprised if you get attitude from one."

I smirk. Oh yeah, have I been on the receiving end of a Shatan's attitude plenty of time.

"Mermaids are the most mysterious. We don't know much about what they do. Where they come from. They abide by the rules. They keep to themselves. They make *our* lives easier."

I watch Ashiya's lips quirk into a smile at that.

"Help us on any investigation we need them to. It often times makes me wonder if they may have something to hide, that's why they're so willing to help all the time."

"Don't fill her head with conspiracies Chief. Let her come to her own decisions," Z jumps in. "Really they're good people. Used to date one," he whispers, with a smirk to Ashiya.

Ashiya laughs silently at that. We come up on the club front and take a right at the side of the building going around back. The Hyper entrance. Opening the back door, I let everyone in first then follow.

There is never muscle at this door. The Shatan's spelled it with an ancient language revered as sacred to the ancient Hypers - one of them being Kwan-Min - to keep those of hyperhood in and humans out. Any human wanting to sneak in will find the steel door rusted and sealed shut with no handle.

A combination of our own cuneiform and sanskrit the spell was etched across the top of the doorframe as by tradition to the Shatans. Their herbs and words would have been enough to ward the door, but writing it across the door is their equivalent of etching it in stone. No Hyper speaks it anymore except for select families who somehow kept the tradition alive. After the *Tragedy of 1849* it became hard to hold on to the old language just like most of Hyper tradition.

I close the door behind me and turn around finding myself back in the burgundy halls of my addictive past. Tiberius looks back at me with uncharacteristic compassion, as I watch everyone down the line wait against the wall for me. My eyes land on Ashiya and I swallow my memories leading the way down the hall and around the corner.

We enter through a door at the side of the bar and I look around as the scent of every Hyper in the room fills my nostrils.

"So, this is what being in a room full of Hypers smells like," Ashiya says, stepping up beside me.

I look down at her and remember when we're in a room with Cassius, Tiberius, Z, and Chief, Ashiya and I still smell human. Amongst the Hyper community I'm known as the vampire without a scent and now that also goes for Ashiya. Even now as I pass a group against the wall my unscented status draws their attention.

"If anyone asks your name say, 'I'm not at liberty to oblige.' They'll respect that," I lean over and whisper in to Ashiya's ear.

She cuts her eyes at me and gives a small smile in answer. We take seats near the middle of the bar, Tiberius and Z to my left and Ashiya to my right. Cassius and Chief remain standing by the door leading down in to the dance hall. The bartender turns around and halts in his usual spiel.

"Prince!" he exclaims astounded. "I haven't seen you here since your injury!"

"I know," I say and wish I had a drink in my hand to down.

Ashiya looks at me out of the corner of my eye and I can feel the question in her stare.

"I heard you went out on your own. Haven't seen the clan around here since either," he says conversationally, taking out a shot glass and placing it on the bar top with a glass clink. He fills the glass to the brim with brown liquor and passes it to me. He takes out another shot glass and fills it. Lifting the glass in silent speech, I lift mine and we both knock them back and slam them down to the countertop. The drink goes down smooth and burns my throat.

Wooh! Now, that is *respect.*

I look up at Vincent as he shakes his head clearing the brown from his senses burning its way down his throat and through his sinuses. Vincent never asks questions and minds his own, one of the reasons why I like him. If others want to divulge that is on them. He listens, he watches, but never comments. He was a good bartender that way. Whatever happened at the White Bar, stayed at the White Bar.

Z lifts his finger and Vincent catches it behind the bar raising a finger to tell him one minute already bent over fixing his drink. He passes Z his drink, along with Tiberius' usual and leaves Cass and Chief's at the end of the bar to get when they are ready and turns to Ashiya.

"Hey," he says, connecting her vicinity to me as association. "It's nice to see a new face around here. What's your name?"

"I'm not at liberty to oblige." Ashiya smiles enigmatically.

Vincent's eyes drop to Ashiya's hands laying crisscrossed on the bar top eyeing her wedding ring and physically backs off, his eyes darting from me to her putting the puzzle pieces together.

"Welcome to the White Bar," he recovers. "I'm Vincent, *Princess*," he adds quietly.

Ashiya beams approvingly. "Nice to meet you, Vincent," she says.

I swing around in my chair looking through the one-way glass blocking the bar from the dance floor below. Across the dance floor on the other side is the Black Key, the "human only bar". From my position I can see the few humans straggling the bar under black lights, their clothes glowing under the florescence opposite in the stark white of this bar. This side to human eyes is known as an "elite only bar". No special privileges. Just very - private.

"Vincent is a Merman. One of the good guys," I speak softly, knowing Ashiya hears me. "Missed his calling in law enforcement. Very observant. Saved my behind a few times."

Out of my peripheral, I see Ashiya smirk. "I'm glad or else that behind wouldn't be mine."

I smile and shake my head with an amused huff.

Vincent chuckles to himself obviously hearing her little comment, as he sets a glass of red liquid before her and adds a lemon peel. *Cranberry juice.* He could probably sense the chemical shift in her body being pregnant despite alcohol having no effect on us. I turn around to him and he smiles excusing himself down the bar to a customer flagging him down.

Ashiya leans over taking a sip of her drink when someone sits next to her bumping her shoulder. I notice Ashiya jerk at the impact looking up at the person. I look over and it's a brunette, who just stares at Ashiya and nothing else. She then turns her back on Ashiya turning to the man next to her. Ashiya looks at me and I know we're sharing the same look and possibly the same thought, mine most likely more colorful than hers. *Shatans.*

Ashiya turns away and goes back to her drink. I don't hear the conversation the two Shatans are having or notice Chief's reaction to the sudden party of bodies congregating at the opposite end of the bar. It's not until I turn back to Ashiya still bent over her drink that I know something is wrong. Ashiya frowns, pushing back in her chair, just before the brunette whips around grabbing her by the hair brandishing a dagger. In an instant, Ashiya spins into the hold grabbing the brunette by the neck slamming her into the counter and snatches the dagger from the brunette's hand, flipping it between deft fingers and plunges it back into the guilty hand.

The man next to her stands from his chair ready to attack and in a flash he's back down, as I whip around Ashiya and slash him across the chest with the sword disguised as the belt around my waist. I turn to check on Ashiya when a dagger whips pass my face connecting with the chest of a Shatan rushing at me. I turn looking back at Ashiya standing behind me arm out post throw.

Z, Chief, Cass, and Ti have their own hands full as they make their way through the line of attacking Shatans coming at them. Cass pulls a volting hand up, balling it into a fist and sends the current down into the floor with a punch knocking the first row back with the blast. Z and Chief take up the sidelines slicing and singeing as they go. Ti disintegrating every limb that touches him.

I look around the room as I watch innocent Hypers who want no part of this hurry out of the way, Vincent helping them get out or at a safe distance from the fight. Ashiya elbows a Shatan in the face, as my sword rips through another Shatan's middle. All I can think is my family is in danger. I don't understand. I don't - I look at the blood splashed across every surface it can reach: the floor, the bar top, the glass looking out over the dance floor, the walls. The White Bar is a *blood bath*.

I tremble with fury as the *beast* takes over, the veins in my eyes throbbing. I tighten my hand around my sword, as I know I'm losing my grip on the thing. Memories of blood stained floors just like this play through my head, as a Shatan breaks through the barricade created by the

Shatans against Cass and his team. They didn't care that they were fighting special agents. They obviously came here to die trying to kill Ashiya. The approaching Shatan pulls a handful of copper dust from his pocket smearing it across his palms I know to be poison and thrusts it at me. He was at the back of the line for this very reason. He was the last contingency plan.

Ashiya is behind me, I check over my shoulder urgently. In an effort to protect her and myself, I cut through the dust watching as the little magical webbing connecting the particles split into two breaking the poisonous strands and forcing it away with the heavy gust of wind created by my sword. In the blink of an eye I'm in his face. I don't give him time to flinch as my sword forces its way up through his chin into his skull. His eyes stare in to mine with the shock of his death. It's almost - *almost* - too cruel to look. After that I black out.

I remember bits and pieces... Cassius and Chief raising their badges, yelling at the remaining surviving Shatans to put their hands up. The Shatans raising their hands and dropping to their knees... Ashiya - *Ashiya laying her chin atop of my shoulder. I remember wrapping my arms around her shoulders on autopilot... My eyes landing on Vincent behind the bar, as he comforts a fellow mermaid. I turn looking out on the dance floor below none of them the wiser of the bloodshed that went down here. I remember feeling angry. How ignorant is their bliss? This could have easily been them. I close my eyes leaning my face into Ashiya's hair blocking out the scent of blood and burned flesh out of my nostrils.*

CHAPTER 11:
Kwan-Min

ASHIYA

1848

She was life. She was magic and at first sight I was in love with her. She was the color of precious ivory. Her eyes the color of blue at dawn, ebony hair spun by the finest silk. Though she wore our garb, she spoke the Queen's language. She was a beacon of light drowning out all the sights and sounds of the bazaar, the vibrancy of the brightest spices. Why would the Louv tempt me so? She was meant to be loved, but loved by another.

The light of sunrise wakes me up the next morning. Orange sunlight filters through the blinds casting an outline of the window over the sheets and blanket. For a moment, I feel like I'm in a Noir Film. I turn over to see Kai sleeping peacefully on his back with an arm thrown over his stomach. I smile looking over him, as I prop a hand under my head, watching him breathe. It's moments like this when I sit back and think, despite everything going on in my life and I thank God for everything. Kai is such a blessing in my life and no one, but God put him here. I can't fathom sharing my life with anyone else. Especially, after last night. I will fight to keep him here.

It was the strangest thing fighting side by side. Him protecting me. I protecting him. It was as if the wildest thing came out of us. It's the vampire - in me. In *us*. It didn't go over my head that the Shatans were after Kai just as bad as they were after me last night. It concerns and confuses me as of why when I've been - *I am* - the target. It didn't make any sense.

Following the play of light on his muscles, I trace the outline of shadows on his forearm with a finger. It was like a road map to the deepest, darkest part of him. The things that he kept hidden and I was aware he had many. I stop in my ministrations my eyes landing on his lips and I lean over kissing him, not expecting him to kiss me back.

"Good Morning," Kai sighs in his sleep, as I lean up.

"Good Morning," I reply softly.

"What time is it?" he mumbles sleepily.

I look up out the window at the glaring sun and say, "Seven fifteen."

Kai moans, whining, "I don't want to get up, yet."

I giggle at him and throw a leg over his torso, straddling him.

"How about this. I'll go fix us breakfast, while you rest and after breakfast we'll take a shower together," I coax him.

"I love you," Kai mumbles seriously, half asleep.

"I love you, too." I giggle and slip off of him and out of the bed.

I turn and stop outside the door thinking about last night. My instincts tell me I'm not wrong. Something else was going on last night.

When we got home last night, we didn't talk about what had happened. We both silently agreed that it was a bad idea. But without that decision I wouldn't have discovered that Kai may be in as much danger as I am. I look up from putting my boots on at the end of the bed to Kai leaning against the doorframe to the closet staring pensively down at the baton sword he saved me with the first night I was attacked. Mounted upon a chess between our clothes it still looks as deadly and beautiful. A silent killer.

In my own pensive thinking, I don't notice Kai look at me and follow my eyes to his sword.

"It was a gift from my clan leader," he says.

I look at him. His eyes reflect a pain I can't describe, as he stares down at it.

"He was a good guy, until he wasn't. He uses people until there is nothing left of them to go on," he says haunted, his voice breaking at points, as if he's trying to keep from breaking down.

He doesn't blink. He doesn't move. I stand up from the bed and walk over, taking him in my arms. Immediately, his arms wrap around me, clutching on to me, as if I'm the only thing he has. His pain. It's crippling. I feel myself almost buckle under the weight of it. I press my face into the side of his comforting him the only way I know how.

For moments like this there are no words, but a comforting presence and someone to lean on.

KAI

Ashiya was now nine weeks along, her skin rounding to show signs that she was with our child and the mere sight of it is a miracle. It is a blessing to see her get this far with everything going on around us. I don't know how she is doing it able to stay so calm in the midst of all the attacks, working on her movie and her book, keeping a happy husband... She is the strongest woman I know. From the

126

moment she found out I was a vampire she has been my strength, keeping me afloat. I don't know what I would do without her.

Today would be the first time I would get to see the baby and as excited as I am, I also don't feel worthy. After last night, after the last *year* I could be this blessed in life and deserve this. I smile, looking over at her in the passenger seat. She truly is my redemption. My gift.

"You ready, Daddy?" the Ultrasound Technician asks, as she turns from the prepared machine.

"Yeah." I smile nervously.

Ashiya looks up at me obviously reading my nerves. She smiles and takes my hand, squeezing it. It's then that I notice the soft throbbing behind my eyes, the grey most likely showing through. I blink and focus, turning them off.

"It's okay," she says softly.

I smile and lean down kissing her on her forehead.

"Okay Mommy, this is going to be a little cold," the technician warns Ashiya, as she gently squeezes the cool gel on her exposed abdomen.

I squeeze Ashiya's hand drawing her attention back to me, as the technician presses the transducer to her stomach giving her an excited smile. The first thing that welcomes our hyper sensitive ears is the baby's strong heartbeat beating a little out of sync with Ashiya's. We both smile unable to contain the happiness welling up within us, as we stare at one another.

"Well, would you look at that," the technician gasps in awe.

Ashiya and I turn to the machine to see a sonogram of two embryos on the screen.

"I didn't catch this before. Twins," the technician whispers, adjusting the transducer on Ashiya's stomach. "Do either of you have twins in the family?" She turns to us.

My voice a little thick, I reply, "No."

Staring at our babies, Ashiya shakes her head.

The technician smiles and turns back to the screen saying, "Well, Congratulations on your first generation of twins."

Twins. Wow. I think, as I stare at the screen. I take Ashiya's hand and bring it to my lips, kissing it. Ashiya doesn't fight the tears that leak from her eyes.

Ashiya and I walk into our apartment only to stop upon entering the living room to see Kwan-Min sitting comfortably on our couch cross legged in a navy blue suit, his suit jacket discarded over the back of the couch. Next to him lays an immensely heavy looking marble case.

"Kwan-Min, what are you doing here?" I ask, stopping Ashiya behind me.

"After the noise you two made last night, you're *really* surprised I'm here?" he asks, pressing his hands together.

"We ordered -" I begin, when Kwan-Min cut me off.

"You forget Kai I know things. You're lucky you didn't garnish yourselves some *unwanted* attention." His eyes land on Ashiya behind me and he stands. "Excuse me, Princess, my manners. I'm Kwan-Min. It is a pleasure to finally make your acquaintance." He bows respectfully.

"It is an honor," she says softly, bowing her head to the man whose family and himself have saved her life thrice, "though I'm curious myself. Excuse me for my bluntness, but why are you here?"

128

"No insult at all, Princess." He turns to the marble case on the couch and heaves it into his arms, turning it towards us. "I come baring a gift for your friend, Niani." He flips the latches on the case and lifts the lid revealing a pair of antique Sais lying in black silk. The blades resemble weathered stone, the lines and cracks filled with burnt orange Blaizinium with his ancient language inscribed into the handles.

I glance at Ashiya's look of refusal and turn to Kwan-Min. "I don't think that is a good idea Kwan-Min."

"Give. them. to her," Kwan-Min insists seriously. He looks at Ashiya and closes the case. "You've been worried about your friends and family, about them getting caught up in the middle of what you're in. All you need to know is that as many enemies as you have, you also have friends."

As if taking his word for it, Ashiya tentatively steps forward taking the case.

"I came to say my piece," Kwan-Min states and turns grabbing his suit jacket off the couch, gently laying it over his arm and walks for the door. "And congratulations on your twins. Oh, and Princess," He stops, holding open the door, as he turns to us. Ashiya and I turn to him.

"*Hala to sa've Me' wi ne lay,*" Kwan-Min says, looking at Ahiya.

"*Or'a louv t'er yongheng,*" Ashiya follows up naturally, when her eyes widen in surprise as if wondering where that came from.

My eyes find Kwan-Min again and he looks at me this time regrettably with sympathy and says, "You'll never be able to lie to her," before walking out.

The silence that follows is too loud to my ears and I have to sit down as it all becomes too much. It reminds me too much of -. Ashiya turns around and just stares at me - at nothing.

"He does that." I sigh.

"I don't doubt that," Ashiya replies.

She looks at the case in her hands and walks over to the couch setting it down and opens it again. Kneeling before it, she looks at the ancient weapons distantly and says softly, "I don't want her involved."

I hear the pain etched in her voice and slide down off the couch, pulling her into my arms. Her head nestles into my chest and I hold her close, pressing my lips into her hair.

"Whatever this is Kwan-Min obviously knows you need her help, but that in return she has Cass."

Ashiya gives a watery sigh as if she's crying, but I know she's not. She's emotional, but her vampire is borderline of feeling nothing. That's the problem with being a vampire. We're always guilty of being detached.

Ashiya then pulls out of my arms and asks, "What was that language?"

"It doesn't have a name. It's a language I only know the ancients and their families to speak," I answer.

"Then how do I know it? Did I put it in one of my books and somehow forgot?" she asks herself the latter.

"Maybe you're having a Harry Potter moment and it was somehow instilled in you when you became a vampire," I joke.

Ashiya cracks a smile, then giggles. "Yeah, I speak Parseltongue for Hypers." Just as she's giggling, she stops. She looks pensive, as she slides delicate fingers made for the ebony and ivory keys across her lips. "Kai, they weren't just after me last night. They were after you. They were trying to kill you."

The certainty in her words make them finite.

I'm unable to say anything to her. Maybe they were, but I was more worried about her than anything else. All I can say is, 'I'm sorry', but the words don't come. I pull her again into a hug and she leans in not fighting me.

I listen to her soft sigh, as we breathe as one. After a couple of beats she pulls away.

"I have to get to casting," she says, sighing heavily, as she closes the marble case and stands.

"I'll drive you," I interject, pulling myself off the floor.

CHAPTER 12:
Shadows and Light

My apartment doorbell rang not expecting anyone to come over. Opening the door, I'm horrified to find Kai fatally injured slumped against the doorframe. He collapses inside and I catch him. He's weak on his feet, dragging as I half carry him into my living room sitting him down on my couch. He groans slouching back into the cushions.

There is a huge gash in his abdomen near his left hip bone, where his hand covers it blood slipping through his fingers. He's panting in pain, his already warm ivory skin looking more pallid and I'm too concerned to cry.

"Here take my blood." I force my wrist to his lips, kneeling at his feet.

He softly pushes my hand away, tears swimming in his eyes.

"No. No. I don't need your blood. I just need you," he says weakly and the tears finally slip from his eyes. "I can't do it anymore. I'm done. I'm leaving my clan."

KAI

"I'm sorry," I say, as I pull up in front of the building Ashiya's having casting calls at today and flip the car in park. "I'm sorry about Kwan-Min. I'm sorry about the many questions I can or don't know how to answer."

Out of the corner of my eye I see Ashiya shake her head and blink, as if to get something out of her eyes, then

I hear her chuckle. I hear the compression of body weight against leather, as she turns herself toward me and I look over to her staring at me, a soft smile on her lips. Slowly, she leans over the console taking my jaw in her hands looking me deeply in my eyes.

"It's okay," she whispers so softly, it's almost hard to hear even in the confined space of the car to my hypersensitive ears.

I smile.

"You are the death of me," I say softly, smiling at her ability to turn a dark situation lighter.

Her smile broadens. That was my equal of saying, "I'm in love with you." She must have got the message, because she closes the distance between us kissing me, *hard*, deeply, pouring every ounce of how much she is in love with *me* into it.

Her hands slide along my neck winding into my hair, pulling gently. My hands find her middle, tugging at her shirt to find any sort of skin on skin contact. She lets out a gasp as my lips find the pulse in her neck, nipping and sucking. She rips herself away from me, trailing needy worshipping kisses down my temple to my jawline. Little satisfied noises escape my lips, as she returns to my lips. My body is humming. The intensity. I feel as if I'm on the verge of an outer body experience, as my senses run wild, when - she suddenly pushes away from me to her side of the car. I watch her eyes look over my shoulder out my window to William approaching the window. I don't have to see him to know he is there, before I'm rolling my eyes. Turning around, I see William bend down to knock on the window.

"I'll be right there," I mumble to Ashiya, opening the door ajar causing William to stand and double back, as I open the door fully and get out of the car.

I cut William a look, as I walk around the car and open the door for Ashiya. She stands from her seat and whispers with a smile, "Thank you."

I return the smile, as she turns to William. I hate this act that we have to put on, 'I know you, but I don't really know you.' The whole acquaintance crap. As she walks around the car to William, I hear her whisper, "I love you and I'll see you later," knowing I will hear it.

"I love you," I whisper in return.

She looks over her shoulder at me wearing a beautiful smile, but my next thought is of him touching her and me breaking his hands.

"Not nice, Kai," I hear Ashiya's whisper reach my ears.

I chuckle, then I realize she read my mind. I watch after her unsure if she realizes she can do this, until they reach the doors and William opens the door for her - *he better* - as he looks back at me with a rival smirk. I smirk myself as I watch him turn to Ashiya, who catches him with a stern look. I laugh to myself, as I open the Challenger door, catching the grin she sends to me, as the door swings closed behind them and I climb back into the Challenger and drive off.

ASHIYA

William and I step onto the elevator and William stands across from me staring at me with one undiscerning expression for a few pregnant beats, his mind devoid of any thoughts. It makes me nervous, the hairs on my arms standing on end, before he turns and presses our floor

134

button. I have no idea what that look meant, but it derails both my security and my senses.

"So, why are you riding with him?" William asks, trying to sound casual only to succeed in sounding resentful, as we look across the elevator at each other.

I almost want to say *he* has a name when I remember William nor Niani know Kai's name.

"I was at the studio this morning and my car wouldn't start. I asked him for a ride," I clip.

"You could have called me. I would have come and got you," William says with too much hope in his voice.

I don't say anything to that.

He stares at me and pushes off of the wall, his mind now full of one thing. I see the action in my mind and reach a hand for the top right dagger hidden in the slit of my jeans, when the elevator doors open to our floor. I don't look at William, as I quickly step off the elevator before him into a large black and wood panel sitting area with an unmanned reception desk, walking straight up to our casting director and director standing in the hallway talking outside our appointed room. I allow them to whisk me away, putting as much distance between William and I. Which I'm grateful for because I can't trust myself around him - not with dagger happy fingers.

With a break from casting, I walk in to the empty break room away from character monologues and performance critiques and grab a water bottle from the refrigerator. Leaning over the counter, I welcome the rooms lingering silence. It's been interesting to see how each actor takes on my characters. Never once did I think I would be turning one of my novels into a movie. *Hoped,* yes. But in reality? It was a far cry from what I imagined. It feels good to be here, going over prop designs with the production team, narrowing down casting, scouting for locations... If I wasn't doing this every day I would think this was a dream spell induced by a Shatan. Am I glad it's not.

Red-Orange

William's aura signature flashes in front of my eyes, just before he walks into the room obviously looking for me. He steps up beside me and I can practically hear his mind whirring with crush induced thoughts. Out of the corner of my eye, I see him sigh and roll his neck trying to vie for my attention. I take a swig of my water ignoring him, as the tight knit collection of muscles bunch in the back of my neck toward my shoulders in annoyance. I really don't want to deal with him right now. I know he likes me, but this is too much. I take another swig of water and William moves around somewhere behind me. Next, his hands are on my shoulders massaging into the muscles. A split second of instinct tells me to turn around, grab him, slam him in to the counter, and break his hands, but I reign myself in. I pull myself from him, turn around, and meet his eyes, *hard,* letting him know this isn't cool. His hands drop to his side, his face contorting in explanation.

"You have to stop doing this. I cannot work with you like this. I know you like me. I get it, but I will not allow you to jeopardize your career nor mine. We cannot afford for someone to walk in here and see what they think they are seeing. You are my partner in this film. My friend and nothing more. There can *be* nothing more."

William's eyes search mine deeply, relenting and determined.

"Ms. Bride?"

I look over to our personal assistant standing in the doorway.

"Mr. Cuaron wants to speak with you for a moment."

"Okay, I'll be right there," I say.

She nods and steps away. I look back at William and he meets me with that same determined stare. I sigh, shaking my head at him and walk away for the door.

"Ashiya."

I stop.

He stays silent for a moment trying to collect his words.

"You looked tense," he says finally, his voice despondent yet strong.

In my chest, I feel my heart constrict painfully with unrequited love. *His love.*

I shake my head sympathetically and reply sincerely, "Thank you," and walk out.

He thinks I'm single and I'm just refusing him. I hate that I have to lie to him, but the truth of my pregnancy will be revealed all too soon. It's unavoidable. I'm just afraid of the fall out.

William stays business throughout the rest of the meeting, if not quieter than usual. We get along as if nothing happened commenting on the actors or laughing over an old inside joke, which feels like a slap in the face to him. Though, all the while I can feel his distance growing.

When it's finally time to leave he stays back talking with our casting director as I walk out the door. It's good that he does so seeing Kai pick me up won't add salt to injury. Although my heart hurts for him, I'm glad I nipped this thing in the bud. Hopefully, he'll remember what I said. It's a long shot but one does not announce they're having someone else's child. He had to see that. I wasn't ever going to be his - *ever*.

"Hey." I smile, as I slide into the passenger seat of the Challenger.

"I missed you," Kai says, leaning over and kissing me.

"I missed you, too," I reply, as he pulls away.

I feel her before I hear her. The sound of her landing on a rooftop reaches my ears and Kai's eyes meet mine. Without a second thought, he turns to the wheel and shifts into drive pulling us out onto the road. Kai grabs his cellphone from the cup holder and presses a number pulling it up to his ear.

"Hey. Yo, Cassius I have a situation. Can you meet me at Edgewood? Yeah. Alright, see you there. Thanks man."

Kai looks over at me.

"You're going to be okay."

I don't doubt it, but it still doesn't help my dagger happy fingers reaching for a dagger.

As we pull in near Little Five Points, I feel her stop and turn back. She's not allowed here.

"Why can't she be here?" I turn to Kai.

"Jurisdiction. This is Faerie area. Vampires can't hunt here," Kai answers, as he makes a left onto Moreland Avenue.

I notice the sun going down as we drive a few blocks down and turn into Edgewood's Shopping District into a parking garage. We park getting out of the car and two parking spots to the right Cass climbs out of his car walking over to us.

As Cass approaches us, I smell her before I see her.

"You brought Niani?" I question.

"We have a -" Cass goes to answer, when Niani interrupts.

"Ashiya?" Niani stands from the car looking at me, as if to ask what am I doing here. She walks around the car to the three of us and a tense silence befalls around us.

"What's going on Kai?" Cassius asks seriously, cutting through the silence.

Kai cuts a look from Niani to Cass, as Niani smirks across from me silently teasing me about the fact that I'm with Kai. The next sentence cuts the smirk right off her face.

"We have a stalker. She's hanging out around the building where Ashiya is doing casting. She likes to keep to the shadows. Tall. Latina. Short violet hair. Since you were with Niani, I wanted to keep you aware in case you see anyone with this description. I'll stay with Ashiya," Kai answers, the flexion in his voice telling between the three of us that there is much more to what he is saying.

"How does she know how you look?" Niani asks me concerned.

"People find ways." I shrug, as if it is what it is, which it was.

Cassius nods with a concerned frown. The faeries four were given the day off, giving Kai and I some alone time with my appointment and casting. But knowing this, I know Cass will want to stay by my side.

"You two go. Don't worry, I'll be with Kai," I say softly. "Cass, take care of her."

"Of course, Prin- Ashiya," he nearly slips up.

I smile and look at Niani. "I'll text you when I get home."

"You better," she says, worry all across her features.

"And have *fun*," I tack on. "Don't worry." I smile.

Niani smiles softly and cuts a look at Kai.

"Protect her with your life, Jung," she says threatening otherwise.

"Always." Kai smiles softly, turning around and opening my car door for me.

I climb in taking a seat and throw Niani a smile over my shoulder, as Kai closes the door behind me. Kai gets in and I toss Niani a wave, as Cassius ushers her around the car to the passenger side door, before Kai pulls out and away.

KAI

We walk back into the apartment, Ashiya slipping her phone back into the front pocket of her wallet after texting Niani as promised. She looks at me over her shoulder, as she walks ahead of me into the foyer and I can see the weight of questions on her mind. I want her to say it, lay it all out for me. She can read my mind, so she has to know I want to answer anything she has to know.

As if to answer my line of thinking, she stops and turns facing me.

"You knew how she looks," she states. "Who is she?"

"Mahina. She is what my clan calls a 'Shadow'. She has the ability to teleport, blend in, and become shadow. A vampire that makes sure the deals of our clan goes down properly. I worked with her distantly."

"How is she able to go out in the sun?" she asks.

"I don't know. My clan leader must be using her to track you down and she's found you."

"What's to stop her from coming in here, right now?"

I smile at that question, happy to our advantage. "She can't track a daylight vampire. She can only go upon sight and sound and something tells me she didn't get much from either. The sun considerably dulls their senses. Now, my turn. How did you know *she* was a she?"

Ashiya stares at me in my eyes and says, "It's been happening since before I found out I was a vampire, maybe by a couple of weeks. I could read people's emotions, sense their thoughts, flashes of their intentions. Now, it's getting stronger. I don't know what to call it. It's like hyper intuition."

"Does it scare you?"

"No." She shakes her head. "It's as if I'm writing a book and I'm delving into my character's lives. It's very similar feeling their emotions, knowing their intentions... It is all the same, except it's - real." She looks up meeting my eyes. "What about you? Were you scared of your power? *Matter of fact,* I don't know what your power is." She frowns up at me, as if to ask, '*How could I not know this?*'

"And it's something I hope you never find out and never have to see," I tell her.

She frowns even harder at my statement and I sigh in reluctance. She's seen me kill. What difference would it make for her to see my power?

"My clan used to call it, 'The Verserker'."

"Like Berserker?" Ashiya asks.

"Yes. Instead of a B they put a V for Vampire."

Ashiya cracks a smile. "Your clan is ironic."

I crack a smile of my own. "Yeah...," I say and fall silent for a few seconds before, "All I've wanted to do all my life was help people. That's why I became a doctor to heal, but not knowing I would become a vampire one day would I learn my true gift." I huff a derisive laugh. "I'm a Protector, alright. In the heat of battle, I lose myself over to my senses so much that in the moment of protecting someone

- I will kill. I have killed. - I like it. For me it's a rush. The power. The adrenaline."

"Kai, that's nothing to be scared of." I frown at her statement. "You grew up doing martial arts. You enjoyed it. You want to protect people. Protect *us*." She takes my hand and places it over her stomach. "You just have to separate the joy of the fight from your fierce need to protect. I understand how your environment didn't allow that type of distinction, but you have it now. You have it in me."

My eyes search hers and I've never been so lucky in my life. I lift my hand from her stomach and grab her at the wrist pulling her towards me and kiss her thoroughly.

CHAPTER 13:
I am WuXia

ASHIYA

Dwayne Johnson finally confirms 'Reign' lead coveted role

'Reign' to get early start filming without full cast

Director teases 'Reign' script with Author-Screenplay Writer Ashiya Bride

'Reign' Author Ashiya Bride promises fans script stays *very* close to novel

I scan through the articles surfacing on the Google News Feed curiosity getting the best of me with the recent release of news on *Reign.* I'm excited Dwayne 'The Rock' Johnson is to be a part of this. I couldn't ask for a better Brendan. I had my sights set on Jared Padalecki, but with a prior commitment to a film it was a no go. So when the team suggested Dwayne I was all for it. He came in and blew my mind in his audition.

Sunset Orange.

Niani's aura signature flashes in front of my eyes signaling her arrival at the office apartment just before I hear the front door open and shut loudly in true Niani fashion.

"Hey! How was your night with Cassius?" I smile, closing out the few articles I have open, as I hear her quick stride coming into the room when a chain yokes me up around my neck.

"Ni-a-ni," I choke, her scent filling my nostrils, as I scrape at her hands and the chain trying to pull it off.

I struggle against her hold kicking my desk and sending my laptop askew, as my chair roles backwards into the living room. Enraged, I stop the chair with my foot, grab the chain, flip the chair from under me pulling Niani down and flip her over me. Her back connects with the floor bouncing twice like a skipping stone before lying flat and I go to stand when a painful cramp knots in my abdomen. I press a hand against the pain and notice Niani begin to get up. I can't fight her - not like this. I pull a dagger into my hand from the lining in my shirt, anyway, despite the pain in my stomach from the effort and hear my gritting moan fill the room.

Niani turns like a zombie on me, her eyes glassy, a film wavering over them like light reflecting off water. I wrap an arm protectively around my stomach, the vampire and me warring to protect the babies with everything we have. My K9's elongate on their own accord feeling a pressure behind my eyes. Adrenaline shoots through my body shaking me with rage. But I can't hurt Niani. I have no choice. I do the only thing I can do. I scream.

"CASSIUS!!" an inhuman scream erupts from my throat and in a flash of lightning Cassius is there.

He looks at me on the floor gripping my stomach on all threes hunched over my overturned chair to Niani standing across from us with hypnotic eyes ready to kill. She darts for me and Cassius immediately grabs her

144

around the neck sending a shockwave through her and she collapses unconscious. He collects her in his arms and lays her gently on the ground. Cassius quickly makes his way over to me and bends down placing a hand against my stomach, where my hand is placed. I watch his face wondering what he's checking for, as he moves my hand aside.

"It's a strain," he sighs, pulling away.

"Lean on me," he instructs, pulling my left arm over his neck and swoops me into his arms, carrying me over to the couch and lays me down.

I look at Niani on the floor her heartbeat strong in my ears. I feel like a savage beast, panting hard, body bristling, and wild eyed. Niani shouldn't have done this. I want to hurt her for threatening me and the twins. Why would she do this? What made her do this?

"Ashiya," Cassius says warningly and I look up at him kneeling over her body. He gets up and comes over to me pulling the dagger from my shaking hand and sits down at my side. "It's okay. It looks like she ran into a mermaid at some point and they gave her the Siren's Kiss, which puts anyone under the mermaid's control. Knocking her out should have severed the line. She'll be okay."

I look away from him and blink. Cassius watches the side of my face intently making sure I don't try to reach for my dagger and go after Niani. I know I won't, but I feel the vampire under my skin pacing to take control unappeased with the results. I lift my eyes to Cassius and watch him lift a hand to rest on my stomach, his thoughts whispering through my mind.

"*You can't move.*"

I nod my head and he smiles knowing I read his mind most likely learning how I can from Kai. He gets up from the couch taking his cellphone in to his hand and presses a number on speed dial.

"Hey guys, I have a situation. I need you over at Ashiya's office," he says and hangs up.

"How high was the voltage?" Tiberius asks.

"Enough to keep her incapacitated for the next hour." Cassius signals a hand to a still unconscious Niani now tied down in my chair.

"It must have been good cause she's still breathing," Chief says, bending down in front of Niani's face inspecting her.

Z stands in front of me obviously standing guard in case Niani wakes up, barrels through the three of them and tries to come after me again. My mind is tired. All of these Hypernaturals after me and now they send my own best friend to kill me. I'm going to have to tell her. I can't put it off whatever Kwan-Min knows about her. I look at her, her head lolling to the side, five black dots in her neck where Cassius' bolts went through her. I have no predetermination to how she is going to react to this, especially towards Cassius. My eyes slide up to him. Things got pretty serious between them fast in the last couple of weeks; I hate to ruin it. Cassius thought Niani was the one thing far removed from his job, but not anymore. Niani is going to have to get involved, most likely even fight for me. He won't be able to protect us both. I shake my head. I can't take up majority of their lives. It's not fair to them.

Suddenly, the front door opens and slams with a bang. All of the faeries turn as one, element at the ready, as Kai rushes into the room dropping to his knees before me, one hand against my stomach, the other on the side of my face.

"Alright, who called the Tyrant?" Cassius sighs in frustration, as he drops his hand dousing the blue bolts sprouting from his hand.

"I did," Tiberius snaps annoyed.

"I had him do it, otherwise I knew you wouldn't. You would try handling things on your own," Kai says, turning to Cassius, as he obviously did.

"And this is the reason why!" Cassius snaps, waving a hand at Kai pointedly.

I turn and look at Kai's face seeing cold blown pupils, his usual silver irises nearly matching the whites of his eyes.

The Verserker, I witness.

I exhale a breath in surprise and Kai turns fixing his eyes on Niani. They're possessive and promise retaliation not unlike my vampire before, but this vampire is not hidden under the skin, but full on in control. Of one mind with Kai. I slowly slide a hand over his hand lying on my stomach. He turns back to me his eyes falling on my hand to my eyes and I plead with him, *the vampire* that Niani is not a threat. Kai closes his eyes, softening, as he understands that if Niani was truly in control of her actions she would be infallible to make this mistake. When he opens them again, his eyes are back to normal.

We hear a pain filled moan fill the room and all of us turn to Niani. Kai helps me stand, as Cassius bends down in close to her face and Niani opens her eyes.

"Cassius?" Niani croaks.

Her eyes roam the room before landing on me in Kai's arms.

"What's - ?" Her eyes drop to the ropes around her wrists and legs and looks at Cassius panicked. "Why am I tied up?!" her voice spikes in panic. "What's going o -"

"Niani, I need your attention," he says sternly.

She stops moving and looks at him. "I need you to look at Ashiya." He points a finger at me. Niani follows his finger looking at me. "Do you want to kill her?" he asks delicately.

"No!" She turns her head looking at Cassius like he's crazy. "Why would I want to do that?"

Cassius pulls up to his full height.

"Untie her," he instructs, stepping back.

Chief and Tiberius both step up to untie Niani. The ropes hit the floor and Niani stands.

"You didn't answer my question." She looks at Cassius. "Why would I want to kill Ashiya?"

"Because you tried to over an hour ago. Because you were being hypnotized." Tiberius steps up.

Niani looks at him up and down like he's short.

"Who are you?" she asks rudely.

"I work with Cass," Tiberius says, rolling his eyes and walks away.

I watch him walk away from Niani standing on the edge of the room, folding his arms over his chest, his pride hit. His mount of insecurities seemed to be hit by that one statement. Though anyone else couldn't see it. I look away from Tiberius to everyone else looking at me in expectation.

Tell her the truth, Kai's voice echoes in my head.

I step forward knowing I owe Niani an explanation. I stop between Z and Cassius becoming consciously aware I feel safer this way.

"Niani, I'm a vampire," I start with this to gouge her reaction. As laughable as it sounded I expected her to laugh, but she didn't. I read her mind. Nothing. She's completely open. "Over an hour ago you did try to kill me,

148

because you were under the control of one of the many Hypers that want me dead. A mermaid. Kai is my husband and the only reason I didn't know this was because he took my memories away in order to protect me, but they're coming back now. Cassius and his team are my protectors and faeries. I didn't tell you any of this because I was trying to protect *you*."

Niani looks at me for a moment lifts a finger and points.

"Vampire." I nod. She turns and squishes a tiny space between her thumb and forefinger at Cassius. "Faerie?"

Cassius looks at her like he's not impressed by her choice of gesture. They did just sleep together the night before.

"Elemental faerie," he corrects.

"Elemental," she repeats.

"Elemental," he repeats and throws a hand out sprouting lightning from his fingers.

Her eyes widen at the spectacle and she turns to me.

"Kai," I call him up, since I can't show her anything physical at the moment still in transition.

Kai steps forward and his eyes glow their haunting silver I love. They go out returning back to normal and Niani looks at me anger wrinkling her features.

"Ashiya, we write about this! Why *wouldn't* you tell me? We know enough when the human doesn't know they get hurt or involved. I'm involved! I could have killed you!" she snaps.

She was right. I couldn't deny that. But I had that stupid rule hanging over my head otherwise I would have told her.

"Or Ashiya would have killed you. Or the hypnosis would have," Z speaks up for the first time.

"That makes sense. That's probably why Cass was able to knock the connection off so easily. The spell wasn't complete. Someone must have interrupted the process," Chief says, talking amongst themselves.

Z nods.

I watch Niani's face as she looks between the two of them. Like she can't believe this is happening or that this is her life, but it is. In front of her face. Then she looks at Cassius like she can't stand to be in the same room with him or anyone for that matter.

"I can't do this right now," she says and walks for the door.

"Cass, go with her," I instruct.

"No." Niani stops turning around, as Cassius goes to follow her.

"The only reason none of us aren't dead right now is because we've had people watching over us. Now, he's coming with you," I snap. "Make sure she gets home safe." I look at Cass.

"Yes, Princess." He nods and follows her out at a distance.

"Princess?" Niani huffs, throwing her hands up in exasperation. "Figures," she says, as she walks out the door.

"Well, someone is about to get some angry sex," Chief jokes.

Tiberius looks at him like he's disgusting. "Chief. Shut up."

"You okay?" Kai asks, coming around to face me, a hand on my arm.

"They went after my best friend. I want this ended soon." I look up at Z's eyes on me.

I look around the living room. The chain once around my neck broken in half on the floor. My laptop askew from kicking the desk in my thrashing. The tracks from the wheels in the rug where Niani rolled me out here. I can't be here. Too much has happened here.

"I'm going to go lay down in the apartment," I inform Kai.

"Okay," he says. "I'm going to have Z go with you. I'm going to stay here and talk to Tiberius and Chief for a moment."

I nod and turn for the door, as Z follows me.

1849

"She's lost too much blood, Indra. It's time. You have to say goodbye." The midwife turned and looked at me over her shoulder sympathetically.

She was one of us unbeknownst to Amita's father standing outside the door. A Shatan. I looked at Amita, the bed sheets stained red from her giving birth. Her shallow breathing rattling to my ears. Her chest rising and falling with great struggle. Tears rolling down her temples.

"This wasn't supposed to happen," a lead Shatan from a local coven said sadly behind me.

She was right. This wasn't supposed to happen. Amita wasn't supposed to marry Dorian. She wasn't supposed to have his child either. That was for me. She gave up her happiness, so my life could be spared. This was my fault. This was my punishment. If only I had done what I was charged and put her with Dorian in the first place she wouldn't be here.

Amita gasped for breath and I went to her quickly kneeling at her head and took her hand. She turned her face to me her eyes dancing with unshed tears that fell when she blinked.

"I love you," she rasped.

"I love you, too," I said, gripping her hand tighter, not wanting to let her go.

She turned her head to the babe in Diana's arms, my guard for my transgression.

"His name is Kiran," Amita said.

I looked on the baby, as if he were my own. That was what we were planning to name our child.

"Watch over him for me. Tell him I love him every day." I turn back to her as her hand loses grip in mine and I watch as her bright blue eyes die out.

Shakily, I reach a hand up and close her eyes. Knowing that she's gone and but an empty shell in my arms, I break down holding her head to mine.

I pull myself awake and instantly curl into my pillow, bawling. The *pain*. I can't. I can't. I hyperventilate. I'm sobbing so hard I can't breathe. It was just a dream, but I can't stop crying. Even though I'm in the comfort of my own bed, I still feel like I'm in that room. The metallic smell of blood in that sterile room with the stoic white walls and dark wood borders. The smell of hot sand in the air that never goes away. The bitter taste of grief in the air. The stale taste of death. The Cupid, Faerie, and Shatan in the room. *Everything*. I feel stained by it. Every time I close my eyes I see the blood, Indra's mournful cries, Amita's dead eyes... I need to get away.

I throw the covers back and walk out into the living room, Kai still not home. I hear his distinct husky bass voice through the walls still talking with Tiberius and Chief. Z lies across the couch with a book over his face. I smile.

"You okay?" his voice echoes from under the pages.

"Yeah," I say, really not.

"I heard you crying. Everything okay?" he repeats.

"Bad dream." I sniffle involuntarily.

Suddenly, he sits up letting the book fall into his hands off his face.

"Come on." He stands.

"Where to?" I ask.

"Out," he says, as if he tacked on an "of course". "You need to get out. You and I have been cooped up in this apartment going on six weeks. I don't know about you, but I need more than just a night out. Come on."

I smile at him, as I follow him out of the apartment.

"So, what was your dream about?" Z asks absently, as he drives through town.

"Dying. Being in the wrong man's hands. Leaving behind Kai and our children," I list. "At least that's what I think the dreams are telling me."

"Children?" Z asks, raising a brow.

I forgot that I didn't tell anyone about the twins.

"Yeah, we're having twins," I say for the first time, a smile flitting across my face.

"Congratulations," Z says, smiling broadly, overjoyed by the news.

"Thank you," I say, my smile dropping.

"Are Amita and Indra, who you keep dreaming about?" Z asks, turning onto the highway.

"How did you -" I turn to Z questioning.

"You were crying so hard, you kept saying their names," he answers matter of fact.

"It feels like it," I answer finally with a sigh.

I lean into the cradle of my seatbelt watching the scenery pass by.

"At first I thought that maybe they were my subconscious' way of projecting my fears, but now - it feels as if it's something else. Kwan-Min made these Sais for Niani that I have to give to her. I can speak a language only the ancients supposedly speak. I write about a world I barely know anything about." I can go on, but I don't.

Z looks at me out of the corner of my eyes and says, "*Hala to sa've Me' wi ne lay.*" I turn to him in surprise. "It means, For heaven and haven, I will not die."

"Indra used to say that to Amita as a promise in my dreams," I say surprised.

"It's a promise the ancients use to tell their love ones that their love for them will never die," Z says. "The love one often returns it with, '*Or'a louv t'er yongheng.*' For our love is eternal. Because you know the language it may be hardwired in your brain," Z explains.

"It still doesn't make any sense." I shake my head, not willing to believe that is it. My hyper intuition tells me that isn't it.

"Hopefully, it will soon," Z says. And that I can believe.

An hour later we're sitting in Little Five's Pizza over a shared half eaten large pie with no cheese and tons of veggies. This is the first time since I've met Z that we've actually had some one on one time. I've hung out with Chief, Tiberius, who is just plain quiet, which never bothers me and Cassius, but never Z. Z, who always seems so collected is actually a ball of light.

I laugh over my half eaten slice at him, as he tells me a story about when Tiberius first joined the team. How Chief constantly played jokes on Ti because he never let up. He was always so *serious.*

"Yeah, we have to break him out of that," I say.

"I guess. But it's all a part of his character. He hasn't changed from the day I met him." Z smiles.

"Poor Mr. Grumps feels like he has a lot to prove," I comment.

"Why?" Z asks, frowning.

"I don't know," I answer honestly. "I guess he feels inadequate compared to his big brothers or feels like he has to make up for something in himself."

Z frowns. "I don't know why. He's great at what he does. He has a lot of experience under his belt in comparison to our years."

I nod. "And honors," I add, remembering the line of pins hanging from his badge. They all had some, but none as many as Tiberius. The likeliest reason he was set with them in the first place.

"So, time for me to grill you Z," I say playfully.

He leans over the table crossing his arms all ears.

"Besides being my protection detail. Do you moonlight as a bartender?" I joke. "Go home to someone significant?"

He gives me a secretive smile. "It all depends on if you imagine me straight or not."

My mouth drops reading between the lines. "You're gay?" I ask.

"Yup. Been dating this vampire whether or not for a couple of years," he admits, taking a bite out of his crust.

"Okay. So not only are you vegan, lactose intolerant, but you're also gay." I tick off with my fingers.

He nods proudly with a smile. "I'm still trying to bring you over to the dark side," he adds, joking over the fact that I quit eating meat since the start of my pregnancy.

I get enough protein from blood alone that I don't actually want meat, but rather crave fruits, vegetables, grains, beans, and oddly the occasional case of coconut water. Actually, the scent of any meat repulses me. Even the scent of anyone else's blood besides Kai's sends my

155

stomach rolling with nausea and considering that in a warped sense he is my sire and the babies' father I will only take his blood. Either that or this was my own version of morning sickness. Good thing we don't need blood all the time, because I wouldn't want to weaken Kai in our state of affairs.

I giggle at Z's comment and take another bite of my veggie pizza for emphasis.

"Yes!" he exclaims.

"So, will I ever get to meet him?" I ask suddenly.

"Who?" Z questions.

"The vampire you've been dating!" I exclaim, as if I need to remind him.

"If it gets serious." He smiles.

"Gets serious?!" I reply. "You've been dating the vampire for two years. Things better be serious."

Z chuckles, shaking his head at me, as he looks up at me under the hood of his dark lashes.

"How are you doing about Niani?" he asks suddenly.

My smile drops as I look up at Z and shake my head.

"Why do you and Cassius ask questions that I feel Kai should be asking me?" I ask softly, placing my pizza down on the paper plate before me.

"Because you miss him and we're your friends," Z answers empathically. "You two have been dealt cards that haven't been exactly fair to you. Kai sees you and knows you aren't taking this well, but decides in making it easier on you, for you. You see it, too. You know he's having a hard time within himself, as if this is bringing back all the demons of his past with the clan."

I lean forward on the table. "What happened Z? What happened to him? To all of you?"

"Too much," he clips, going no further.

His bright blue eyes are haunted, swimming with trauma. What happened to them? His eyes lift up to mine and again he leans forward verifying the seriousness of this.

"Think of your children when I tell you this, Ashiya. You don't want to know," he pleads.

A hand instinctively goes over my stomach and he's right. I don't want to know.

NIANI

I'm in the apartment for all of twenty seconds when Ashiya walks in. She stops when she spots me on her couch inside her and Kai's apartment and I watch her hands instinctively move for the hidden daggers at her hips, her eyes darting around the apartment for things unknown. Immediately, I throw my hands up in a show of peace. Kai warned me that the vampire would still be gunning for me after what happened earlier. No matter under what control, I had broken the bond Ashiya's vampire associated with me and with Ashiya feeling suspicious of me it isn't helping my case with the vampire symbiont.

"What are you doing here Niani?" Ashiya asks, still not making any moves to pull her hands away from her daggers.

"Kai let me in. I came to see if you were all right. Cassius and Kai explained what happened earlier. What's happening *to* you and I wanted to know if you were okay. If the babies are okay." I inch a smile at the last sentence. Wow. My best friend - my sister - is having twins.

"We're fine," she replies guarded. "I'm sorry." She frowns.

"I feel like I should be the one apologizing for what happened earlier even if I didn't have control over myself," I say.

Right then, her demeanor changes and her eyes soften making her way over to the couch next to me.

"I'm sorry," she says softly. "Are you okay? I threw you pretty hard earlier."

"I'll live." I smirk. "So - our books that good, huh? We have every *Hyper*natural creature out to get us?" I joke.

She smiles. "No, just me. Sadly, you were just a pawn in my demise."

"Wow, you demote me down to a pawn?" I comment sarcastically.

"I'm the one wired with the brain for the Hypernatural." She points at her head. "How are you and Cass?" she asks.

I shrug. "We'll work it out."

Ashiya shakes her head obviously frustrated by that news.

"It's not your fault, Ashiya. I understand why neither one of you could tell me. Right now, me and Cass have to navigate the supernatural part of our relationship."

Ashiya looks at me with downcast eyes, shaking her head. "I'm sorry."

"Trust me, we're going to be okay, Ashiya," I assure her. "Now, I know I'm only human, but are you sure there is nothing I can do to help?"

Ashiya looks at me, a light flashing in her eyes as if there is. She gets up and walks upstairs to the second level of the apartment and brings down with her a heavy looking marble case.

"These are for you," she says, as she takes her seat beside me and moves the definitely heavy case to my lap.

"*These* are mine?" I ask skeptically, looking up at her.

"Yeah," she answers. "Me and Kai's weapon maker told us to give these to you. They were made for you."

I look at Ashiya. I know her. With her giving me these she thinks she's sending me out for the slaughter. That me getting involved will somehow ruin the life I could have had. That I could die.

At least I'll have reasons behind why I die. To protect her. To help these two to be drop dead gorgeous babies come into this world. I turn to the case and bring my hands to the latches flipping them open with a flourish not willing to let my fear make me hesitate. I lift the lid consciously aware I'm holding my breath and inhale as my eyes take in the contents inside.

On black silk lay a pair of antique looking Sais. The three prong blades are sharpened to the upmost peak and I know without much effort on my end I can slice through flesh like butter maybe even bone if the Hypernaturals have anything to do with it. I run my fingers over the deep bronze handles feeling the exotic inscription underneath my fingertips. Suddenly, I can't move them. My fingers are stuck over the inscriptions, as if magnetized. I'm ready to panic and ask Ashiya what's going on when my head feels funny and under no control of my own I start muttering words I can't understand.

"Hala to sa've Me' wi ne lay."

"Hala to sa've Me' wi ne lay."

"Hala to sa've Me' wi ne lay."

"Hala to sa've Me' wi ne lay."

"Hala to sa've Me' wi ne lay."

I can't stop myself from saying it as I repeat the words over and over again. I say it so much I start to remember it. I black out and images flood my brain in fast forward.

A handsome Asian man I know somehow as Kwan-Min sits on the floor of a calligraphy room in ancient silk robes at a table repeating back to me the same words I still hear in my head. I look down onto the table where he's writing in an unknown dotted, swirling language and I see the same words, the same inscription on the Sais along the paper glaring back at me.

"Je t'er yerda charuju."

I look up at him as the words leave his lips, when he suddenly jumps the table striking out at me. I throw my arms up over me in a feeble attempt to block his attack. When I don't feel the impact, I bring my arms down to see I'm in a bazaar. A true Indian bazaar, cramped and elbow to elbow packed as stall owners yell their wares for the day, customers haggle potential purchases, and the scent of spices and fresh made bread waft in the air with the sparse peppering of a British soldier. Like the white rabbit, my eyes are drawn to a young Indian man about my age standing down the way and I watch as he ducks behind a stall.

I follow him and tail him as he secretly watches a woman with beautiful ivory skin, bright blue eyes, and ebony hair covered in a sky blue silk sahri that matches her eyes draped over her head. Her eyes lift up catching mine and I see into a life that should have never been:

She and the Indian man leaning against a tree, him standing over her, their hands intertwining intimately as they talk quietly.

The two of them in the grass kissing under a tree by a large river under a dark canopy of forest, the late afternoon sun hazy with their romance. Friends lounge nearby on rocks looking over the river or swimming, smiling over their friends teasingly.

Everything feels so light, beautiful, *sweet*, until it becomes very dark. I watch her scream and fight a much older man, as he busts out the front door of a house with a rifle and points it at the Indian man taking the shot. I scream, a hand covering my mouth, as he collapses to the floor blood sprouting from the wound in his shoulder.

As she lay broken with a man she did not love and given vows to whom they did not belong to.

The Indian man healed and well at her side after her giving birth, the sheets stained with her blood. Her skin pale and sickly, as I watch them talk quietly, the room filled with the somber resolve waiting for the inevitable. I watch as she gives him her last "I love you" to the baby in a woman's arms and falls silent forever. I gasp tearfully from where I stand in the room wanting to run, get away from this as I watch the Indian man breakdown. Suddenly, I'm back in Ashiya and Kai's living room and I can't breathe as I choke on my sobs crying harder than I ever have before.

I feel Ashiya beside me unsure of how to react. She lifts a hand to hug me, touch me, something, when I throw a hand up and tell her to give me a minute. I stop crying and look at Ashiya my eyes now wide open to the truth. I look down into the case and lift a Sai slowly into my hands.

Suddenly, I feel my mind snatched. A load of information downloading into my brain, a flash of fast forward maneuvers and mixed martial art moves second nature to my unaccustomed limbs. When I open my eyes, my left hand is bleeding where it was holding on to the blade in a death grip. I open my palm surprised that it doesn't hurt.

I look up at Ashiya to see if my blood entices her, but she looks ready to be sick.

"I guess that answers my question, my blood doesn't tempt you." I smirk.

Ashiya slowly swallows and shakes her head, appearing to get her nausea under control. I turn back to my case.

"I failed in killing you. The mermaid will come back. First after me, then you," I state, taking the other Sai from the case.

I feel them in my hands, the handles solid and the weight distribution perfect. I flip them in my hands and notice the inscriptions imprinted into my palms and fingers with no sign of going away. Along my palms is tiny gold iridescent glitter running up my fingers and arms.

"You got that just before you started chanting and this pulsating energy bubbled from your Sais," Ashiya explains.

"Magik," I comment looking at my arms. I look as if I've just been glitter bombed.

"Are you okay?" Ashiya asks in concern.

"Yeah." I sigh, turning to Ashiya.

"You smell different," she comments.

I smile, trying not to laugh. "That's because I'm a Hyper, now. I'm a WuXia."

CHAPTER 14:
Amita

ASHIYA

Niani and I force our way into the office apartment bypassing Kai and the Faeries Four sitting in the living room going straight for our office. Kai stands up following us in concern along with Cass, but before they can cross the threshold Niani throws a finger up making them both stop. "Don't come in here. You don't want to see this."

Niani and I pull books off our shelves throwing them on the floor. Those we worked on together, read for research, or wrote on our own. We get down on our hands and knees flipping through chapters and passages, reading, coming to small conclusions before coming to Niani's newly released manga flipping it open and stop.

In a bonus picture we see Kallea, red hair thrown over her shoulder, nearly scantily dressed in a slitted skirt and bra top showing off her midriff with Sais in her hands in a seductive stance. To her right in a dialogue box:

"*I* am *WuXia.*"

Niani and I slowly sit back on our behinds. I look up at my books still lining my bookshelf. All my research. I feel Niani look at her drawing station, her wall filled with her artwork as if they betrayed her.

"Ashiya, what's going on?" Kai asks.

I look back at the picture before me.

"I wasn't the only one writing about Hypers," I say slowly, looking at Niani as she looks at me. "You are, too, except, you are drawing them. But why would they make you a WuXia if -" I stop and look up at Cass standing outside the door remembering what he said about what Hypernaturals exist. WuXia wasn't one of them. "If you were meant to be the only one," I state finally.

"Don't I feel special," Niani cracks sarcastically.

She then looks at the drawings on her wall and stands up going over to them. She stands there for a moment looking them over in silence.

"I was warning you," she says suddenly with a frown turning away from her wall. "If you look at the date on any of these you'll see they were right before we started a book, finished it, or - " she throws her hands up in exasperation, "half of these were during the time you were dating Kai."

I frown.

"But if this was going on since - What? - *we* met, then where is any of this coming from? *Whisper* was based off an idea you came up with. I ran with it. We worked on it up until college? Between that time I was working on *Reign*. You were working through Animation classes. We hadn't even published anything yet. What could you be warning me about? Between work and school we had no time for -"

"I've got a headache," Niani whines, putting her head in her hands.

"Girls, you want to explain what's going on?" Chief asks over Kai's shoulder.

"It looks like some Hyper made a sick joke of our lives turning me into a Chinese knight and Ashiya in to a Hyper life whisperer!" she exclaims.

164

All the guys look at her with raised eyebrows, as if they don't want to touch that with a five foot pole.

"What's going on is that none of this is making sense. The Sais that Kwan-Min gave Niani turned her in to a Hyper. A WuXia, a mystical Chinese knight in term. As much as I've been writing about this world, Niani has been *drawing* it. She's been warning me. We just never knew it."

I walk over to the wall of drawings, the guys following me in. Manga artists and J. Scott Campbell have always inspired Niani, so a lot of her work reflected those influences. I look at a drawing of two heads, a man and a woman kissing dated on 3 November 2012. The day before Kai's birthday. The girl's long hair floats in an invisible wind, as her head angles just right, the man's hair windswept sexily as he leans in. I frown as it easily could be Kai and I.

"Hey Kai, it looks like she got your hair just right," Chief jokes, pointing out said picture.

"Shut up," Kai remarks.

"Okay guys, let's step away from this for a moment," Cassius coaxes.

We all walk away into the living room taking seats on the couch, chairs, or parking it on the floor in utter silence. Things just became absolutely weirder. When Niani mentioned what she was I remembered the name somewhere from one of our books and how one of them featured the WuXia, not until I remembered the book isn't out *yet*. Not until July next year. I didn't expect Niani to be so wrapped up in this. I didn't think she would play a role, but the Hypers had another thing in mind.

I look around the room, everyone lost in their own thoughts. We were an eclectic group, four elementals, two daylight vampires, and one mystical knight. None of us were going to be able to sleep tonight.

I sit up on the couch, everyone's eyes falling to me at my movement.

"I think it's time you explain to us what parts of my books are fact," I say, looking around at the faeries four and Kai.

Some minutes later we're sitting at the kitchen table around a pot of coffee and decaffeinated tea for me. Cassius sits in front of me, his hands wrapped around a cooling mug.

"When you were in college a faerie discovered," Z begins, drawing our attention to him at the sink, as he rinses out his mug, "a short story you wrote for the creative magazine that helped us discover and craft Blaizinium. Everything you wrote about it being in Europe and Asia, how it is created, where and who would find it was true. You saved many lives in a time of great rivalry and unrest between the Hypers. Hey, you mind as well helped us stop a war. You put that in *Reign*."

"Everything you wrote about most of our occupations, how we move, how we conduct business is what has everyone in an uproar. We live in a world where we have to live with humans, but not be upfront about who we are, because some humans are not going to be as openhearted as you and Niani have been. We are literally scared for our lives. Afraid one day someone is going to put two and two together and then it'll all be over," Tiberius explains uncharacteristically sympathetic, leaning against the windows.

And I gave them the ammo. Niani and I look at each other across the table. The shame couldn't be more permeable.

166

"Baby doll," Chief leans against the table between us leveling his eyes with mine, "Us telling you what is fact will not prepare for what you will see. I know you're trying to find answers, to why, to how, but as a writer you know that you cannot be *told*, but shown," he advises.

I sigh and feel a large hand touch my cheek and look back up into Chief's brown eyes.

"Don't be sorry, because everything happens for a reason," he says sagely. I close my eyes and nod. He leans down and kisses my forehead whispering, "Don't worry," before pulling away and turning to Niani. "You too, firecracker."

I smile at the nickname and turn to Kai, who's been quiet since we sat down. His eyes meet mine and he smiles softly. He looks tired and I remember what Z said earlier about all of this bringing back all the demons of his past. If there is anything I want more is this to be over for him.

"Let's call it a night, guys," I say, not looking away from Kai and he smiles.

Chief catches the exchange and tosses the rest of his coffee back and places the mug down on the counter. "Alright guys, I know that look. Let's give these two some privacy."

One by one everyone gets up, Niani tossing me a small smile before they all make their way out. When the door finally closes behind Ti, Kai sighs from his chair.

"I need something stronger than this," he says, standing and walks over to the corner of the counter where Niani and I keep a bottle of red, uncorks it, and fills his mug.

I walk over to the counter near Kai and lean across it.

He looks up eyeing me from over his mug, as he takes a sip. I move around the counter and lean back against the countertop across from him. He steps forward and presses up against me and puts his mug down behind me, trapping me within his arms, his hands low on my hips. Suddenly, his eyebrows are twitching into a frown.

"I know I haven't asked this yet and I am sorry, but how are you doing with all this?" he asks concerned.

"I'm not fine, but I am okay. If that makes any sense," I answer, huffing a small laugh.

"It does," he says softly.

I stare into his eyes and say, "I love you."

"I love you, too." He smiles broadly.

NIANI

Everything is different now.

I can feel the earth move, inch by glorious inch, the sun's ultraviolet energy charging every cell in my body, the moon's gravitational pull. I can feel gravity circling through my veins up and down dragging me down to earth, yet ready to fly off at any given moment. I've been changed. Through alchemic properties I was now something extraordinary. I don't think anybody was aware of how different.

I spent better part of the night in my living room scrolling through every form, maneuver, and counter strike the Sais downloaded into my head like a manual. I knew nothing of martial arts before yesterday besides what I have read, but now I was like Bruce Lee without the training. Physically, I not only feel different but look different, too. The imprints and iridescent glitter on my palms, fingers, and arms had not gone anywhere. My muscles more defined.

I don't know whether to feel overwhelmingly scared which would be totally in my right mind to feel, but knowing how heavy things can get. *Will* get. Any nerves I have don't outweigh the duty I ultimately feel to Ashiya. Next to dating an elemental this is by far the most epic thing to happen to me. A complete 360 to how I was feeling last night. Today, I can deal.

Like now, as I turn out of Jonah's office, one of the lead animators on the *Reign* project with me. After going over the layout design notes with him. It feels normal.

Suddenly, a hand lands on my shoulder as I close the door behind me and immediately I can tell *he* isn't human. I turn pulling a mini cyclone of fire orange energy between my palms, lock it between intricately poised fingers and thrust it from my right palm hitting him square in the chest. The force of the blast sends him slamming into the wall behind him, citrine metallic fire burning off his cotton shirt, as blue electricity sparks off as it connects, when a familiar moan reaches my ears. I throw my hands down pulling out of stance to see Cassius frantically patting the fire out on his shirt, hissing in pain on the floor as he does so.

"Cassius?!" I exclaim.

"Ah! What was that?!" he gasps painfully, finally putting the fire out.

I don't say anything. It's against code to talk of the way of the *Xia*. Without a word, I bend down and pull him up.

Checking out the commotion, one by one people start sticking their heads outside their offices, including the door I just came out of. Jonah looks down at me asking, "Everything okay out here?"

169

"Yeah," I sigh, "we just ran into each other." I turn to everyone else down the hall. "We're good," I say, waving a hand with a sugarcoated smile.

They all duck back into their offices closing the doors behind them and I turn back to Cassius.

"What are you doing here, Cassius?" I ask.

"I came to check on you," he says, his eyes running up and down my body catching on the Sais attached around my thighs like leg braces peeking above my thigh high boots. "We didn't get to talk yesterday after -" He nods towards my legs referring to the elephant in the hall regarding my new status as a Hyper.

I roll my eyes and grab his hand dragging him into the closest empty conference room. I close the door behind us and turn to him.

"Are you okay? Are we - okay?" he asks self-consciously.

My eyes dart to nothing around the room, then I sigh.

"My best friend is a pregnant vampire, who has Hypers after her for things she can't control. She has you and your team to protect her, but no that's *my* job. I wish I could share the things that are going on with me with you, but I can't! I'm all alone in this and *yes* we are fine." I hear the tremble in my voice and I know I'm more emotional than I care to be.

Cassius steps forward placing his hands along my arms and his beautiful fair green eyes stare into mine.

"You're not alone," he says softly, "because you have me and I'm not going anywhere."

I can feel the current of electricity through his skin under my fingertips and I don't know what takes over me. It's erotic, like smooth velvet under my skin. Humming. Restless. I can feel his heartbeat in my skin beating within

170

my palms, as if I hold his heart in the palm of my hands. I breathe him in literally tasting his sweetness on my tongue, as his lips fall prey to mine. But just as quickly as I'm victimizing his lips, I'm pushing him away.

"Ashiya!" I gasp.

"What's wrong?" Cassius asks in alarm.

"Ashiya's in trouble." I back pedal and move around Cass closer into the room.

"Come. I can get us there faster." He grabs my hand and pulls me with him to the door.

"No." I pull my hand from his. "I can," I say and look toward the window realizing where I was headed.

"No," Cassius says, as he follows my eyes to the window and back.

"*Yes*," I say with a smile, making my way towards the window. "Meet you downstairs," I add, pulling the window open before hopping out.

KAI

Z opens the door for Ashiya into the apartment and she walks in digging in her purse searching for a possible sticky note she may have written on at some point. I otherwise would find it cute knowing she takes to writing on any hard surface she can find and taping it inside a book once she gets home. If it weren't for the current situation I were in. It doesn't occur to her that she shouldn't be here, until I see her eyebrows knit together into a frown and her steps slow, then she hears my voice.

"Ashiya, don't move."

She stops and looks up, the look of dread already on her face. I watch her eyes flit around the room to me sitting in one of the chairs, the curtains drawn tight behind me blocking out any sunlight from getting in, to the two others standing in the room. To my back, Marcus, a handsome young dark-skinned vampire frozen in his 30's dressed in an expensive all black suit to Mahina, the tall Latina vampire with bob short violet hair standing at the end of what used to be our coffee table, to Niani and Cassius sitting on the couch.

I watch her eyes survey the mess Niani and Mahina made of the room. On the floor of the fireplace there is broken glass everywhere, the candles having fallen off, the mantle broken, the marble smashed. The banister to the stairs broken leaning haphazardly for dear life on its own splinters waiting to impale someone. The coffee table shattered.

Mahina is holding up better than she looks with a bloody lip, paling skin and a few deep decaying slashes on her torso, left arm, which includes a badly hanging shoulder and thigh gash after Niani took it to her. Everything else healed before the Blaizinium could take effect slowing her healing factor considerably.

Ashiya's eyes land on Marcus behind me staring at her as if he wants to possess her with his dark eyes they could be black. Beside her, I watch Z step up on her right. For a moment, I'm hopeful. He won't stand for this.

"Hello beautiful," Marcus says in a smooth voice and a sure charismatic smile, his aura black as night demanding respect.

I notice his eyes go pass Ashiya to Z.

"Hey handsome," Z answers.

The world stops, as so does my heart. *What?*

I watch as Ashiya's face crumbles in betrayal, as she stares at Marcus across from her and I wish I could read her mind in this moment. Z barely gets two steps passed

172

her toward Marcus, before Cassius shoots off the couch catching Z in the face with his fist.

"You brought him to her?!" he yells at Z's broken form on the floor. I watch as a wad of blood dribbles from Z's mouth, as he lands on his hands and knees. "This is who you've been - ?!" He can't get it out he's so hurt. "Kai's ex-clan leader?!"

At his words, Ashiya for the first time looks at Z in shock.

Cassius lifts a leg to kick Z while he's down, when Ashiya says, "Stop."

Cassius stops looking at her, as if to ask why should he, when she looks at Marcus, as Z climbs his way off the floor.

"If you're not here to kill me, what do you want?" she asks fiercely, clearly reading Marcus' thoughts.

That bit of information makes me exhale a sigh in relief.

Marcus steps forward and I snap from my seat, "Marcus, if you touch her. I will kill you."

Marcus stops where he stands and smirks. He knows I will make good on my threat. He made me this way anyway.

"I'll say getting faeries to protect her. I'm very proud, Kai. Especially, with that one," he nods toward Niani.

"Stop wasting time. You have a clan member dying over there," I snap.

He barely glances at Mahina, as if they've been through all this before as many times as they have. Then his eyes land back on Ashiya.

"I would never hurt a daughter of Amita," he says with an enticing edge.

173

Ashiya's eyes widen a fraction in recognition and I frown. Her mom's name isn't Amita. Who is Amita?

"Amita is a woman from my dreams," Ashiya says to Marcus. "She isn't real."

She never told me about this.

Marcus' smile lingers, as he ducks his head as if to hide his laughter.

He picks his head back up and looks at Ashiya. "As real as that necklace around your neck." He references the short teardrop abalone pendant I bought her in Hilton Head sitting on her clavicle.

He then pulls out a chain hidden under his waistcoat and holds out a pendant I recognize of a ruby teardrop within a silver circle around ornate filigree in three spaces where the circle and tear don't meet, but on closer inspection it's not a ruby at all. It's blood inside a vial shaped into a teardrop.

He looks at the pendant longingly in his hand and for a moment there he looks almost sad, before looking up at Ashiya.

"Ever wondered why you were attracted to the teardrop - *that* necklace?" he asks, pointing to the pendant around her neck.

"The rain? The *darkness*? How from the moment you were born your life has been a *constant* lament." He pushes forward, his voice growing stronger, angrier with passion.

He takes a step forward to gauge her reaction and he doesn't lose. Her breath hitches in truth and my heart squeezes painfully in my chest never knowing her pain was this deep. Afraid of this from the very beginning that she would be attracted to this darkness, the darkness that still was embedded in my heart. She was perfect for his world. From the moment we met I could see it. The way

174

she dressed in dark laces, sheers, and vests as if she came from two different periods in time, a modern, but bygone era. How when she found out I was a vampire, she seemed to settle far better into us than I ever seen her. As if she belonged. As if my darkness was her light.

I feel my heart ache for me. Marcus is going to take her away from me.

"I've been trying to find you in order to protect you, and before you say I have enough protectors only her and myself are supposed to be your guardians." He nods at Niani again. "The faeries have always been his," He points to me, "Extendedly yours."

"And how are *you* my guardian?" Ashiya asks, as if testing him.

"I was there when Amita died. I was there when your Sais or *mili* were crafted," he answers, looking at Niani. "I know how your stories connect." He looks at me.

"Okay," Ashiya says without a second of hesitation.

"Ashiya!" I exclaim.

"Kai, I've been looking for answers. This is my answer." She glances at Marcus from me.

Cassius and Niani look at the side of her face, as if she has lost her mind.

"We all go," she finalizes, making it clear that she is not going anywhere without us.

"Great!" Marcus chirps, as he picks up his jacket from the couch and throws it over his arm, waving Mahina on a little too excitedly.

Ashiya cuts a look at Z, as she turns Cassius and Niani falling in line with her, flanking her on either side, as they walk out. We turn out of the apartment, all of us, running into William standing outside the office apartment. Right now, it couldn't be a worse time for him to show up.

"Right now, isn't a good time William. Call me in two hours," Ashiya orders, as we walk by.

I watch his eyes flit from face to face over our dangerous looking group. I know he feels it that weight on his shoulders that makes vampires feel intimidating to humans, when his eyes land on Mahina.

"Is she okay?" he asks, when suddenly she collapses into his arms.

"Bring her," Marcus orders flippantly, not looking back as he walks ahead with an arm thrown over Z's shoulder.

No. I watch Ashiya turn to stop William when I stop her and she looks at me. I shake my head at her silently. She understands. The less he knows of what is going on, the less danger he will be in. She turns into my arms with Niani and Cassius on either side of us and follows Z and Marcus on to the elevator. William collects Mahina into his arms and follows us on to the elevator.

As the door closes, Marcus flips a hood over his head hanging from his suit jacket and looks at me with a smirk when he catches me looking.

"Courtesy of Kwan-Min," he gloats.

If I didn't want to murder Marcus right then, Kwan-Min would be first on my list. Then Marcus looks around me to William.

"She has a sun allergy," he says, nodding his head to the hood hanging from the back of her neck.

William looks down at her in his arms and carefully maneuvers her in his arms pulling the hood over her face and picks her back up in his arms. To see the gentility he puts into her surprises me in opposition of his pursuit toward Ashiya.

I do not like where I see this going.

CHAPTER 15:
The Tragedy

ASHIYA

"What do you think?" Marcus asks proudly, as we walk down a dark hallway of his contemporary style gothic mansion.

The decor oddly reminds me of the hallway into The White Bar, which makes me think he might own it. Matter of fact I *know* he owns it, digging in his mind. Which also makes me think that Kwan-Min was right. We should be glad it didn't garnish us some unwanted attention, unless it had given us our current situation.

I cut my eyes at Marcus and say, "I'm not staying," reading his underlying thought to get me to stay.

"I expected that as much," Marcus says, shrugging indifferently. "Well, there is always a room for you and Kai here." Marcus looks at Kai over Z's shoulder.

Kai scowls at him and I look over at Mahina in the back of the group looking up at William, as she hangs weakly from his arms. He's been quiet since Marcus told him to bring her in, not that anyone would answer his questions on the limo ride over. He wonders if this is going to be where he dies. If Kai, Niani, and I were somehow involved in something bad due to Cassius. My "protection detail". I roll my eyes at his thoughts.

I turn back around and look up at the high Cathedral raftered ceiling. It's hard to believe we're still in Atlanta, instead of an old 18th century English manor. The contemporary style smoked glass sconces shaped like stemless wine glasses lining the hallway highlight the dark purple wallpapered walls giving it a modern touch and I look over at Marcus. It takes a certain character to have such a style mansion and I don't doubt that he is definitely a character. He has a certain flair for the dramatics, which I can see given his manner of speech and an appreciation for the arts, as I read his thoughts about his next home improvement project: carving the rafters.

I barely contain rolling my eyes and shaking my head at him. I look up at Kai staring ahead of him, as he holds me close to his side and I wonder what this has to do with him. What Amita, who I thought was a woman in my dreams has to do with Niani and I. I'm prepared to know I'm not going to like the answer.

We reach the dark wood door at the end of the hall with a rectangular stained glass window and Marcus opens the door with a smile back at us. We step into an oversized den filled top to bottom with vampires. Overhead they stare down at us leaning over banisters of a staircase, lounging on chairs and couches set up around a Persian rug in the middle of the room.

"Welcome," Marcus says dramatically, walking into the room around us and sweeping the room with wide arms.

The room is identical to the hallway outside with the same matching purple wallpaper and dark stained wood moldings, live plants spattering the room, as stained glass windows showing Hypernatural figures circle the den: a kneeling angel cradling a heart, a man standing on fire, a dragon circling a lotus flower and a ball of fire, a mermaid laying seductively at the bottom of the ocean, and a man and woman standing back to back in Greecian clothing under a ray of light. The only ones I don't see memorialized are the Vampire and Faerie.

I turn around to find Marcus staring at me.

"We need to talk," he states, stepping up to me and reaches for me as if to force me along.

Kai quickly pushes me behind him before Marcus can touch me and I see the anger cross Marcus' face. He's grown tired of Kai's constant interfering and I can see in my mind's eyes his means to attack him if he had the upper hand. Choke him out and break his neck so that he can get a moment alone with me and I just react. Anger flaring in my chest, I duck under Kai's arm, grabbing Marcus by his throat, using all the speed I possess, my momentum lifting him off his feet and slam him hard into his varnished wood floor, splintering it. Over my left shoulder, I see William jump in shock.

"You forgot something," I growl into his face.

In an instant his clan is on their feet and I turn throbbing eyes on them, Kai by my side.

"Ashiya, your eyes," Niani whispers in awe.

I cut my eyes to the full-length mirror across from me seeing my eyes glittering green into mercury with bright crescent moons shining in the pupils looking back at me. *Beautiful.* Marcus laughs under the pressure of my hand hard and deep, delighted and I turn back to him. I look back at his clan and they don't know whether to attack or back off. They're sizing Kai and I up and confused to their leader's reaction. They look at me. They look at Kai. They look at our team. Cass and Niani at the ready. They see our eyes. They see our power. I took down their leader. Finally, Marcus waves a hand at them to back off and they all settle down, taking their seats. Kai and I turn back to Marcus.

"I'm sorry, I didn't mean to startle you. I only want to talk," Marcus says, under the strain of my hand.

"You have another thing coming if I'm leaving her alone with you," Kai grits through his teeth.

"That," I nod towards Kai, "and her," I say, nodding toward Mahina in William's arms over my shoulder, as if to remind him.

Marcus raises an eyebrow at me when a moment passes and I still haven't taken my hand from around his neck. Not done with him yet, I get closer in his face adding pressure to my hand around his neck hearing muscles pop and Marcus winces.

"If I were you, I would watch my *thoughts*. Do we have an understanding?" I threaten.

"Okay. '*Kay*,'" he says hoarsely, putting his hands up in surrender.

So unlike myself, I smirk at that. I force my hand away from around his neck and stand up. Marcus pulls out of the imprint his body made in the floor and looks down at it, sighing in frustration. He waves a hand at no one in particular and it's my turn to flinch, as the familiar figure rounds the staircase. Those *eyes* stare into mine unflinching, as the day I first saw him in the lobby over a month ago.

"I see you've met Wilson already," Marcus says. "I had him tailing you for a while before you went underground. Doesn't talk much, but a great healer."

Wilson, a faerie, I notice by the scent of hot chocolate and cotton candy coming off of him, as he walks over to William taking Mahina from his arms. He turns to walk away with her when William speaks up.

"Can I go with her?"

And once again I'm surprised by his concern for her. I can feel it. Something there new and warm blossoming in the sun of it. Wilson looks at me, as if to ask for permission.

"Yes," Kai steps up and answers for me, "but he comes back the same."

Wilson nods and William follows after him, as he carries Mahina out of the room.

Once they're gone, Marcus pipes up, "My guests, follow me."

He turns and leads the way through two dark wood doors off the den, closing the sliding doors behind us. It's a study, simple with bookshelves taking up a full wall, cherry wood furniture, and a roaring hearth in the corner with diamond pane windows open to a large green backyard. But what makes the room is the set of three stained glass windows, each depicting a woman: an angel holding a heart up to the heavens, a woman with a crown levitating above her head dressed shoulder to floor in red, her hair cascading down her back, wrists out turned exuding power in her stance, and next a woman holding a ball of light in between her in turned palms, light rays covering her naked body. All of them depict women of African descent.

I walk over to the window with the woman in red and turn to Marcus, as he takes a seat on the leather couch, laying his hooded suit jacket to his left.

"This is me, isn't it?" I ask, sensing something familial about it.

"Yes." Marcus smiles proudly. "Have a seat, Princess," he directs politely to the couch across from him, where Kai and Cassius are already seated.

181

I walk over to the couch, taking the seat between Kai and Cass. Niani stands not for a second delaying time off an attack if she had to stand up from sitting down. Marcus watches her and smiles for a moment, before turning to me.

"Before we get started, we took care of your mermaid problem," he says, looking at Niani.

Niani doesn't say anything, but stares at him.

Marcus then fixes me with those intense black eyes of his and I look anywhere but him around the room, unnerved by his attention.

"I'm sorry, I don't mean to make you uncomfortable," he says reverently, looking at me emotionally like a proud father would at his daughter as a grown woman, "but give me a moment. - I remember the day your parents brought you home, so small and beautiful and watching you grow up. - There were so many times I wanted to take you away."

A flash of emotion strikes across his eyes, as I tear up seeing his memories of me in my mind. Me laughing with my drama castmates outside the stage doors on the middle school sidewalk after practice nearing nightfall. Me, hurt and depressed under a dark sky threatening rain, as I walked around my neighborhood after a fight with my mother in high school. I remember wishing it would rain, so it could match what I wanted to do, but couldn't - cry. Sitting in the front row watching me play my first viola solo at my orchestra concert. My parents weren't there going through an emotional break-up, but he was. My dad wouldn't have been able to make it. He was out of town on business, but my mom - I push away from all the memories and look at Marcus.

"Then why didn't you?" I ask him.

A heavy hollow feeling weighs down in my heart and all sorts of emotions I can't explain come to me at once. Is it elation? Surprise? Betrayal? Anger? I think about all the things that could have been if he had. I could have been with Kai a long time ago. I could have escaped my mother's abuse a long time ago. I could have been happy. I could -.

"I would have - I was - but certain *politics* kept me from making that happen," Marcus says, annoyed by the memory, suddenly leaning back and throwing his right arm behind Z across the back of the couch. I watch his hand idly massage at the nape of his neck.

I can feel Niani, Cassius, and Kai's eyes bounce between me and Marcus wondering what was transpiring between us unable to see what I could see.

"What do me, Kai, and Niani have to do with Amita?" I ask.

Marcus looks at me for a moment, before answering.

"Amita is your great, great, many greats grandmother," he explains. "On her deathbed, before you were even thought of, you were promised to us. Amita was a human, who became romantically involved with a Cupid named, Indra. Cupids are sent to protect and lead chosen mates to each other. Instead of Amita falling in love with her chosen, she met and fell in love with Indra. Indra tried to fight it, but Amita wouldn't. She didn't care if she was chosen for another or what Indra was, she loved him." Marcus eyes drop sadly to the pendant lying in his lap.

"Indra soon stopped fighting his feelings for her and they became inseparable. The Hyper community fell in love with her. She was kind, beautiful, and you remind me

183

of her," Marcus' voice becomes a whisper thick with the fight to keep from crying, as he stares at me.

I can see into his memories of Amita. Him helping her sneak out of her house to go dance the night away with the Vampires and Indra. Her kind interaction with those she knew secretly as Hypers in the day, breaking bread with those in need on the street, when her father would look upon them with disdain.

"We had plans for those two. Children. Half hyper and half human. Until her father found out about Indra and it turned out the same man he wanted Amita with was the very man Indra's company wanted her with. To save Indra's life from her father killing him Amita gave up her love and did as the company foretold and married -"

"Dorian," I fill in the blank feeling Kai's stare on the side of my face.

"Yes," Marcus agrees. "Soon she gave birth to a baby boy, but there were complications. Sadly, she died in Indra's arms and her midwife, who was actually a Shatan was outraged. She felt it was unfair that Amita was taken from us. That she should be with us no matter if she was human. That Indra was cheated of a life he should have had." Marcus stops and schools the anger clearly on his face. He's quiet for a moment before continuing.

"In that room. On that day with Amita's body laying right there in that bed, Evangeline, the Shatan, cast a curse on Amita's bloodline that every girl born of her blood would be attached to the supernatural. Based on the design of the curse, three from Amita's line will be promised to different Hyper communities. When they called me to witness I should have known when she passed me a teardrop shaped vial filled with Amita's blood that one of you would be vampire." He smiles

184

ironically, as my eyes fall to the pendant hanging from his neck again. "There was a time I would have changed you myself, then Kai came along and I saw a whole new possibility for you. Then he decided to leave not knowing he had you all along and my plans changed. You were the reason he was leaving. I should have known not to go against fate." He laughs as if he is the Mad Hatter himself.

I'm not with him. I'm thinking of the other two girls of Amita's bloodline. My sisters. Still in high school. I feel a hand close around mine and look over at Kai.

'You okay?' he mouths in concern.

I shake my head and turn back to Marcus. There were only men born on my dad's side of the family until me and my sisters came along. My father's bloodline. Amita's bloodline.

"What about my sisters?" I ask.

"We'll see about that together, won't we?" Marcus smiles smugly, telling me without telling me he doesn't know.

"What about Niani and Kai? How do they play a role in this curse?" I ask, feeling lower then low every time I hear the word. *Curse.*

"Like Amita, the Shatan knew you would face opposition for your choices so they in placed a guardian. One to guide you and another to protect you. That protector is Niani," he answers and looks at Niani. "That is why the two of you are friends. You would need someone that would stay close. Your mutual love for fantasy kept you attached to the Hypernatural and your writings and drawings guided you to us." Marcus' eyes travel between me and Niani.

"I know you have questions Niani," Marcus says, looking up at her, "but to answer one of them - they made you a WuXia because it best fit your physicality and natural affinity. She wanted you to be different, but not alone. They may go by a different name, serve a different code not so different, but they are just as much *knights* as you are." He nods his head to Cass next to her.

Cass and Niani share a look, one of mutual love and respect.

"And Kai?" I ask, turning from them back to Marcus.

Marcus smiles at that question. "The one thing about this curse is that you were promised love."

"And *you*?" I ask.

"I have been entrusted to guide you into this world. *Your* community," Marcus states.

I feel Kai's hand tighten around mine in anger.

"I'm assuming none of the rest of the Hyper community know of this curse. Otherwise, they wouldn't be trying to kill me," I state, acknowledging that this needs to be over for Kai and for me.

"Sadly, we call it the Tragedy of 1849 because that was the year Amita died. All the Hypernatural community knows is that it changed things for us. They may not know why -"

"So, what you're saying is we're dealing with a warped Romeo and Juliet storyline. No one knows why everybody is fighting," Cassius speaks for the first time.

"Yes and no," Z speaks up, sitting up. "They know that some Hypers revere humans as special. That's because of Amita. She changed the way Hypers saw humans - in India, but not the rest of the world. There were still being wars fought, Hypers and humans being enslaved, human empires taking over Hyper land. Now we're in the present and we're still hanging on to those old prejudice. Some find it odd and a betrayal that we would place in law to protect the humans when they aren't like us, when by all nature they are. All of us are made equal by blood and created from the same source that created the earth. Human and Hyper alike for years have been trying to make that separate distinction."

"So, what now?" I ask.

"We introduce you to Hyper society." Marcus smiles. "You do know Sara Collins?"

"No." Kai's voice cuts through the air like a knife, even I feel cut by it. I look over at Kai and find his eyes blazing silver they're almost white.

"Kai, this could protect -" I start, when he cuts me off.

"This is a decision for my family and I to make together, not you," he growls, not taking his eyes off of Marcus.

"I understand," Marcus says quietly, not fighting Kai on this.

"Are we done here?" Kai demands.

"Yes, you are welcome to leave when you are ready," Marcus says. "Lelin will take you back."

Kai gets up immediately and I stand myself, ready to get him alone so we can talk about this.

Cassius and Niani follow us out of the study into the den, where William stands outside the doors waiting for us. Immediately, I notice the room is empty and he looks - *enlightened*. He smiles as we approach and says, "Mahina is "recovering", as Wilson put it *and I love how you staged this*," he adds with a whisper.

I breathe a sigh of relief. Of everything I have learned in the last hour, this I can smile about elated that he thought this whole thing was staged in inspiration of *Reign*.

"Are we ready to go?" Kai asks softly, his anger now dissipated.

"Yeah," Cassius says, almost immediately and I can feel his anger quiet, simmering under the surface, as he walks ahead ready to get out of here.

William turns from me watching as Niani follows after Cass and he follows after her, Kai and I bringing up the rear.

CHAPTER 16:
Coup

We pull into the parking garage, Kai helping me out of the limo as everyone else climbs out on the other side. As soon as I'm standing on solid ground, I pull away from Kai and make my way over to William.

"What you needed to talk about earlier was it important?" I ask.

"No, it's nothing that we can't talk about tomorrow. I can tell your minds are someplace else right now," he says, looking around the parking garage at Niani, Kai, and Cassius.

"Are you sure?" I ask, almost wishing for anything he had to say to take my mind off of what I've learned.

"Yeah." He nods. "We'll talk tomorrow. Take care of what you've got to."

He glances over at Kai as he watches us before giving me a soft compassionate smile and turning for his car.

Cassius then steps forward slipping his cell phone into his front pocket. "Tiberius is upstairs waiting to fix whatever that was broken."

"Okay. Thank you." I turn to him.

Suddenly, he frowns appearing conflicted.

"Me - and Niani - are going to go," he hesitates to explain.

I glance over at Niani looking our way, her embarrassment in her stance telling me everything I need to know in the distance between us. She couldn't come to me personally to tell me she was feeling a certain way about what she had learned. About me.

"No need to explain," I turn back to him. "I understand." I smile reassuring him that it's okay.

"Okay." He bows, something that he's never done before and walks away over to Niani.

Kai steps up beside me watching as Cassius and Niani walk over to her car and climb in, before they too drive off. I look up at Kai and turn to walk inside, Kai right behind me, when we notice the limo is still there. Kai leans down into the open passenger side window to look in at Lelin.

"Lelin, you can go on and head back to the Manor," Kai informs him.

Lelin turns to Kai in the window and says, "Marcus asked me to stay just in case the Princess or yourself decided to change your mind." He smiles, knowing Marcus' message would get under Kai's skin.

Murderous and annoyance crosses Kai's face at the same time.

"We haven't changed our minds. *Go* Lelin," Kai says, barely containing the threat in his voice.

Lelin smiles wider pulling the limo into gear before driving off.

Tiberius is there waiting outside our apartment when we get to our floor. He doesn't say anything as we approach the door just nods to us in silent acknowledgement understanding that we've been through enough tonight not to ask questions. He comes in sliding his hands over shards, splintered wood, and dust lifting and rewinding it back in to its restored earthly state. Then he's gone just as silently as he came.

I walk up the stairs to Kai practicing his sword strokes. Shirtless and beautiful, he looks like a dancer in his element. He turns and strikes hard, his mind someplace else. With each swing of his sword the candles flicker along the wall. I notice the incense burning on the end table in the corner. Nag Champa. His choice of incense usually reflects his mood at the moment of training. Today, he's having fun. He starts to slow down getting ready to transition into meditation. I walk up behind him and snatch the sword from him, surprising him. He turns around and smiles as I tuck the sword behind my back.

"How do you always do that?" he asks.

"A girl never divulges her secrets." I smile.

"Come on. You can tell me if you've had training," he just about begs.

I just shake my head and Kai reaches for the sword. I dodge out of his reach. He chuckles and goes for it again. I dodge him again.

My own laughter fills my ears, as I come out of the memory opening my eyes.

"You okay?" Kai asks concerned, running a strand of my hair behind my ear.

I nod. "Memory."

Kai lies under me across the couch as I sit on his lap straddling his waist. After Marcus' neither of us wanted to be alone. Kai laid down on the couch and I crawled into his lap, his arms instantly making their way around me. I'm glad it's still in us to lean on each other as we did in the past when times got rough. The comfort of each other's silence and our presence is our safety net knowing we can rely on each other. Something as finding out you're cursed and your whole life has been mapped out for you often times would send couples to the opposite ends of the city or house.

"You've been quiet ever since we got home," Kai notes.

I don't add that he has been, too.

"How do you know Sara Collins?" I ask, remembering how he reacted after Marcus mentioned her.

Kai drops his gaze squirming under me then points indicating that he wants to stand up.

I crawl off of him and he stands walking a couple of paces before stopping with his back towards me.

"She was a patient," he says and the silence that follows screams for him to fill it with what he's not saying.

"Kai?" I question.

He turns around, facing me.

"She was the one who turned me."

I frown unable to answer for a moment, horrified.

"*What?*" I say finally.

Sara. Sara Collins. Academy award winning actress and one of Niani and I's friends from high school is a Vampire?

"One morning, the sun hadn't even come up yet. Sara came into the hospital with an allergic reaction from a bite. It didn't appear to be rabies but I had to draw her blood to be sure. She went into a seizure on the table and in her thrashing she knocked the needle into me with her blood and I - became infected," Kai explains. "She's not like me, but she is the beginning of me. She's the first person to ever be found allergic to the vampire venom. She's not quite human, but neither is she a vampire. Her reaction made her merely a ghost between the two. Her reproductive organs are frozen, she has some of our strength, she is sensitive to light, but she is mortal."

Kai's memory plays through my head like a flashback in a movie. Fast, intense, and emotional. Sara bleeding from a wound between her neck and shoulder as she begged for help and exclaimed how she was attacked. Her seizing on the table as her flailing limbs knocked into Kai, as he tried to remove the needle from her arm causing him to stab himself through the glove. His horror of not knowing what he had been injected with.

I drop my head nearly sick to my stomach knowing that attack was the catalyst that sealed hers, mine, and Kai's fate to jump start this curse. Sara was pregnant over a year ago. It was never discussed how her and her boyfriend had lost the baby, but the timeline fit. Her allergic reaction to the bite made her loose her child. *Oh my goodness.* The realization hits me making me want to vomit. I did that. Because of this curse, I made her loose her child. I can't help but think what if that was me? That was why Kai had reservations about changing me in the beginning, because Sara's mutation ran through his veins. It all made sense now.

I close my mouth to swallow the bile climbing up my throat. I can barely breathe correctly as a heat flash flushes my skin with perspiration and my hands shake. My eyes well up with tears. I can feel Kai looking upon me worried as he watches me breakdown. His emotions becoming mere shadow to me. Then Kai is there taking my hands down from their entanglement in my hair looking at my face as the tears leak down.

"Why did they do this to me?" I whimper.

And Kai pulls me into his arms, hugging me tight.

"I'm sorry, baby. I'm so sorry," Kai gasps tearfully.

Kai runs his fingers across my scalp silently, as I lay with my head in his lap. The glistening of the crescent moon reflecting through the blinds like that of my eyes catch my attention and I notice the time. Pass twelve. Where did the time go? I ignore it and concentrate on the motion of Kai's fingers, the soothingness of them.

"Kai?"

"Hmm?" he hums.

I quiet again and I sense he wants me to look at him, so he can get a good look at my face. I sit up and face him.

"She lost her child because of me and can never have another one," I say. "There was a time when all of this made sense. When it was just you and me. And now - " I look at everything around me. "I feel violated. Tainted. I feel like all of my choices have been made for me and everyone's whose lives I have touched. I *am* cursed."

My eyes burn as the tears well up in my eyes and a knot twists in my throat. I sniffle trying to rear it all back in, but it doesn't work.

"I know it's not my fault and that Shatan was only trying to do a good thing, but I don't see anyone seeing it that way. But out of all this I'm worried about *you*." Kai stares at me, unflinching. "I'm not blind that you went through something and Marcus *broke* you," Kai looks away from me tears welling up in his eyes, "and you think whatever you can't tell me would make me look at you any differently? It can't. It won't, because nothing can beat what I've seen. What I can imagine. I know the vampire I vowed to spend the rest of my life with." Kai looks back at me, a tear rolling down his cheek slowly. "You can tell me. Just start slow."

I reach up and take his face in between my hands leaning forward gently kissing the tear where it left a trail. At the contact, Kai closes his eyes a few tears escaping and opens them soft silver looking into my jade green and mercury.

He can't.

He can't. Not tonight. And I understand.

KAI

I'm already up the next morning, unable to sleep from the previous night, when Ashiya walks into the kitchen. I smile when I see the ivory satin and black lace slip she's wearing, her nearly ten-week-old belly adorable as it peaks against the fabric.

I spent most of the night with the twins, caressing and whispering softly, as their mother slept against me. Promising that I'll be there for them. I love them. And I'll protect them with everything that I am. I love their mommy. How beautiful she is and that we're sorry we're putting them through this and they're not even born, yet.

I couldn't get Ashiya's words out of my head. "I'm not blind that you went through something and Marcus *broke* you." I fought hard to put what Marcus put me through and my own choices behind me, but it looked more like I put a band-aid over it. The cuts and burns were still there festering without the process of healing. Without Ashiya's powers she could see that and sought to make it right. Help me get passed it. As much as I wanted to - get it out. Talk to her last night. It's still hard to talk about.

Ashiya smiles as she approaches obviously hearing my thoughts as she steps into my personal space wrapping her arms low around my waist. I still can't get used to that. I smile, pulling her into me.

"Get used to it." She smiles, pushing up on her toes and kissing me.

I smile, as she pulls away, dropping my head in amusement, my eyes landing on the mail in my hand. More specifically, the expensive translucent envelope on top in a shimmering silver stamped with my name and address in metallic maroon ink and return address from a *Sara Collins*. The same Sara Collins Marcus mentioned yesterday. There is another here addressed in Ashiya's name. I found it slipped under the apartment door this morning carrying with it Niani's scent.

"Niani dropped this off for you earlier," I say, handing Ashiya the invitation with her name on it.

I watch Ashiya's eyes cut to the invitation with my name on it reminding us both of what had transpired yesterday with Marcus. Ashiya opens the envelope carefully and pulls a thin cream card from its depths. Reading over it quickly, she tucks the invitation back into its envelope and places it on the counter as if she never saw it.

Complete silence follows after that. I look at Ashiya in concern wondering what is going on inside her mind as I watch her eyes drift someplace else. I can't let it go on like this.

"We're going," I order.

Ashiya's eyes slide up to mine.

"I spent most of the night wondering about what Marcus said and if introducing you to Hyper society will guarantee you and the twins safety, I won't argue with that."

Ashiya turns to me on the stool.

"Kai, I won't make you do this if it makes you uncomfortable being near him," she says compassionately. "I can have Cassius or Chief go with me."

196

"I can handle him one night," I say. "After that - " I shake my head refusing to think about it.

"Okay," she urges, "but if there is a moment you are ready to get out of there, we are gone."

I nod, smiling in appreciation of her.

"Now, what's her theme *this* year?" I ask, knowing Sara makes no exception of making every party just as extravagant as the last.

"Vampires." Ashiya smiles.

"How appropriate," I snark.

ASHIYA

I swing the door open to find Chief on the other side, as he muscles his way into the apartment. I close the door behind him and immediately his big hands are on my stomach.

"How are my Godsister and Godchildren, today?" he asks.

I smile in exasperation.

"We're fine, Chief. You've done this every day since you've been over the past few days. You don't have to walk on eggshells around me. I'm not going to breakdown under *the weight of my emotions*," I say the last part playfully.

Understanding he's being overbearing Chief bashfully takes his hands off my stomach.

"Anyway, I should be asking you how you're doing. I'm not the only one Z - betrayed." It's still hard to say knowing Z only did it so I would finally know the truth.

"I couldn't tell you. I haven't seen him," Chief says darkly.

I silently listen to the emotions he isn't telling me. He's hurt, angry, but that anger hasn't settled in yet, not until he sees the culprit of his affliction.

"How about you? You'll be basically *coronated* into Hyper society in a few days," he asks. "After this, everything you have been through will finally be over."

I look up at him thinking otherwise and turn walking into Kai and I's living room, Chief following.

"I don't think once this is done the life I lead will allow that. I will be associated with Marcus, *The King of Darkness.* Niani is soul bound to protect me for as long as I shall live and I won't die for a *very* long time," I say, turning to Chief, "Even if they were to find out why I divulged all those secrets to the world, Hypers won't forget what I am. What I can do." I bring a hand over my abdomen and Chief follows my hand, sighing with crushed realization.

He sits down on the couch almost defeatedly, but keeping some strength about himself.

"Have you shared this with anyone else?" he asks, looking up at me seriously.

"No," I answer. "Besides Kai, you're the only one I've seen in the past few days. Niani isn't talking to me right now. Tiberius is on a case and Cass is most likely working or with Niani."

As if it's a crying shame, Chief drops his head shaking it and looks up at me.

"Talk to me. What are your other concerns?" he states.

"I'm worried about Kai," I say, "All of you. About what this may be doing to you all since finding out."

Chief stares at me with quiet decision his hands clasped together at the knees, as if he understands what I'm purposely omitting.

"I think you need to go see Kwan-Min," Chief says finally. "We as brothers may have vowed not to talk about it, but Kwan-Min was there with us. He might be able to divulge what we can't. Or won't. This is not intentionally to worry you, Ashiya, but reliving that is simply not what we are willing to do." He stares into my eyes, unflinching in his resolve.

I nod.

The sun is high and bright in the sky shining blindingly down off of car hoods, as Chief pulls us inside the H-Mart Shopping Plaza off of Pleasant Hill Road in Duluth stopping in front of a store named, *Hero's Artillery*. I recognize the spot having passed the plaza a couple of weeks ago scouting for mansions in Suwanee for *Reign*. The unmistakable name *Kwan-Min* blares out at me in white Hanja decal letters from the store window and I turn to Chief. He gives me an encouraging smile.

"I'm going to go find a parking space. You go on ahead. I'll be right out here," he says.

"You're not coming in with me?" I ask.

"Kwan-Min's is protected ground. If anyone infringes on his property is signing their death certificate," he answers with a cheeky smile. "And if anyone be so bold is utterly stupid with all of those weapons in there."

I sniff a laugh at his explanation.

"Go," Chief insists.

I open the door, stepping out of the car.

A bell rings overhead as I step inside the store and customers lining the front counters turn my way in the light of the doorway giving the dim lit store a dark seedy feeling like the saloon of a western film. I let the door swing close behind me, as they go back to their purchases and their window shopping, my eyes taking in the glass display counters lining the front of the store filled with sharpeners, sheaths, knives, and daggers ready for use. Swords, sticks, shield supplies, and endless assortment of guns in caged glass white cases cover the walls all the way back to round tables and chairs in the back of the store. Incense smoke lifts from Sandalwood scented sticks sticking out of brass bowls reminding me of a place I wrote in *Coup* the second book after *Reign* like déjà vu.

I frown. It feels weird being in a place I, myself wrote about. I know the place so well it feels like coming home.

'Why not get a coffee while buying a few firearms while you're at it?' I remember the stroke of inspiration I gained while sitting in a cafe over a year ago.

I approach the counter, a blonde Chinese woman dealing with two female customers turns to me immediately interrupting the sell to say, "Kwan-Min will be right with you," unsurprisingly low in Korean.

"Gomabseubnida." I nod with a warm smile.

She excuses herself from her two customers disappearing through a beaded doorway behind the counter. The two women turn to me appraising me as if to wonder, 'How am I so special?' The one on my left squares up as if about to say something and I watch as blue veins map across their skin. *Mermaids.*

They assume I'm human, otherwise they wouldn't dare step to a Hyper like this. I take pleasure in letting my adrenaline bleed into my eyes showing off my jade and mercury orbs for them. Showing them how *inhuman* I am. Their mouths form into surprised holes and if we weren't interrupted by their sales associate returning I can imagine them scrambling to say their apologies and maybe even bow. *Good.* I'm glad they don't, because I don't need any more attention. I walk around them over to the wall of guns.

Many are engraved with the Hyper language or with English words, tigers, dragons, or flowers. Some even gold or with mother of pearl handles.

"Which one do you like?" a familiar wise voice asks.

"I don't know. I'm pretty partial to the chrome Desert Eagle up here and that Beretta."

"Wonderful choice, Ashiya." And I turn my head to find Kwan-Min standing next to me. He's wearing a soft smile, but his eyes tell me he's not too happy about the turn of events that brought me into his store today.

"Let's talk, Princess," he says gently, directing with a hand to a round table.

I follow him to the table farthest away out of earshot of most of the customers and take the seat offered across from him.

"I'm aware of why you're here," Kwan-Min begins softly, "But I must begin by telling you I am not willing to betray your husband's confidants, but what I can tell you is that the very thing your husband is trying to keep buried is still alive."

"Kwan-Min, I know Kai would like to tell me at some point about his past but the way I *feel*," I try my best to describe what my Hyper intuition is telling me, "by the time he does it will be too late. For what? I don't know, but I know that you are the only one that may be able to help me understand even if you can't tell me."

Kwan-Min sits back in his chair silently assessing me with his eyes before sitting up.

"Your husband and his brothers dealt with a piece of history that should have *never* been repeated. If I should speak for them, it's something they never want you to witness because once you've seen it, it can't be unseen. Below our world is a darker underworld, where the corrupt, the vile, the deadly work. A world Marcus was once a part of, your husband reluctantly, but instrumentally - as well. Some of those things not so hidden in the human world."

'Nothing can beat... what I can imagine.' I remember, my words coming back to me.

An angry tremor quakes in my hands, as Kwan-Min's words hit home. Not because I found out Kai was a part of something illegal, but because Marcus dragged him into it. My husband who was now broken because of him.

"Princess," Kwan-min says, bringing me back to him and I look up into his face, his forehead creased in a painstakingly serious frown, "trust me when I tell you it will not always be this way. There will come a time when you will know peace."

Suddenly, Kwan-Min waves a hand above his head and the woman that greeted me before walks over to the table bringing with her a small flat velvet box. She smiles placing the box down in front of me before returning back around the counter to her customers. I watch after her, seeing the white-hot ball of energy in her chest dripping with liquid fire.

Wow. Her power.

I turn back around to Kwan-Min and the velvet box before me, Kwan-Min waiting patiently for me to open it. I lift the lid with a creaky snap and see an oval stone carving inside, a little bigger than the size of my palm. Hand carved and pastel painted with a blooming pink rose with a hyacinth on its left and a vanilla on its right surrounded by intertwining vines in its background.

"Press here." Kwan-Min points to the head of the rose over the top of the box.

I press the rose head and like a puzzle the petals separate and the stone seamlessly opens like a book, whipping out two blades on each side like the petals of a lotus engraved with intricate intertwining flowers matching its cover. It looks like a boomerang.

"With one throw of this piece you can kill every person in this room, if you wanted to," Kwan-Min explains.

I look around the room of every hyper and human then back down at the beautiful boomerang in my hands. Already seeming to understand the mechanics of the object, I press the hyacinth noticing the protruding buds on the weapon like a button and it folds shut with a snap releasing the scent of hyacinth in the air.

"How much is it?" I ask, looking up at Kwan-Min.

"Nothing. It's yours. I made it for you," Kwan-Min says.

"Kwan-Min -" I look at him, taken aback. "I would rather pay you -"

"I make more than enough in my night rush that I don't even need to be open right now," he interrupts. "I can afford to get rid of a few instruments or make them for respectable Princesses."

I deflate in my concern, as I stare at him.

"Thank you, Kwan-Min," I say softly.

He nods with a small grin as I stand acknowledging my departure and he walks me to the door, where I can see Chief waiting for me outside leaning against the trunk of his car scrolling through his phone. I turn to Kwan-Min and he fixes me with a pensive stare. Even within that look I can feel the protectiveness exude off of him.

"Be safe, Ashiya," he says.

I nod with a small smile, lifting the velvet box to let him know I have it covered and walk out of the store with the sound of the bell overhead.

"Did you find out what you were looking for?" Chief asks, as I approach the car.

"Not yet. Not all of it," I reply, as I climb into the passenger side.

CHAPTER 17:
The Fall

My mom's name lights up for the third time across my cellphone disrupting my meeting with my cover illustrator and agent. I place the cover samples down and excuse myself from the table, stepping aside.

"Hello?"

"So, you forgot you had a mother?"

I sigh silently, rolling my eyes.

"I'm in the middle of a meeting with the cover illustrator and my agent. Can I call you back?"

"No, they can hold on!" She snaps. "There is no way you can be so busy that you can't pick up the damn phone to call your mother!"

"Mom." I press the pad of my thumb against my forehead. "There is a lot going on right now that you won't understand," I say, trying to be civil.

"Won't!" she snaps.

"Yes," I interrupt her, before she can interrupt me.

I know exactly what she will say without having to read her.

"Tell me what's so important going on in your life I won't understand. Come on. Tell me." And she will go on to compare my life to her years of experience at my age, but she will never win this one. Not with what I have going on.

"Now, I have to go. I love you," I tell her firmly and hang up the phone.

I know it wasn't the right way to handle not talking to my mother after a month, but it was the only way I could excuse what has been going on and get back to my meeting without becoming unprofessional in front of my peers. Walking back to the table, I return to my partners and resume the meeting.

It's not until later, as I'm leaving the outdoor cafe after the meeting that I get a text message saying:

If you would call more often you would know that your sister is having trouble.

The only time she refers to "my sister" is when she is talking about Anisse, my middle sister and by her words she's still salty about the way I ended the call earlier, trying to guilt trip me for not keeping in touch with her as of late. But playing a game of one-sided phone tag with no call back on her end for a month, only for my sisters and dad to tell me she is okay, and she is the one upset.

I drop everything remembering the curse and call Anisse. She picks up on the third ring and claims that everything is fine. It's all about some rumors at school, nothing she can't deal with. By her voice I can tell she's telling the truth, but there is something else. It's sugary sweet and laced with a thickness even I feel pulled under by it. *Love.* I know it because it's exactly how I feel for Kai. Bringing it up, we talk about the young man in her life and she doesn't give much away but that she met him during her time in Maryland at the family reunion. The one I couldn't make because of casting and somehow he ended up moving to California and they have been dating for a couple of months. It's all genuine without a doubt and I don't know what to say. Of course, the big sister - slash - mom in me comes out and I tell her I know she'll make the best decisions and take things slow, but I want her to be careful not just with her heart but with everything. *Be safe out there.*

As the words leave my lips, I know it's already started for her. The curse. I make a decision right then and there that as soon as I get the chance I am going to go see her.

I reach my car and catch Chief and Tiberius on the other side of the street at the curb staked out in their car, watching me. Tiberius throws a peace sign out the driver's side window letting me know they have me and I quirk a smile, opening my car door and slip inside.

The smile slips from my lips, as I slam the car door behind me. I don't know how I'm going to do this with my sisters. A part of me wants to be there to guide them, explain them through this, *be* there for them but knowing that this is far from over on my end, I can't. I realize I can't be of any help when I don't know the first thing about what this life, this curse means myself. The only one that can help, though I can't trust him as far as I can throw him is Marcus. He is supposed to be my guide in this world after all. He is the only one that knows how this works. That is where the problem lays. As much as I can't trust him, my vampire does. I can't do this without him.

I start the car and the song I was previously listening to before I got out of the car flips to the next and I cut my eyes out the front windshield knowing the song well. Dirty drums and down tempo bass... Kid Cudi's 'Maniac'. I reach over and turn it up to drown out my thoughts.

That's more like it.

Pulling on to the road, Z and Tiberius right behind me, I head towards home.

I step out the front door of the apartment building as Niani approaches the steps from her car parked out front along the sidewalk. She stops when she sees me, her face immediately darkening with an annoyed frown.

"You sensed I was here?" she accuses.

"No, Cassius called me letting me know you were on your way," I answer cordially.

She conceals the impulse to roll her eyes at Cassius for opening his mouth. I look up feeling the awareness of eyes on me and a pressure against my chest. I look over Niani's head to see Marcus' limo parked across the street, Lelin leaning an elbow out the window casually as if he has nowhere else to be. Niani follows my eyes over her shoulder and I step down off the stairs walking across the street. Niani right behind me.

I lean down in front of the window and Lelin turns his head to me with a devil may care smile from around the navy blue hoodie he's wearing sparkling with hidden Blaizinium in the fabric under the sun.

"Princess," he greets, his eyes swinging over to Niani at my side, "Warrior."

"Lelin, what are you doing here?" I ask.

"Marcus said you might want to see him. I came by to see if that were true," he says matter of fact.

I look away from him thinking back on how I previously thought I couldn't do this without Marcus. I barely regard Niani standing next to me when I hear her say, "Ashiya, what are we doing?"

I look back at Lelin and watch his hand lying on the window seal dip back down into the car and press the lock

208

button, the drum of the back doors unlocking making its loud bearing presence known.

He smiles wider if possible as he looks at me and says, "Get in."

I turn and climb into the limo, Niani dutifully behind me. As I get comfortable in the back seat, I look up to Niani eyeing me angrily. I can tell she's biting at the bit to get at me, angry that I dragged her along without her consideration, I think guiltily. She still isn't happy with the arrangement of things.

Lelin walks us into the manor. Immediately, Z coming in from the next room stops us short of the foyer into the hall. I didn't know what I'd expect to feel when I saw him again. I didn't expect to feel anything. Seeing him again now, I didn't expect this. I didn't expect to miss him.

He hesitates in his nervousness to speak.

Finally, he asks, "Can we talk, Princess?"

I watch Niani step up out of the corner of my eyes, her Sais lifting up threateningly into her palms. I place a delicate palm up to placate her. She cuts her eyes at me angry that I stopped her and back at Z.

I turn my head and look into Niani's eyes. "Give us a moment."

Niani reluctantly averts her eyes and drops her Sais back into her holsters. Z nervously takes a step back and leads the way into a room off the foyer and closes the door. It looks like a drawing room with a simple sanded wood desk against the wall strewn with papers unkempt atop and littering the floor underneath for the purpose of effect. Even dusty silk chairs are in the room in front of a sooty fireplace that appears as if it hasn't been lit in ages. Nothing else. An old desk and a few dusty chairs. It's cold and unwelcoming to anyone that dare come in here and knowing Marcus this room was specifically made to be this way.

Z turns to me fixing me with his baby blue eyes.

"Ashiya, I didn't set out to betray you or set you up."

"I know," I say, "But you could have told me. Told your brother differently. You know what he's going through."

Z nods, admitting his guilt. "I know I should have, but when I met you and I saw how happy you and Kai were. I couldn't. I decided to let things fall the way they were supposed to, but then when Niani attacked you and I heard how badly you wanted this to be over I knew it was time to tell you."

I look at Z understanding his predicament, remembering how he looked at me that day.

"I didn't always know about your family's curse," he says unexpectedly. "But when Marcus and I started our relationship I stumbled upon some information about Amita, Indra, and the curse and Marcus was *forced* to tell me about it."

I find it odd Marcus being forced to do anything, but if Marcus didn't want to lose Z he would tell him anything he needed to know. I smile. I wonder if Z knows how much Marcus loves him.

"I understand," I say into the silence. "But no more secrets. I have enough of those and talk to your brother. He needs you four."

"Yes, Princess." He bows.

I didn't know how much I would miss hearing those words come from his mouth.

"I missed you," I admit and step forward enveloping him into a hug, which he receives with open arms.

We step back out of the hug and Z's eyes drop to my stomach peaking against my button down shirt under my vest. He lovingly places a hand over the twins.

"This hasn't changed, right? I'm still their Godfather?" he asks, his hope and love for them evident in his voice.

"Nope." I place both my hands over his. "You're still a Godfather."

Z grins all teeth. "I'll take that as your forgiveness."

I smile softly. Z takes my hand and tows me out of the room. We step out into the hall and expectantly see Marcus walking up to us with Niani behind him.

Marcus smiles as he sees us, his eyes landing on me and Z's hands clasped between us.

"Ah, I see we are on good terms," he says.

"Yes, we are. You and I not so much," I say.

Z and Niani both cut him a stern look as if to ask, "What did you do now?"

Marcus smiles mischievously as if he's used to it. "Maybe we can talk about it and see if we can come to terms?" he requests charmingly.

I let go of Z's hand and wave a hand for Marcus to lead the way. I stop before Z and Niani can follow and turn to them.

"This needs to be a private discussion," I say, hoping they understand the importance, as I look between the two of them. My eyes find Niani's and I say, "I'll find you after we're done."

Niani looks away from me angry she can't disagree otherwise, her respect and duty to me too strong. I drop my eyes guiltily and follow Marcus into a dim sunroom closing the door behind us.

"I'm surprised you're up and about I would expect you to be asleep," I say, noticing the dark rings under his eyes and the heavy lids.

"I have to keep up with you, so I must keep to your schedule," Marcus replies. "It's been a week since we've last seen each other. What have I done this time to receive your ire, Princess?"

"We will get to that. Right now, I just want to talk."

"Isn't that what we're doing?" Marcus asks, raising his eyebrows.

"No, we're talking in circles," I answer and take a seat on the floral couch offered behind me. Marcus takes a seat in the chair across from me.

"I hope you've noticed the attention come off of you. Since Kai sent word that you would be attending Sara's party, I've gotten word out about you. The Hypers are curious, willing to set aside their anger now that you have been made one of us."

"And you're sure about that?" I challenge.

"Sweetheart, I am *The King of Darkness*. They wouldn't dare challenge me," he says, gloating in pride of his namesake.

I look him in his eyes letting him have that. A name. And I know he knows it, too. Knowing people better, I don't tell him that Kai has been pulling out extra patrolling shifts not for a second believing that because Marcus said so that Hypers would suddenly stop wanting to come after me and they do want to. Walking down the street I could see it in their eyes, they didn't trust me enough to be a part of their community no matter what reason Marcus may have given then.

"Thank you," I say instead. "I don't know what you said to make Hypers less aggressive and ready to kill me, but I'm glad for it."

Marcus looks away from me and sighs, knowing I was the one able to get under his skin and turns back to me - and *smiles*.

"You're welcome.

"The girls would like to prepare you tomorrow. They have gone through preparing everything from your dress to your make-up. It would give them great pleasure for you to be here. You and Niani. Niani has already given me her consent."

I try not to think that she said yes to spite me.

"I personally don't see a problem with it, but I will have to discuss this with Kai," I answer.

Marcus nods, tapping his fingers against the arm of the chair. "As I would have guessed."

"Now I want to talk," I state, Marcus' eyes locking onto mine. "I know that I can't do this without you. You know what this curse means for me. You know what being a part of this life means but I want to make one thing clear. You may be my guardian but my sister's lives come first. I want you to protect them. Whatever Hyper connections you have, use them."

"Done," Marcus states.

"I want to know what that means, your *sobriquet. The King of Darkness.* What does my life mean being associated with you?" I ask, sitting up.

Marcus sits up, wringing his hands, his elbows on his knees as he averts his eyes shamefully.

"What has Kai told you about us?" Marcus asks, looking up at me.

"Nothing," I say. "We kept that part out of our lives."

213

Marcus nods, unoffended. "Then that gives me reason to explain myself.

"We are a Mafia. I understand Kai disassociated himself from this life with you. When I found him and discovered his ability to walk in the sun, I was intrigued. I pushed him to see how far he could go. Matter of fact, I encouraged it. My methods were - unorthodox and for that, I regret how far I let it get. Kai *is* like a son to me and I pushed him into someone I barely recognized until he met you." A sad, yet tender smile pulls at Marcus' lips. "I own the Faerie unit of the police and do what some would consider very unsavory things in the human and Hyper eye for money. Needed someone gone? I took the hit. Needed a drug pushed? I provided the handling for very good reason. You want to know what being associated with my name means? It means having the *respect* of every Hyper in the world. They call me dark because I will do *anything* for my family. I take care of my family and Kai may have bare witnessed to more bad than good, but *you*, those twins," he points at my clothed stomach, "and Kai will be *very* well taken care of."

I'm left speechless by his heart-filled admission.

"Is there anything else you would like to know?" He sighs, that explanation seeming to have taken a lot out of him physically. He's been holding on to that for a very long time.

"No, I think we're done here," I answer.

I would say more about how he hurt my husband and how it's going to take me some time to trust him, but I think he gets that.

"Good," he says, "because there is something I would like to add." I meet his eyes at the seriousness of his words. "No matter what you write. If Amita and Indra had ended up together or not you would have chosen this life, because this is where you feel you belong. You are as worthy of this world as anybody on the street that makes this choice. Forget about the curse. You are as much one of us as Amita was being human. *You* make your choices. Do you understand?" he asks softly.

I nod at his fatherly tone.

"Now, we have a very angry friend out there. We should go deal with that," he suggests with a smile.

I smile agreeing with him and stand to go find Niani in the manor. I find her in a hall staring through a large window down into a double sized training gym below. Over a dark mat stand weight machines, a boxing ring, in a corner hangs a few punching bags and enough floor space for six people to spar, where there are weapons lining a wall. No one is down there but it keeps Niani's attention.

She looks up as I approach and looks back down as if my presence annoys her. This has gone on far enough. She needs to start talking, because I'm not going through this with her.

"Niani, we have enough going on not to be talking," I say.

As the words leave my lips, Niani spins on me. "*We* have enough going on?!" she snaps. "How about me! Where were *you* when I needed my best friend?!" She reverts back to the night we stopped talking.

Anger burns hot in my chest at her accusation.

"I was there! I gave you space! You think I don't understand?! You had just learned that you were soul bound to protect me by a curse and all of your choices had been made for you! You can't even make a decision because you feel this uncontrollable duty to me! You think I don't get that?! Where were you?!"

She bristles at my assertion and acute description of what she is going through and points out, "You think you understand because of your powers, but you can't just give people what they want because you can read their thoughts!"

"We made a mistake!" I scream and I feel my eyes throbbing furiously. "Because of this curse, I didn't even know if my feelings were real for my own *husband!*" She hushes in surprise at my rage. "Because of this curse I have killed! Sara lost her -" I feel the tears brimming in my eyes, the emotion welling up inside me at the memory of Sara's loss, choking me, and I turn away. I take two steps away from Niani, when I feel my heart lurch in my chest causing me to stumble.

"Ashiya?!" I hear Niani exclaim in concern and run to me.

I press a hand against where my heart is as I feel my body slide down the wall. Niani catches me, as my back nearly connects with the floor. I - I can't breathe. My heart punches against my breastplate, beating fast, as if fighting to stay alive. I try to speak, but my voice catches in my throat. All I can hear is the drum roll that is my heart. My breathing coming out in sharp gasps. My fingertips growing frozen numb, snaking its way up my skin. I think about the twins. How they could possibly survive this. A tear leaks down my face, as I stare into Niani's frightened eyes. I wait for my brain to shut down, for my heart to stop. Pretty soon, she complies. My eyes grow blurry. I can't hear Niani's screams to tell her what's wrong, though I can only just read her lips. My heart stutters to a barely there staccato...

Then I take my last breath.

NIANI

Ashiya lies motionless, eyes open in my arms. I feel the panic rise up in me at her still figure. I don't want to shake her, because of the twins. I gather her in my arms and pull a hand up under her nose to check if she's breathing. Nothing. I check her pulse in her neck. Nothing.

"Marcus!" I scream. "Marcus! Marcus!"

In an instant, he's there.

"Ashiya!" he panics, seeing her lying motionless in my arms and rushes over.

"She collapsed. We were arguing and she just collapsed. What's wrong with her?" I ask, as Marcus checks her over.

"She's dead," he answers, as he collects her into his arms and stands.

Suddenly, my blood runs cold at those two words. I feel dizzy. The world catches up with me, as I watch him walk away with her out of my parenthetical vision and get up walking after him.

"W-wait. Where are you taking her?" I ask, as I catch up to him. "I have to call Kai." I remember suddenly, as I reach down into my pocket for my cellphone.

"Don't call Kai," he states.

"Wha- Why?!" I exclaim, as if he's crazy. My best friend just died in my arms and he expects me not to call her husband?!

"Because she is a vampire," he says easily.

Then it catches up with me. She is a vampire. She's dead, but she's not dead. Meaning she will wake up.

A few minutes later, I'm standing in front of a large window much like the one to the training room staring

217

into a room of Indian decor. The walls of paisley metallic gold wallpaper are a highlight to the wooden floor carved with mehendi and mandala designs under Ashiya. The room is bare, except for the speakers mounted in the four corners of the ceiling emitting music. Ashiya's body floats in the middle of the room above a large carved mandala.

"Why is she floating?" I ask, Marcus standing next to me.

"Her body is now more spirit. Her vampire finally taking over," he answers.

I remember how her vampire reacted after I attacked her under the Siren's Kiss.

"Will she be different?" I ask, afraid the friend I knew will be gone.

"You two were arguing," he says rhetorically. "You were angry with her, but you didn't know exactly where that anger was coming from. Your feelings were valid, but you weren't exactly as angry as you felt. We call that *Them*. Like a Shatan, you are closest to human as any Hyper. A vampire's spirit is intimidating to humans, so their first reaction is to combat in any way they see fit. Yours and Ashiya's reactions to one another were simply a battle between being Hyper versus being human. You were angry about Ashiya taking control over your life, but you know that is not her fault."

"Of course, it's not her fault," I retort.

"It was until you were faced with her death," he states.

I don't have a reply for that. He is right.

"So, to answer your question, "Will she be different?" Yes and no. She's been through a lot and those changes will affect her vampire as well as her human side. It all depends on which side wins out."

At his words, I look over at Marcus in surprise and turn looking back into the room at Ashiya. Through the glass I can hear the ghostly gentle r&b vocals of James Blake filling the room from the speakers with the soul graced voice of Justin Vernon from Bon Iver over a minimalist electronica and gospel influenced track.

"Why the music?" I then ask.

"Music speaks to the soul. It shapes the heart, vocalizing what otherwise cannot be expressed. Ashiya's been hurt in her life. She needs a reason to hold on to the person she is and the vampire she will be. The last thing she remembers of her human life is crying and arguing with you. It's not a good memory to have when you wake up a vampire. The music will help her heal - and focus on her humanity."

His words are a bullet to the chest. Our argument was a part of her last breath as a human. That's a hard pill to swallow. All she was trying to be was understanding and I gave no thought to what this was doing to her.

"How do you know you chose the right music?" I ask, trying not to cry for the shame I'm feeling.

"Because Kai made it," Marcus answers.

Again, I look at Marcus in surprise.

"He made a drive for Z, Chief, Tiberius, and Cassius to carry around at all times in case of this very reason. He knows her. Now it's up to her," he states firmly, staring at Ashiya through the window with faith and hope.

We watch Ashiya for what feels like hours, but really may have only been one. Kai's music a soundtrack to the scene when I notice Ashiya's foot flex then her hands move. Slowly, Ashiya curls in on herself as if turning over in bed and delicately sits up on air. It's the most beautiful thing I've ever seen, as the white gown Marcus had me

219

change her into bellows around her. She looks like a dark angel. Marcus moves away from the window to enter the room when I grab his arm stopping him.

"Let me go in," I request.

"No," Marcus states. "It needs to be me."

Seeming to understand a deeper meaning to his words, I let him go and watch him enter the room through the door at my side. Ashiya looks his way as he enters the room and as Marcus stoops down before her I watch them stare at each other for a moment, before I see what I never expected to witness: Ashiya throwing her arms around Marcus and breaking down into his arms. Marcus catches her, as her body collapses back to the floor, holding her like a baby as she cries. That's when I get it. Ashiya's given up a lot. She nearly stopped speaking to her parent's afraid that her contact with them would bring them closer to danger. They don't even know about the twins. She needed a parent and Marcus is the closest to a parental figure she can get. He is her guardian.

When I'm finally able to see her, she's changing back into her clothes in the bedroom Marcus had me change her in. That was the most life altering experience, changing my technically dead best friend's clothes like in a funeral parlor. Never say I didn't do anything for you Ashiya.

"Are you okay?" I ask, stepping into the doorway.

Ashiya turns to me before the bed with a grace I've never seen on her before. And I can see it. The vampire. She looks the same, but - different. Her skin glowing, her silver green eyes entrancing, but something is off... she's not talking. She's just *staring* at me.

"Don't take offense. She's really not talking to anyone. Though, she may smile," Z explains from a corner chair, not noticing him there before.

He looks at Ashiya, as she turns back around to the bed buttoning her vest.

"Is that normal?" I ask.

"Marcus says Kai was like this too when he woke up," Z answers. "I guess it's like when a baby is born. Some cry and some -"

"Don't," I finish his sentence staring at Ashiya.

I look at her trying to find a semblance of my best friend, but I can't. She is like a blank slate, a vessel of my best friend. At least she didn't look at me as if she didn't know me. I try to take comfort in that thought.

"Marcus said, "her first show of her humanity was when she cried in his arms," I say.

"Yeah," Z agrees, "as long as she is smiling. She is communicating." At that Ashiya looks up at Z and smiles at which he returns. "When she finally speaks that will be a different story."

"It feels weird to be talking about her as if she not in the room. So, she is just standing here listening to us?" I ask uncomfortably, afraid she'll snap and murder us both like an escaped science experiment in a sci-fi film.

"And listening to our thoughts, seeing our intentions, feeling our every mixed emotion," Z says and I feel bad for my last thought. "She shouldn't be able to hear my thoughts. Elementals have the natural ability to disturb energy to keep Hypers with psionic abilities from reading our minds but Ashiya can. It goes to show how powerful she is." He looks at Ashiya endearingly. "We need someone like her in this world. Someone that can read between all the bull in it."

221

I turn from him looking back at Ashiya as she takes an elegant seat on the end of the bed. Suddenly, Z stands drawing my attention back to him.

"I'll leave you two to talk or - just you," he says with a sassy raise of his eyebrows as he passes me out the door. *He's been hanging around Marcus too much,* I think, as I watch after him.

I turn back around to Ashiya as she stares off at no particular spot on the floor at her feet. I look at her prone figure sitting on the edge of the bed. A newborn to this world. I exhale a steely breath and take a step forward.

"I don't know what you're going through inside your head, but I understand," I begin, as Ashiya's eyes lift up to mine. "I'm - *so* - sorry. I can't tell you how sorry I am. You've given up so much and I *see* you." I get down on both knees in front of her as if to beg her. "I *see* you. I don't care about this uncontrollable duty I have to you. I give up my life to you. You're my sister and I love you."

Ashiya stares absently down at me, when her jade mercury eyes suddenly fade to their original brown. I'm hopeful for a moment that she will say something, but deceptively she doesn't as her eyes find the wall. I close my eyes and drop my head in frustration, a rogue tear escaping my eye.

I don't know how I'm going to return her to Kai like this.

CHAPTER 18:
The House of Marcus

Lelin pulls us up in front of the reinforced steel studio door and parks. I look at Ashiya staring vacantly out the window with a small smile before climbing out of the limo, then reaching back in and guiding Ashiya out. Slamming the door shut behind her, I turn and press the doorbell on the intercom box mounted up beside the door while keeping a hand on her.

A woman's voice then comes over the intercom greeting, "Harwood Studios."

"Jung, Studio B," I answer in to the box, pressing the speaker button.

A buzzer sounds and I turn the knob, letting us in. Tossing a hand up to tell Lelin goodbye, I lead Ashiya through the door letting the door swing closed behind us. From the exertion of leading her around I sigh winded, as we stand in the foyer of the recording studio.

I look around never having been in a recording studio before. Tiled stone floors and industrial wooden walls create clean lines and a grounded atmosphere. Plaques of Aaliyah, OutKast, Romeo Santos, Common, Linkin Park, and AWOL Nation hang across the walls. Not needing to stop and get distracted, I follow the instructions Cassius gave me over the phone in the limo. Turning left, I lead us down a hall and to the right bypassing two soundproof doors into a private section of the building: An open hall with a full house kitchen through a glass sliding door on my left and on my right through another soundproof door 'Studio B' on a monogram plaque. A set of stairs in a corner lead up to the studio manager's office and a few meeting rooms.

I pull Ashiya through the soundproof doors of Studio B walking in ahead of her. Kai sits at the console pausing a Zedd like track talking to the producer I'm guessing in the next chair over. Kai stops mid-sentence obviously sensing our auras and swivels around in his chair toward us. His eyes barely train on me, before they're on Ashiya widening at the sight of her. He pulls up from his chair standing slowly.

"Kai," I hear whispered softly behind me.

I make a face in exasperation. *So, now she decides to speak.*

"Hey Frank, give me a moment," Kai says to the might be producer.

"Yeah. No problem," Frank says, standing from his seat, "I was just getting ready to have Jesse order me something from the Indian spot. You want something?" he asks, as he walks to the door.

"No, thank you," Kai says distractedly, his eyes not coming off of Ashiya.

"You guys?" Frank asks, turning to Ashiya and I.

"No," I answer for the both of us and taking that as bond, Frank disappears outside the door.

Without a word, Kai steps forward meeting Ashiya as she passes me taking her hand and leads her through another two sound proof doors separating the control room from the recording room around the mixing board. Through the glass window into the recording room, I can see Kai approach the grand piano in the middle of the room and take a seat.

ASHIYA

I let my eyes wander the spacious recording room of varnished wood and foam paneled walls, as Kai takes a seat at the piano and begins to play. He knows I need it still teetering between the trauma of dying and being truly undead. I recognize the melody as Meshell N'Dedgecello's, 'Outside Your Door' caressing my ears like an extension of Kai's skillful fingers. I smile, loving to hear him play.

I can sense Niani's eyes on us, as if through a rearview mirror in the back of my mind, as she watches us through the window into the mixing room. I can feel her concern, hear her thoughts, taste their essence like melted chocolate on my tongue. Her words for me back at the manor are still an echo inside my mind. Even if I wasn't all there, I could still hear her. A part of me was glad that she understood my position in all this, but the other part of me understood that I needed to apologize for thinking because I knew what her WuXia side wanted that I knew what *she* wanted. I won't make any excuses of it, but this Hyper situation had us all messed up. We haven't had much time to talk since her becoming a WuXia and with our argument we had a lot to discuss, mainly where we stood. Especially now, that she finally accepted her fate as my protector. It would take a lot to break this friendship, I think with a slight smirk, but at least I knew we would be okay.

My eyes land on Kai's acoustic guitar on a stand in the corner. I remember when he used to play it for me when we dated. Even when he brought me here one night and played a private concert of nearly every song he's ever written for me. The same room he told me for the first time he loved me. Usually, when Kai writes music he uses the piano, but the acoustic is strictly reserved for me.

Dying and coming back to life brought the last of my memories back in one swift stroke. I turn back to Kai still playing, swaying seductively to the music, his eyes closed, fingers playing across each key tenderly and intimately. He lifts his head obviously feeling my eyes on him and reaches a hand out for me to come over, as his other continues to play. I walk over taking Kai's hand and he guides me down onto his lap returning to play around me, this time softer.

"Hey," Kai says softly, brushing my neck with a kiss.

"Hey," I return, leaning back into him, as I slide my hands up his arms over his hands and he stops playing wrapping me in his arms.

"How was your day?" he asks softly.

I sigh heavily and shake my head.

"That bad?" he asks, drawing me closer.

"I got a call from my mom," I say, expanding no further on the issue, "then I went to see Marcus -" I feel Kai stiffen in my arms. "I had to. It was about my sisters. It's already started for Anisse," I tell him, turning to look him in the eyes. His face softens as he understands. "Niani and I got in to a *horrible* argument, then - I died," I say, still feeling hazy in the head.

"I figured," I hear Kai say quietly in my left ear, as he pulls my hair from over my shoulder behind my ear. "I can see you," he adds with a husky timbre. The true me, he means. My vampire no longer a symbiotic entity living under my skin, but in my skin. Of one mind, one body, one soul. A power so dark and seductive it flows through my veins, lacing its way through my mind, my limbs, my chest, my very soul. I have to close my eyes. I'm dizzy with intoxication. And I understand that this is what Kai has been so scared of. The temptation of something so dark twisting you into a different person. Something that you've never been. Stronger. Stronger than you are. The ego. The belief that you are better then you've ever truly been. Because I am. I am *her*. I am *me*.

"Thank you for the music," I say, turning around and straddling Kai about his waist. His hands settle low on my hips and I can hear the *'You're welcome,'* in my head, as his eyes search my face thoroughly looking as if he's finding reasons to fall in love with me all over again.

"How are you doing?" he asks softly in concern.

I run a hand down the side of his face.

"Alive," I say, nearly a whisper.

Kai closes his eyes, placing his forehead against mine, thanking God in his mind for me. I could cry from the mere feeling.

"This is what it was like," he says, his eyes still closed.

"What was?" I ask.

"You asked me once, "what was it like when we were together". This is what it was like," he answers, his eyes now silver searching mine, endearingly.

And I know it. I remember. It was. I smile. "It was," I say.

Kai's brows bow in confusion. "Y-you remember?"

"Yes. I remember everything," I say.

Kai takes my face in his palms, as if he can't believe it and brings my face down, kissing me. I return the kiss just as tenderly feeling every pressure and move, as he pulls at my lips as if enhanced and slowed. He lets go of me slowly and I know I have to cut the moment short, but also that there will be more moments like this to make up for it.

"Marcus asked me if I would come by to prepare for the party tomorrow. That it would be a pleasure for the girls to dress me," I say, searching his eyes for a sign of protest.

"It's tradition," Kai says. "When a new vampire enters the clan and is to be introduced to society the women dress the female and the men dress the male. It's um -" he stops, looking uncomfortable, "their way of saying welcome to the family."

I watch Kai's face go cold with that last sentence, remembering what Marcus said about taking care of his family. How Kai, our twins, and myself would be well taken care of, because to him we were family. Kai was family.

"I think you should have this experience." I look up meeting Kai's eyes. "You've witnessed the good, the bad, and you may even witness the ugly," he explains. "But no matter my relationship with Marcus I can't keep you from this. This world is as every bit of yours, as it is mine. I remember my induction and it wasn't half bad." He smiles for comedic relief.

I smile myself.

"Okay," I say softly, taking his face in my hands, silently telling him I'm here. He smiles softly in response.

"You want to hear the last track?" he asks suddenly.

"Yeah!" I exclaim, pulling away excitedly.

Kai chuckles, knowing I love getting a preview of the songs he writes for artists, especially now that he was writing for a new girl group debuting in South Korea. I stand up and Kai follows me back into the control room

228

with his hands stuck low to my hips, where Niani waits for us.

Steel boning hugs my back without remorse, as the back of my dress is zipped up leaving a plunging V down the middle of my back. Crimson dark as blood drops to my feet. A silver tiara darkened by time is placed upon my head, as candlelight dances off opalescent moonstones. I look at myself in the floor length mirror, as Mahina and Gayle take a step back. A replica of the stained glass window in Marcus' study stands in front of me. The crimson red gown, the oxidized silver tiara on my head, and the power radiating off of me as I stand before myself.

The door to the room opens in the reflection of the mirror and Tracey, one of the ladies of the manor attending to Niani tonight stops in the doorway, her eyes landing on me.

"Wow, Princess. You look - beyond words," Tracey compliments in awe.

"Whatever else did you think we were going for?" Alana, the effervescent blonde comments over her shoulder already dressed in a gold gown. "Was there something else you wanted to inform us?"

"The men have returned," Tracey answers, skillfully ignoring her comment, as a flash of blues strike across my eyes. *Kai.*

Alana turns and looks at me. "Are you ready to show them that they don't mess with the Princess of the House of Marcus?" She smiles dangerously.

Whether or not I belonged to the House of Marcus, I was ready to get this over with. I look at Alana through the mirror once more and nod. When I woke up this morning I didn't imagine my day going like this.

From the moment Kai and I woke up, we were separated. We hadn't even got breakfast in. Chief, Cassius, and Tiberius came by and dragged Kai away, promising to have papa vampire back to me by time for the party, courtesy of Chief. Then Niani dropped in, pulling me from the apartment to Lelin parked out front behind the wheel of the limo ready to whisk us off to Marcus'.

Not too soon was I being paraded into the dim sunroom surrounded by the female population of the manor including Mahina for morning tea and breakfast. *Blood* in their case. It was unexpected, but I appreciated their trying to make a good impression.

It was strange. I didn't know what to expect, but they truly did act like a family and all of these women were Kai's sisters. They treated Niani and I as if we were both family and poked fun at Kai like a little brother. They tried coaxing Niani to take off her Sais claiming that she wouldn't need them with them. That we were safe here, but they understood that part of her that was hardwired to protect me wouldn't let her.

They cooed and awed as they touched my stomach feeling the twins' heartbeats and questioned me about how I felt when I found out and told Kai, how it felt being vampire and pregnant. How amazing it was that I was and their own dreams and stories of raising their own children at one point. I noticed then that half of them were in different stages of their childbearing years, but neither had the chance or did before they were changed.

The subject then moved on to our "re-birth" stories, a roundtable of exchanges as to how we became WuXia and Vampire. Mahina's story was the most surprising and emotional of them all. Others were changed during various times of war periods, accidentally from a vampire on a hunger strike trying to deny what they had become or a rogue's attack on a blood binge. Mahina was twenty-two in college in the 1950's when she was changed and the only one in the house to be bitten by Marcus.

It was her birthday and her uncle who lived closest to her college had picked her up under the pretense that he was taking her out to lunch, but surprised her at his home with a surprise party with her parents and extended family members. On her way back to her college that evening, her and her uncle ended up in a fatal car accident. Marcus came across the scene and knew the ambulance would be far too late for her. Her uncle would survive, but she wouldn't. Marcus couldn't waste a life of potential and gave her the choice to live. A life eternal and she took it. Her parents never knew what happened to her that night. It became a cold case that her body was never found, dragged off by some animal or somebody.

After Mahina's story it left our breakfast a bit morose, but luckily we had a schedule to keep to our minds quickly changed by the oncoming party and that is where we end up here.

I turn from the mirror, looking at myself once more, and face the ladies in the room.

"Let's go," I order.

We walk out into the hall, my attendants trailing behind me, when I stop. At the end of the hall, standing in the wings away from the landing overlooking where the men are waiting is Niani with her attendants and she looks *incredible*. Niani turns to me sensing my presence and I get a full view of her gown. It's royal blue with bronze floral applique across the whole halter top. Her skirt is loose, flowing, and functional with two long slits at the front showing off her Sai handles peeking above the thigh high strapped heels she's wearing. One can barely tell they are weapons thinking they may be part of the shoe. I smile, thinking Hypers think of everything, as I feel the boning holding my daggers pressing against my back. Her locks are curled and pinned with bronze hair sticks dangling with flowers and a few paper cranes like a crown around her head, matching the swaying earrings dangling from her ears. She looks like the true embodiment of a warrior princess.

"You look *beautiful*," I compliment, as I walk up to her stopping in front of her.

"You took the words right of my mouth," she comments, looking me up and down. She smiles. "Princesses don't look like you."

I smile at her compliment looking down at the off the shoulder chiffon gown running with ruby crystals. Oxidized chains strung with small moonstones to match the tiara hang off my shoulders, as a black rhodium collarette necklace dripping with dark crystals and molded metal roses adorn my neck. My hair teased and wild swept is curled and pinned to the back. No, Princesses don't look like me. A bride of death and darkness, pun intended.

Suddenly, Niani frowns.

"Where are your daggers?" she asks, her voice pitching in concern.

I turn around for her showing off the back of my dress, where my daggers line the back of my gown like the split vertebrae of my spine. Niani smiles with an impressed huff.

"They do think of everything," she says.

"My thoughts exactly." I smirk, turning back around and hold up my pinky, as if in pinky promise.

Niani looks at the offered pinky in surprise and into my face, remembering our little handhold we haven't done since we were in high school. She cracks a smile looping her pinky around mine and we turn walking out onto the landing, where the men turn and look up at us from below. Niani turns looking at me, a small smile of enouement on her face as if she is giving me away and her pinky slips from mine.

I frown, looking down at our once joined hands and into her eyes. The slight smile tinged with a bittersweetness and that's when I understand. She *is* giving me away to my future as a Hyper a part of this world and saying good-bye to the innocence of our past, when we knew nothing about this. She's letting me go. Because nothing can stay the same and nothing can go back to the way things used to be. I figured that out a long time ago. This was for her. This was for her closure.

Chief was right. This is my coronation. I feel the tears well up in my eyes, as I lean forward taking Niani's face in my hands kissing her on the forehead. A *thank you* for all that she has done and will do. A gratefulness for having gotten back on good terms on the ride home last night. Glad that I can experience this night with her beside me aside from Kai. After all this night isn't all about me. This is her night, as well. A declaration that she is a Hyper, a WuXia. My Knight.

I pull away from her and we lock eyes for a moment, before she gracefully curtsies. At her grand gesture, all of the hall and the men down in the den bow. The loyalty I feel at their gesture humbles me, yet fills me with pride. Niani stands and they follow suit. I nod at Niani resolutely and turn at the top of the stairs, my eyes landing on Kai below, as one by one we descend the stairs with me at the lead. I feel like Rose on the Titanic, as Kai watches me from the bottom of the stairs. I'm surprised when I realize old habits die easy when my first thought isn't to hide or drop my gaze, but to hold my head up high.

Cassius' eyes don't hide his astonishment either at Niani's beauty, as his eyes follow Niani behind me. Before I can reach the bottom of the steps, I catch Chief nudge Cassius beside him teasingly. My heels hit the floor and Kai steps forward taking a loose curl between his thumb and forefinger, running over it lovingly.

"You look beautiful."

"Thank you." I smile softly, looking up into his striking brown eyes bordering on hazel, as his silver fights to break through.

He looks gorgeous in his high collar burgundy damask waistcoat over a white dress shirt purposely missing two buttons showing off a bit of skin and black slacks. His only piece of jewelry, a pin attached to the left breast pocket of his matching jacket with three chains hanging from a silver encased hexagon quartz. He smiles watching my eyes roam his body appreciatively, when Marcus steps forward taking me into his hands.

"Grace Kelly would be proud," Marcus compliments.

I huff a laugh and say, "Thank you," accepting the compliment humbly.

Behind him Z smiles at me.

"Should we be on our way?" Niani steps forward at my shoulder, as the last of the women descend the stairs. "I know you vampires have the rest of your lives, but some of us don't have eternity on our hands and want to go party."

Marcus chuckles at her statement and turns, "You all take care of the manor while we are away," he says, as Mahina and Alana head out before us.

Not everyone was going with us. Just Mahina and Alana as extra hands in case anyone wanted to get stupid. At Marcus' command everyone in the room bows silently. Kai takes my hand cupping it at the crease in his elbow and leads me out. Niani, Cassius, and the others follow us two by two toward the car garage.

CHAPTER 19:
Nocturnal Animals

By the time we arrive, the party is already in full swing. The bygone era ballroom looks like a rave meets a gothic ball with red bulbs lighting the dark room with flashing strobe lights blinking through a machine-made fog. BANK's 'Warm Water' blasts from the DJ's booth underneath an archway. Large crystal chandeliers hang from the ceiling, as ivory candles light every surface in long candelabras around the room and small votives across the tables. Hypers are already on the dance floor, sitting and talking around flute glasses on red chaise lounges under the french column archways lining the ballroom, and the elaborately decorated round tables covered in black velveteen filigree tablecloths skirting the dance floor.

"So, where do we start?" Chief jokes. "The bar or the buffet tables?"

Arm in arm with Kai to my right and Chief on my left we follow his eyes to the line of food laden buffet tables covered in white table cloths and black rose petals, lining the back side walls out of the way underneath the separating column archways. Cassius steps up behind us arm in arm with Niani and Tiberius on her other side.

"Let's not lose focus," Cassius orders seriously. "We still have a room full of possible assailants."

"Calm down Cass," Chief says. "I was making a joke. You know making light of the situation."

"Let's go mingle," Marcus pops up and pulls Z with him into the crowd.

"Well that gives us permission to party, right?" Tiberius asks in a voice unlike himself.

We all look down the line at him surprised by his comment. He looks up at us and shrugs his shoulders, unassuming. Kai and I turn and look at Cassius with identical raised brows waiting for him to respond to Tiberius' question.

Cassius rolls his eyes exasperated and says, "Go have fun, children."

And just like children with excited grins, Chief and Tiberius separate into the crowd leaving Kai and I with Niani and Cassius. And right there is where I see Cassius' weakness. It's Tiberius.

"Well, I guess we should do as Marcus said. Let's go mingle," Kai says, none too happy with admitting his orders.

Cassius leads Niani into the crowd, as Kai pulls me onto the dance floor with a smile on his face taking my hands in his. Hearing a sudden undercurrent high pitch sound pierce through the air, Kai and I turn to the DJ booth before most of the audience is aware that he will make a speech.

"Thank you, ladies and gentlemen, and welcome to Sara's Rebirth Day bash!" the DJ exclaims through the mic and the crowd around us whoops and hollers.

"This is a thing?" I ask, leaning into Kai.

"Only with Sara," he answers with an amused smile.

I huff a laugh and pull away.

"So, to kick off this affair with all you fine people let's welcome our rebirth day girl, SARA!" The DJ swings his arm out wide and a melodramatic cello solo sounds from the stage behind us. Turning to the stage, the lights cut up to a dim setting and the satin red curtains on the stage rip away revealing Sara, smoky eyed in this skintight floor length black gown with a dramatic train that would even leave Morticia Addams jealous. She smiles and white fangs aligned perfectly with her white teeth stand out. Kai looks down at me with an amused expression finding it all ridiculous, as the crowd around us claps and wolf-whistles. A young man dressed in a suit comes onto the stage and passes Sara a mic.

Sara stares out at the crowd and takes a breath before speaking.

"Two years ago today, I met two amazing men who saved my life and both changed my life. I do this every year inviting all of you to remind myself of the amazing gift I was given that day. The gift of life and the gift of a supportive, extended family I couldn't live without. Though I may not be like you, you all made me one of you."

"I see you, baby!" A man's voice from the back of the crowd yells.

The crowd laughs and Sara smiles bashfully bringing the mic back to her lips once she collects herself.

"Ignore him," she says playfully and the crowd laughs once again.

I turn my head and notice it's Jason her then boyfriend, now husband. I look at him, noticing when I get no Hyper reaction from him that he's human. I lean in to Kai once more and ask, "Does Jason know?"

"Yeah," Kai sighs in frustration. "It's one of the perks of being under the protection of Marcus."

I look at Kai and frown still unclear of what that means when we have the *rule*. I turn back to the front as Sara continues to speak.

"It just so happens that I get to share this stage with an old friend, who also celebrated her Rebirth day yesterday and I am honored to have the opportunity to use my Rebirth day as her introduction into this community, who made me one of them. Marcus," she calls to the stage.

I see Marcus walk up onto the stage and up to Sara giving her a hug and a kiss on the cheek, before taking the mic Sara holds out to him. Sara steps to the side giving Marcus the stage.

"Good evening," Marcus says, bringing the mic to his lips.

The room falls deafeningly quiet. A pin can drop and no one would hear it under the thrall of Marcus' command.

"Over a hundred years ago I met a beautiful young woman, who many of you here are unaware of changed our world. This young woman who gave up her life to save the life of a Cupid she loved. Unknowingly, many of you know of this story as the *Tragedy of 1849.*

I look around the room at the many faces some frowning angrily knowing their perception is about to be changed, others hanging off every word Marcus speaks.

"Believing their love to be done a great injustice, the Shatan, Evangeline," At the mention her name I hear whispers around me telling me her power must proceed her, "cursed this young woman's bloodline to be attached to the Hypernatural. That night I was given the task of bringing her descendant into our world. Over the last

239

week - no," he corrects himself, "- over the last three years you have heard of this young lady, been angry with her, who beyond her control was given the gift to communicate with us and see us beyond human imagination and tonight I present to you this wonderful woman and her protector, who I take under the aegis of my house. Ashiya, Niani, Kai, may you come up here, please?"

Whispers can be heard rising around the room. Their words fill my mind, if not my ears.

"Kai, the Prince? I thought he left?"

"I see that is Cassius, but who is the woman next to him?"

"Is that her?"

"No. Marcus wouldn't just leave her with anyone. She must be with the Prince."

"... But really, Evangeline? Making an accusation like that is a sure-fire way to a pain filled death."

At Marcus' request, Mahina and Alana situate themselves at opposite ends of the stage stairs. My eyes immediately cut across the crowd to Niani heading for the right side stairs with Cassius. I feel Kai's hand tighten in mine and I don't know whether it's in support of me or vice versa. I can feel his pulse quickening and it might just be the latter. I squeeze my hand in his, letting my strength be his anchor and my eyes bleed into their jade green and mercury. Hyper eyes trail behind us as we head for the end where Niani and Cassius stand, and I let Niani go ahead of me. Cassius tries to hang back, because Marcus hadn't called him up, but Niani drags him along anyway, daring Marcus with a look to say anything because she wasn't coming up here alone. I smile at her act of defiance in amusement, as Kai and I ascend the stairs behind them. As I pass Sara, she smiles encouragingly even if I can't knowing what I cost her. I nod my head instead and make my way in place beside Niani. Marcus gives us four a proud smile, before turning back to the mic. Looking out onto the crowd, I open my mind to every curious, uninvested, angry face.

"You must understand my friends, these two new additions stories are unlike anything we've known before," I feel like a roadside attraction the way Marcus is speaking of us. "First, I have Niani Chevalier, magic born of the Shatan Evangeline and the Ancient Kwan-Min, we have our first ever WuXia, mystic Knight to Ashiya. Vouching for her on behalf of my house is, Cassius Laurel."

Cassius bows fully at the hip, as Niani gently bows her head with the slightest dip of a curtsy.

"Next, I present, Ashiya Bride, blood cursed by the Shatan Evangeline, sired light vampire, future mother of the next generation of vampires, and wife to the *Prince of Vampires*. Vouching on her behalf is none other than, Kai Jung. May you respect them and welcome them into the fold."

Kai and I step forward together and bow. As I stand up, I look out onto the crowd. Skeptical, unwilling faces to believe what Marcus said about me is true look up at me. Because how can they believe a woman married to the *Prince of Vampires*, who left his clan suddenly strategically returns with a story of her bloodline being cursed and a line of assuming evidence that she has been connected to the Hypernatural and written about it. I turn to Marcus and reach out for the microphone. Surprised that I want to speak, he hands it to me and I pull it to my lips. I can feel the room take a breath at my willingness to speak out.

They might not believe Marcus, but they will respect a voice of the Ancients.

"Aneho Miynao. Me' cereima yerda wi ne' mitou aiye', bou Me' de'solte vor de'tressor Me' demontre'. Me' de'solte. One' re'spect aiye'o jichi to paus Miynasou." I bow.

"Good evening everyone. I know you won't believe me, but I am humbly sorry for the distress I have caused. Humbly sorry. Please respect my house and pass us."

I stand and Kai gently takes the mic from my hands. In tense silence, I wait for the ballroom to say something. *Do* something, until little by little I see people in the crowd kneel. There are those that stay standing, but I can respect that. At least they're being honest, not like the few snakes I feel kneeling within the crowd desiring to get close to the *Princess,* so they can stab me in the back. I smirk. They don't know that I've developed a taste for blood.

Sara steps up taking the mic from Kai and holds it up before her.

"I think this party is in need of a little reminder," Sara says, as those in the crowd stand and Niani, Cassius, Kai, and I exit the stage. "LET'S GET THIS PARTY STARTED!" she screams, and the crowd goes wild.

Chief and Tiberius meet us at the bottom of the stairs.

"Keep your eyes open guys. They may not act now, but we have a few snakes in the building," I warn.

"Don't worry. We got you, Princess," Z says, stepping up to us.

Out of the corner of my eyes, Sara walks off the stage as Justin Timberlake's 'Suit & Tie' blasts through the speakers from the DJ's booth.

"Alright men, you hear the song! If you came here with your lady, show her a few things and if not grab a woman and show her how it *is*," I hear the DJ say over his mic.

Kai turns to me.

"Do you feel safe enough to stay?" he asks in concern.

"Yes," I answer, taking his hand with a squeeze of reassurance. "They may be vengeful, but they're not going to try anything here." I look at the crowd of Hypers. "Let's try to have a bit of fun while we're here." I turn back to Kai.

Kai squeezes my hand in his and smiles, leading me between Z and Niani and back onto the dance floor. He turns to me with a swag filled expression staring into my eyes, grooving to the song; his dance moves emphasizing every verse.

Making me giggle, he throws the tail of his jacket out behind him and glides around me being silly. He slides up against me wrapping his arms around me from behind, swaying me to the music. With a smile on my face, I move with him to the music. Suddenly, the music changes melding into something old school, but still keeping with Justin's lyrics, designating a change in songs.

"That's right ladies, show your man who he belongs to... *or could*. BODY PARTY!!!" the DJ yells.

I sway my hips against Kai, as we rock to the song, the temperature around us spiking. I wrap a hand around the back of his neck, as he runs his nose up my neck and I close my eyes against the chill running down my spine. I turn my face into his and our lips are a mere millisecond apart when Kai claims my lips in a way I never knew I was craving until now. It feels like forever since we've had a moment like this. I turn into him putting my hand at the small of his back and pull him flush against me with a

243

rugged smile against his lips, so that we're touching thigh to thigh, middle to middle, and chest to chest and Kai chuckles.

"You're so getting lucky tonight," I say softly against his lips.

"You want to leave now?" he asks enthusiastically.

I laugh and wrap my arms around his shoulders, rocking to the music in our own sweet little bubble. A couple of songs in a familiar voice cuts through.

"Can I cut in?"

I slowly pull away from Kai and turn at the voice.

"William?" I frown and my eyes swing to Mahina standing a couple of feet behind him. "What are you doing here?" My eyes slide around the room filled with Hypers and now *two* humans.

"I'm Mahina's plus one," he answers innocently, not knowing what he walked himself into.

I send Mahina the calmest glare I can muster and fix William with a tight smile. The last we were alone together he tried to forcibly kiss me and with my vampire no longer under my skin, the sensations I experienced from him, the memory of his intention, his fantasy of what it would feel like inside my mind, he mind as well have. I try to think of a few choice words that will tell him how much I don't want him to cut in, but my bubbling anger keeps me from finding the right words in order to be nice about it.

Instead, Kai speaks for the both of us.

"I don't think that's a good idea," he says, his voice etched with anger, as his arms wrap tighter around my waist.

Not one to give up, William steps up to Kai putting a hand out. Kai looks down at his hand and back up at his face, anger setting in the lines.

"I respect her too much to lose her," William says sincerely. "Thank you for taking care of her." I feel him emotionally step down knowing Kai is the one in my life.

Then as if the DJ understands our situation the song changes overhead to something softer, symphonic. The anger dissipates in the lines of Kai's face and he takes William's hand shaking it and pulls him toward him hard.

"Try anything like what you did on the elevator and I will break you. No matter if we're in front of all of these people," he whispers in his ear.

He pulls away from William looking him in his eyes.

"Got it." William nods his head knowing that he earned that.

Kai's eyes swing over to Mahina standing in the same spot behind William. Looking in her eyes, I can tell she was aware of William's feelings for me, but now things are different.

Kai steps back away from him, dropping his hand and places a hand out for me to go to him. For a moment I'm confused as to why Kai is allowing this, but when I look up at William I understand that I would much rather have him as a friend than to lose him to a crush that can go away. William steps forward and tentatively takes my hands in his, leading me in a slow waltz. Kai steps back and I look at him over William's shoulder and mouth a 'thank you'. He mouths an 'I love you' and gives me a gentle smile. I notice Chief step up next to Kai and whisper something to him, but then I'm pulled away from ease dropping by William.

"So, you and Jung, huh?" he asks, moving in closer to me, but is stopped by my baby bump. Shocked, he drops my hands and pulls back looking me up and down.

"Twins in March," I answer his unspoken question and twist my left hand around to show off my wedding band.

"Why didn't you just tell me?" William asks, his eyes following where my hand drops at my side.

"I did," I say, smiling as all the hints dropped over the last three months dawn on him.

"So when you went off on me that day, you were actually telling me the truth?" He grins.

"Yes." I nod my head with a curt smile. I move in taking his hands back in mine continuing where we left off on our waltz. "Who randomly blurts out they're having someone's child? You know I like to keep my life private."

"Point taken," he takes the point graciously.

"So, you and Mahina, huh?" I smile.

"Yeah," William glances over his shoulder at her. "I don't know what's going on there... She said it's been a long time," he turns back to me, "since someone showed care for her the way I did outside your apartment. I feel -."

KAI

"Your wife is beautiful."

I turn from watching Ashiya and William dance to a glamorous blonde in all white standing behind me to my left. Her hair is parted to the side in a 1940's wavy style wearing a satin white gown with a lace bolero cape. Glitter is brushed upon her skin enforcing the image of an angel inside my mind. The first thing I smell is her delicate scent that reminds me of Victoria's Secret *Halo* perfume Ashiya used to wear. *Cupid*. No wonder. The ethereal features and affinity toward soft colors is a dead giveaway.

246

She steps forward, stopping beside me and turns toward Ashiya dancing. I watch her unnaturally blue eyes dance, as she watches Ashiya move across the dance floor trying to tell if there is any amount of threat in them. I don't pick up on anything and her heartbeat is steady in my ears.

"I wish I could have known Amita, the way Indra used to talk of her," she says.

"You knew Indra?" I ask, looking her up and down. She didn't look a day over thirty-two, but didn't Cupids age? "How are you not dead?"

"How is Marcus not dead with the enemies he's made?" she counters.

I frown at her comment. What was she trying to say? "You said the way Indra used to -"

The Cupid turns to me. "Missing. Last I saw him he was headed out on a *Threading* and never returned. I assume after losing Amita he couldn't be in the business of love anymore," she interrupts.

"I didn't get your name," I state.

She fixes me with her unusual blue eyes they're borderline lavender.

"It's Diana," she answers. She looks one last time at Ashiya and says, "Good night, *Prince*."

I watch her turn and walk out of the ballroom, leaving. I frown watching after her wondering what all of that was about. The song ends and I turn back, as William pulls away from Ashiya and approaches me. Ashiya behind him.

William smiles a genuine smile, as he stops in front of me and says, "Congratulations man." I look over at Ashiya and watch her hand lay over our twins and I understand.

"Thank you." I smile.

Without a beat, William bounces on his heels and excuses himself, "Well, I'm going to let you two be and go be with my date. It was good seeing you again Ashiya. See you on Monday," he reminds me of the last day of their casting, as he places a hand on her shoulder and he leaves us both going over to the guest surrounded tables off the dance floor, where Mahina stands talking to a Shatan.

"Mrs. Jung," I say, bringing Ashiya's attention to me and she looks up, "can I get you a drink?"

"Yes," she says with a bright smile, taking my offered arm and we walk over to the bar.

"I'm honored to have had you share your story with me, instead of hearing it from a third party. Let me know if there is anything me and my clan can do for you."

"Thank you, Wila. Your confidence is a great assurance." I nod at the Hawaiian brunette from our Hawaii clan.

"You're welcome, Prince." She bows and stands looking at Ashiya. "Princess."

"Thank you," Ashiya smiles and bows her head in respect.

Wila nods and walks away.

"Cool or snake?" I lean into Ashiya's ear and ask.

"Cool," she answers, turning to lean over the bar counter. "One of the few, who still don't have it out for me."

We've had a few approach us wanting to meet Ashiya, drop their congratulations or inquire about her cursed connection with her writing and learn her story from her mouth, such as Wila did. I was glad to have a lie detector for a wife. It helped weed out the ones that wanted to do us harm and the ones that actually wanted to do us some good. We turned it into a little game to see who would play into which side. Luckily, we had more cool than snake.

I look over at Ashiya and smile. She looks up feeling my smile on her and smiles asking, "Having fun?"

Looking around the room I turn back to Ashiya and look at her, only her, and say, "The best."

Reading into my emotions, she smiles even brighter and leans into my shoulder.

"Oh my gosh! Kai! Ashiya! You two are hard to get alone!"

We both pull apart to see Sara with her mega-watt smile walking over to us from across the ballroom.

"I didn't know you two knew each other! And married?!" she exclaims, reaching us.

We're both taken aback by her loud energy, but that's Sara for you. Blonde, blue-eyed, and ballsy. You can't help, but love her.

"It's about time you came to one of my parties. I've been inviting you forever." Sara turns to me, swatting me on the arm.

I grin. "Sorry, for the first time I had time away from the hospital."

"Don't worry, I forgive you," Sara replies, smiling up at me, as if the sun shined on me. "Anyways, you're here now."

I sniff, finding this funny and turn taking a sip of my cranberry juice. Then as if finally remembering Ashiya's there Sara's eyes slide to her, as I turn back around.

"Look at you Ashiya, trying to look better than the rebirth day girl," Sara compliments looking her up and down. "Marcus knows how to take care of his people."

"Thank you." She smiles.

Ashiya and I as if reading each other's minds turn looking at each other, as if to check on each other at the mention of Marcus' name.

"I'm sorry, was I interrupting something?" Sara asks, backing up a little bit, glancing between us.

"No, not at all. We were just talking," Ashiya says, turning back to her.

Sara settles down and says, "It's been a long time, Ashiya. You, Niani, and I need to get together."

"Yes, we should," Ashiya says.

I turn, looking through the crowd my eyes landing on Chief. He looks up from the champagne he's sipping talking with a Faerie, meeting my eyes immediately. I nod my head and he excuses himself from his friend, walking over. Leaning into Ashiya's ear, I whisper, "I'll be right back. I'm leaving you with Chief". She nods and turns giving me a chaste kiss on the lips, before I turn and leave, as Chief steps up leaning against the bar giving Ashiya and Sara space to talk. Cassius, Niani, Z, Marcus, Mahina, and Alana's eyes lift around the room, as I leave the ballroom, watching my back, while also being mindful of Ashiya's.

CHAPTER 20:
Immunity

ASHIYA

"Thank you," I thank the bartender as she hands me the glass of Moscato for Niani.

Careful not to bump into anyone, I weave my way back through the crowd toward where I left Sara at the other end with Niani. I can clearly see Chief standing close enough by without hovering, when someone bumps my shoulder nearly knocking the glass out of my hand. Stilling the glass, I keep a single drop from falling.

"Oh, I'm sorry," I hear a smooth masculine voice apologize, though he's not.

I look up seeing the man is tall, slim, and Caucasian with full angular features. Handsome, but on the pretty side. Layered brunette hair brushes his shoulders, as manic bright blue eyes stare into mine. Taut muscles cover his nearly shirtless slim frame, as most of the buttons are undone on his button down tucked into cobalt blue pants under a matching suit jacket making him look agile as a cat, but dangerous as a lion.

He is dangerous, my intuition tells me.

His presence is like a two-ton weight on my shoulders. Something about him tells me I should get away from him now. Don't spend another moment in his presence. I look over his shoulder at Chief making his way towards me, as the glass of Moscato drops from my hand to the floor, shattering. Everyone turns at the sound towards me. The man looks down at the golden puddle at our feet and back into my eyes dangerously, seeing right through what I did.

Suddenly, I'm pulled back and gently pushed behind Kai, as he and Chief slam the man together back into the bar top.

The man looks passed Kai to me. "I see why you left the umbrella of Marcus' dominion. She's even more beautiful in person. A *ripe* gem," he says smiling manically, as his eyes trail down my body stopping over my clothed stomach. I place a hand over my stomach, adrenaline shooting through me at the prospect of having to fight. Marcus comes up beside me taking me into his arms.

"You've been busy." The man turns to Kai, raising his brows suggestively.

"What are you doing here?" Kai grounds out, trembling with anger.

"Why Kai, you're not the only one that runs in the higher circle," I hear the man say silkily sarcastic with a thick accent. "I heard about the Princess and came to pay my *respects*."

I look around the room, as everyone's eyes train on me heavy with fear. In fear of this man. Music is still playing from the DJ's booth. With the scene we've made I'm surprised the dee jay's record didn't scratch, except now the song changes to Far East Movement and Marshmello's 'Freal Love'. I frown suddenly feeling malice, when vampires amongst the crowd start attacking people, stabbing and slicing. Z, Cassius, Mahina and Alana react as fire, lightning, and a body slamming to the floor can be seen through the crowd.

I see one of Niani's Sais fly from her hand into the crowd hitting a vampire in the chest from where she stands now behind Chief. The vampire becomes burned flesh on the marble floor, as the Sai flies back into her hand. In the vampire's hand, a dagger once held high above his head clatters to the floor.

"Marcus get Ashiya out of here!" Niani screams, as she rushes into the crowd, ducking punches.

A flash of green and gold energy flies from her hands, as she joins up at Alana's side.

Kai looks over his shoulder, hearing the screams.

Chief and Kai both turn at the man in their arms. The culprit.

"Stop this!" Chief orders with a yell, shaking the man.

"You all deserve this!" the man screams in Chief's face and I believe how much he means it.

Angry, Chief balls up his hand metal coating his skin and brings his fist down ready to punch a hole in the man when he disappears. Chief's hand connects with the bar top breaking a chunk out of the marble.

"We need to go," Kai says, as he turns around in a panic. His eyes are the brightest silver I've ever seen them, scared. He puts his hand out and I take it without question.

Run. His thought echoes through my head.

We race to the ballroom entrance, until I pull Kai to a stop just as we're about to reach the doors. He turns to me with wild eyes, clearly asking me why.

"Niani," I say, turning and looking back into the crowd.

"She's right behind me. Go," Mahina rushes up to us.

We turn and rush through the red curtained doorway into the hall, slowing to a stop, when the elevator dings before us. Sensing vampires on the other side, Marcus and Kai place a hand out for me and Mahina to stay back, as the elevator doors open.

Marcus and Kai glare eye to eye with the vampires inside and it takes nothing but a breath for the fight to break out, as Kai launches himself into the elevator kneeing a vampire in the abdomen and slamming his face into the wall denting it. Easily matched and evenly skilled, I watch as both Kai and Marcus break their opponent down to the floor.

Footsteps. I hear them before I see them and look to my right. I reach in between my breasts and pull out my boomerang knife, pressing the rose head, releasing the blades and throw the knife. As soon as the vampires step around the corner, my knife catches their throats ripping them open and they stop not understanding what's happening to them until it's too late. Their skin burns away until there is nothing left of them, except a residue of sleet on the floor. My knife swings back around and I catch it pressing the vanilla and it closes up.

Mahina sees two vampires coming her way on her left and rushes at them, sliding against the floor cutting one down at the ankle and locks her body around his neck until she strangles him to capacity, before stabbing him in the heart with a curved blade. She stands turning on the other when he rushes her against the wall, pinning her. Mahina eats the hit and takes her elbows driving them down into his neck making him let her go and stumble back. While he's dazed, she grabs his head and using the wall she kicks off launching herself into a spin over his head breaking his neck all the way around, before releasing him with a swift stab to the heart with her sword.

I don't even need to look over my shoulder to know he's there, feeling the wind against my back, as he steps out of the curtains into the hall and reaches into his pocket for the chloroform soaked rag. Too fast for his eyes, I pull a dagger each into my hands from the back of my dress and turn around slashing across every vital vein, artery, and tendon in his neck, arms, and legs with body shattering speed, before stabbing him in the lower abdominal, where it hurts. I stare at the pain in his eyes, the same pain he wanted to deliver to me, my babies and I twist, until he is sleet in my hands. I turn flipping the daggers back into my dress and look at Kai staring at me from the elevator, if not in horror, in awe.

I turn around feeling shock and fear cold in my veins to William standing in the curtained doorway looking on the scene in shock. I notice Niani isn't with him and remember Cass. She might be with Cass. Needing to get William to safety, I grab him by his jacket sleeve and drag him into the elevator with us.

I'm grateful for William's silence, as we descend to the ground level of the hotel, because I wouldn't even know how to explain any of this. Not now. This isn't how I wanted this night to go. Me standing in the ashes of someone's dead, already dead body, running from I don't know what, with the vampires who want me with them. I run my hands over my face and just breathe. *Breathe.* I feel the throbbing pressure behind my eyes die down and take my hands down from my face, taking one last deep breathe. I feel a hand against my shoulder and jump, nearly reacting when I feel Kai's presence.

"You okay, babe?" he asks softly.

I turn and look over my shoulder at him and nod, not really trusting my voice at the moment.

KAI

It's eerily deserted of anybody, as we walk through the main lobby of the hotel.

"Stay close," I whisper, my eyes searching the room, as I pull Ashiya closer to my side.

"They made everyone leave, so it would throw us off and slow us down. Keep moving," Marcus says.

Marcus waves us over to a wall out of the way of the glass revolving doors, where two valets are standing outside.

"Wait here," I say and sneak around Marcus and Mahina through the revolving doors up to the two valets outside.

"Hi," I say, as I walk up to the two valets.

"Hey," the valet on the left says, as they turn to me.

I reach into my pocket and pull out my valet ticket all the while watching my vicinity for any sign of an attack. "I need to get my car. It's a black BMW i8," passing the valet that spoke my ticket.

The valet takes it and looks down at the ticket turning to his partner when he sees the numbers. I notice the exchange and before they can react I pull the pin from my jacket, punch the valet on my right in the throat, then his solar plexus making him drop to his knees breathless. The other lunges at me and I pull the chains away from the quartz turning it into a garrote, wrap it around his neck, spinning around his back, and pull him against me, hard, strangling him.

"Now, I want you to get my car and stop at this worthless attempt of a fight," I say sarcastically.

"And mine," Marcus joins in, stooping down before the valet on the ground holding out his ticket.

The valet weakly takes it and I spin back around the other valet, unraveling the garrote from around his neck and let him go.

"Go." I nudge the valet and both, albeit injured run to get our cars.

I turn to Ashiya stepping out the revolving door alongside Mahina and William and frown noticing her frown. She looks around the area, as if sensing something, but too far to pinpoint.

Ashiya? I reach out to her mentally.

"We're out in the open," she says, speaking in code. Meaning, they're watching us. Ashiya looks at me and mouths, '*They're going to follow us.*'

I nod. At that moment, our cars pull up in front of us and immediately the valets jump out of the cars throwing Marcus and I our keys.

"Thank you," Marcus wisecracks, walking around his car and gets in, as Mahina jumps in the passenger seat.

Ashiya and I climb into the BMW with William in the backseat and my foot hits the gas before the doors can truly close. We gun out of the parking lot following Marcus and I sense *them* follow us.

A car pulls up, racing alongside us and Ashiya and I look out her window at the driver. He stares straight at us not watching the road. My skin crawls, as I look in his eyes, deep, dark, and sunken in with spider veins around them, as if someone punched his eyes in and hollowed them out. I look in my rearview mirror to see another car with him. I turn looking back out Ashiya's window to see him turn his wheel sharply, his car heading straight for Ashiya.

"Hold on!" I yell, throwing an arm across Ashiya and throw the car in reverse, jerking the wheel to the left and hit the emergency break, drifting the car around backwards. At the same time I see Marcus's car in front us do the same. Ashiya looks at me realizing we've done this before. The car ready to collide with us swerves into our lane in front of us, missing us by inches, as he rights the car riding with us, as we speed backwards down the road. His company pushes forward closing in on the right side of my front bumper.

I'm getting boxed in here. Come on, Marcus step in.

I notice Mahina smile in my rearview mirror, her eyes flaring to their bright red plum and she smirks, tipping her head to the side like a maniac. Next thing I know, she disappears into shadow and appears in the car's backseat in front of us.

With the swift deliverance of her sword she kills the men in the backseat and pushes up in the seat behind the driver and I can see the knife edge of her sword plunge through his neck from the back. The car swerves uncontrollably without a driver to control it and clips his partners car, sending them both veering off the road at uncontrollable speeds, flipping over five times before landing like crushed cans. Mahina appears back in the passenger side of Marcus's car and they look over at each other sharing identical smiles. We drift our cars back around front and take off down the road.

I reach over and turn on the radio to listen to anything besides the swallowing silence in the car and immediately the last minute of Linkin Park's 'Somewhere I Belong' greets my ears. I close my eyes a moment nodding my head to the rhythmic guitar before opening them. As the song goes off, the DJ comes on introducing the station, until I hear -

"Oh wow. This just in, -" Something in his voice strikes a chord in me. He can barely get his words out, his voice deeply mournful and sympathetic.

"It's been released that Niani Chevalier, writing partner of local author Ashiya Bride was found attacked in their shared apartment. She was taken to Northside Hospital, where nothing is being said on her condition yet, but her assailant is said to be in the wind. Ashiya Bride was not home when it happened, but I hope everything turns out okay."

It couldn't be a trick, could it? We left her at - I look at Ashiya, as her cell phone rings and she picks it up bringing it to her ear. It's Cassius.

"Ashiya, I need you at Northside Hospital. It's Niani," he says.

"I know," she says and hangs up.

She looks at me and I know immediately. I turn onto the highway going towards the hospital, Marcus following me.

ASHIYA

We step up to the receptionist desk and the receptionist looks up immediately with a sweet smile on her face asking, "How may I help you?"

Her smile instantly helps relieve some of my stress.

"Hi. We're here to see a patient named, Niani Chevalier," Kai answers her, leaning against the counter next to me.

At the end of the counter, I notice a male doctor writing down something in a chart look up at the mention

259

of Niani's name. Closing the chart, he walks up to us saying, "I'm the doctor over Niani's case."

"Is she okay?" I ask.

"Anyone here family?" he asks first, looking around our little group.

"I'm her sister," I answer.

"Okay," he looks down at me, skeptically, when his eyes find something behind me. "Kai? What are you doing here?"

"Niani's my sister-in-law," he says, backing me up. "Is that her chart?" referring to the chart in the Doc's hand.

"Yeah," the doctor says, passing it over to Kai.

"She has a neck wound?" Kai asks alarmed, looking up at the Doctor.

"Yeah. Two puncture wounds to the left side of her neck. Someone took vampirism a little too seriously," the Doctor answers curtly.

And Kai's head whips around to me knowing I heard him. I see his face change from shock to concern, as I feel myself fall apart. I know my eyes are changing by the way he hands his friend back the chart without looking and takes my face in his hands, placing our foreheads together.

"Baby. Baby, it's okay. It's okay," he says low, petting my hair.

"What's going to happen to her?" I ask, looking into his eyes, as I fight the whimper creeping up my throat.

"I don't know, but you can't beat yourself up about this. You had no idea this was going to happen," he whispers.

"Yes, I did. I knew what her being a part of this would bring and I left her out for the slaughter," I say.

"But she's alive, baby. She's alive," he whispers full of hope.

I look into his eyes, as I pull myself together long enough to consider his words. I nod my head, feeling my skin pull against his at the movement.

Kai turns to his friend and asks, "Josh, can we see her?"

We reach Niani's floor and find outside her room an officer guarding her door. I'm grateful for it, as we get closer smelling the familiar scent of sweet carrots. *Faerie*. He nods as we get closer to the door, respectfully and I notice his eyes land on Marcus behind me.

"Sir," the officer says unkindly.

"Ben," Marcus returns evenly with a smirk on his face.

"Only one person is allowed in at a time," the officer says, looking ahead of him as if we're not even there.

William and Kai look at me nonverbally agreeing I go in first. I didn't need volunteering I would have gone in first anyway.

I walk into the room and Cassius jumps up from the recliner in the corner fast. He looks worse for wear in his undone bow tie and disheveled hair and if his lifted hand sprouting a current of electricity from it is anything to go by protecting Niani is all that matters. Recognizing it's me he drops his hand and sighs in exhaustion.

"What happened?" I ask, looking at Niani lying unconscious in the hospital bed.

"It was so much going on. I saw her go after Mahina trying to get back to you, when a vampire caught up to her. I saw her fighting him. When I looked up again she was gone. Ashiya, I am so sorry," he begs, tears welling in his eyes.

I put a hand up.

"It's not your fault," I assure him. "She knew what she was getting herself into when she decided this. Did everyone make it out of the party okay?"

He sits back down in the recliner and looks down at his feet before looking up at me.

"We had a few people hurt. Jason and Sara are fine. We lost Alana, but Chief, Z, and Tiberius are okay."

I nod, feeling numb to it all and look up at Niani. I step up to her, her beeping monitors hammering further into my mind how close she came to dying. I look at her under the covers, her skin pale and gaunt from blood loss, gauze wrapped around her neck. Under the gauze, I can see a bit of bruising sticking out above it. I smell the different scents of hospital staff, Josh, two nurses, and another obviously the vampire coming from the wounds on her neck and body.

I look at the bandage around her neck and I know. I know without even having been there what happened. I see it in my mind's eye.

He forced her into the apartment demanding for me. He thought he could threaten her into taking him to me. As soon as they were behind closed doors, Niani turned and attacked him with a Sai slicing him across the middle. She went to stab with the other, but he retaliated grabbing her fast around the neck and slamming her up against the door making her drop a Sai. Kicking him off of her hard, she sent him crashing into the foyer table breaking it and with it sent a fireball from her hands setting him on fire. She grabbed her Sai from the floor and threw it stabbing him through the thigh. He pulled the Sai from the deteriorating wound despite the fire burning him and threw it aside, burning his hand on the Blaizinium in the process.

She doesn't know he's coming, not someone this fast. He grabbed her, turned her head aside, and bit into the exposed flesh. With one last fight in her, as he drained her lifeblood away Niani twisted her Sai in hand and stabbed him straight through the side of his head. If not from the blood loss, the concussion is what knocked her out.

I take Niani's hand in mine feeling the imprint of engravings from her Sais in her palm. She fought hard.

"Good job, Niani," I say low, leaning down and kissing her forehead. Pulling myself back up, I turn to Cassius and ask, "You want to send Kai in?"

In chairs around the room Cassius, Kai, and I watch Niani lost in our own thoughts, locking ourselves away from the outside world for as long as we can. From the journalists wanting to get the story, human officers wanting to know why Niani had Sais, even TMZ wanting to get a glimpse to see if I would visit Niani. Unfortunately, we just bought ourselves a whole load of attention that won't help me with the Hypers, who haven't made up their minds about me, yet.

"What's going to happen to her? She's a WuXia. She can't suddenly become a hybrid, can she?" I ask.

"I don't know. We probably shouldn't do anything," Cassius says, staring at Niani. Meaning, he's probably already thought about it.

Kai and I turn looking at Cassius.

"The venom is in her system and they are giving her a blood transfusion of human blood, but what about your blood?" he asks, somewhere else.

And I look at Kai. Our blood may be the only thing able to counteract the venom, but what are we thinking? We have our own venom. We have no way of knowing how it will affect her, WuXia or not.

On the same page, Kai questions, "But we have our own venom, who's to say it won't do something we don't expect it to?"

"Who's to say it won't give us the exact results we're looking for? You, her, and Ashiya are a different breed of Hyper. If she was any other Hyper, she would be sick by now or dead. And neither have happened. The most that can happen is she won't be able to go out into the sun as long," Cassius counters looking at Kai. "I believe this can work."

"I'll give her my blood." Kai stands unquestionably.

"Kai," I stall him, hesitant at the repercussions of this decision.

"Baby," he says, turning to me, "I'm not going to have her walk around like this nor a constant reminder of a guilt you don't need. We have to try just to be sure."

"But what if she's immune?" I ask. "Just as you said Cassius, if she were any other Hyper, she would be sick or dead. And neither is she either." I look at him.

"You're the writer. What do you think? I could just be talking out of grief," Cassius says finding himself in that sentence.

Kai looks at me and I look Niani.

"I say we wait. Let her heal. She's a Hyper, so we trust that," I say.

"Alright, we'll know by morning." Kai sighs looking down at Niani.

"I'm going to stay with her a little while longer," Cassius says. "You guys going home?"

"No," Kai sighs again, "not yet. We have to take care of something," he says, obviously talking about the man at the party.

Cassius frowns in concern at that.

"I'll tell you how it went in the morning." Kai says, approaching Cass and giving him a brotherly hug. "You be good, okay?" Cass nods. "She's strong."

Cassius looks at Niani and back to Kai, nodding once more.

"Good night." Kai pats his shoulder supportively and turns for the door, opening it.

"Good night," Cassius returns frowning down at his feet.

"Good night, Cassius," I say, coming from around Niani's bedside to give him a hug then follow after Kai.

"Good night, Princess." He squeezes me, but I've never felt farther from it.

There was no clock about to strike twelve and no fairy godmother to take all this away.

CHAPTER 21:
Begin Again

"This wasn't supposed to happen," Marcus says to no one but himself, as we walk in to the manor den, where Chief, Tiberius, and Z are already waiting.

Suddenly, Kai grabs Marcus by the collar and slams him up against a wall.

"How else would he have found out about her, except through you?!" he yells.

"Kai," I say.

He barely glances at me over his shoulder, as he holds on to Marcus.

"We won't find out anything if you kill him," I tell him.

He lets Marcus go and steps back.

"The only people I told were those in that room. Those representing their clan and their guards," Marcus explains.

Kai looks at me for my opinion.

"Cool," I say, bringing back our little game. "Who was he?"

Chief, Kai, Tiberius, and Z all look at each other, but none of them say anything.

"Someone better start talking," I snap coolly.

"His name is Ryo," Kai says reluctantly.

Marcus' eyes slide to mine and I remember the name deep from the recesses of his memories with Kai.

"Remember what I told you about this clan?" Marcus asks.

Kai looks between Marcus and I in disbelief.

"You told her?" he asks betrayed.

He looks at me, tries saying something but finds himself speechless.

"Imagine a vampire," Marcus says, bringing his attention to me, "who promises he will help bring thousands of Hyper immigrants and refugees across waters and borders to escape civil war and famine in their countries only to be delivered to the rendezvous point, where they think they're headed to the land of freedom only they are huddled and killed? Imagine a hate so strong, he would turn you just to kill you."

I frown reading between the lines of what he's saying. I go back to the first night I was attacked and look at Kai. We thought it was Marcus, but it was Ryo.

"He's a vampire purist and a prolific psychopath," Z explains angrily. "He and his clan feed on humans, though it's against the law. He believes Vampires are the superior race and hates any other species and their sympathizers. If it was his way he would have every Hypernatural species eradicated and leave the humans for food or turning if only they see fit."

"Then why is he still on the street?!" I ask incredulously.

"Evidence wise, we can't catch anything on him." Tiberius shrugs helplessly.

"How is that possible?" I ask. "You know he's doing it. Look what he did tonight!"

"Tonight, we can catch him on. But we will have to take down his whole operation," Chief explains.

"Then let's do that!" I push, looking around at them. Then I stop, connecting what Marcus just explained and what Kwan-Min said about them witnessing a piece of history that should have never been repeated. "Wait. Is this what you've been keeping secret?" Once again, they're all quiet.

"Marcus?" I question, turning to him.

"We were a part of transport, until one day we decided to go and check out the rendezvous points and instead found shoes and the burned flesh of Hyper men, women, and children for who knows how long it's been going on."

Horror and sympathy flood my heart.

I turn to Chief. "Why did he say you all deserve this?"

"Because remember when I told you Faeries make the laws? He hates that we impede on in his mind is the natural order vampires should live and - he's made it his career of going after Kai," Chief answers.

I look at Kai.

"He said he would stop what he was doing if we killed Kai, but we weren't about to do that. We rather take him down using the extent of the law. We couldn't just catch him on bribing an agent. We wanted to catch him on murder and that is what we've been trying to do. Now it appears he's found a new target. You."

That's what they've been doing this whole time every time they alternated, while they were watching me. That's where Tiberius and Cassius disappeared off to do last week.

I shake my head and turn to Kai. "And why is he so hell bent on coming after you?"

Kai looks down at me shamefully and sighs sadly, rolling his eyes up to the ceiling and looks back at me. "The night Marcus found me, I was jumped by some vampires and not knowing I was becoming a vampire then, I put them down. They were a part of Ryo's clan and they reported about me back to Ryo and they have been after me ever since. They couldn't touch me because I was under Marcus' house. Because I am faster, stronger, better than his version of a pure vampire race he wants me dead."

My eyes blaze into their green and silver, angry.

"Leave us."

Knowing not to fight me on this, Marcus signals everyone to leave the room. Mahina drags a shocked William out, as Chief, Tiberius, and Z follow Marcus into the study. As soon as the door slides close behind them, I ream in to Kai.

"You had the Nazi of all vampires after you and you never thought to tell me?! After I told you someone was trying to kill you?! And you're mad at Marcus for him telling Hyper society about me? This is as much on you, Kai. Secrets is what got us here."

"I didn't know it was him! When I left this life I thought I had left it all behind. I wanted to tell you, *tonight*!"

I look at him, remembering what I said to Kwan-Min about knowing Kai wanting to tell me about his past and about it being too late when he does. I shake my head, disappointment replacing my anger. I know he meant well, but -

"I love you, but I am so mad at you."

A consuming silence settles over us as we stare at each other.

"I am sorry, Ashiya," Kai says pleadingly.

"You know what needs to be done, right?" I ask. "About Ryo?"

"He needs to die?" Kai answers seriously.

"Exactly. Waiting for the extent of the law isn't going to cut it. That's too many years and too many lives at stake. He needs to go."

"Are you sure you want this on your conscious?" Kai asks.

"Am I sure I don't want to look into Hypers' faces and see that fear in them again? *Yes*," I state forcefully. "I'm the Princess of the Vampires for a reason. I mind as well start acting like one and protect my people."

Kai looks down at me, as if he's found a whole new respect for me.

"Okay," Kai says.

I turn and yell, "You can come back in now!"

The study door opens immediately and Chief is the first to walk out with a smile on his face.

"There she is! That's what I like to hear!" Chief exclaims. "So, you want to get rid of him?"

I turn to Chief, as the rest of the group joins him.

"We have to or it's just going to be a constant battle and that's a race we can't afford. Not with my children involved and not my husband," I answer.

"You're second in command Chief. What do you think?" Tiberius asks.

"I think we do as the Princess says," Chief says and turns to Marcus. "Marcus, you're just as involved with this as we are. You think we could use some of your men?"

"You can use the whole damn camp. I want him gone. He ruined a perfectly good evening," Marcus says flippantly.

"So, we meet up here? Let's say, 8 o'clock?" Chief asks.

Everyone nods.

"Okay. I'll go call, Cass," Chief says, pulling his phone out of his pocket and walks away.

"I think we have one more problem," Mahina says from a corner standing beside William.

We all turn to her and she nods her head at William.

"He knows," she says.

"He stays human," I order.

Mahina looks at me then at Marcus.

"I kept Jason human, because I wanted to honor Amita and put my trust in humans that they can hold our secret. Mahina, he stays human," Marcus answers with a definitive nod.

William walks up to me and stops before me staring into my eyes. "I always knew you would change my life," he says softly.

I smile and William pulls me into a hug.

"You go ahead and take care of what you got to. I'll be here," he says supportively low in my ear.

I hold on to him tighter, thankful for this.

William stays behind at the manor with Mahina to become better acquainted with the clan, and also to ride him back to the hotel to get his car.

"Where are we going?" I ask Kai, as I notice we passed the turn we usually take going towards home.

"You'll see," Kai says, giving me a sidelong glance as he drives.

I sit back and wonder what this little surprise is.

Twenty minutes later we're pulling up to a grand ornate wrought iron and gold gate with the crest of a kneeling angel looking down on us, as if it's watching us ominously. Beyond the gate I can see miniature mansions lining the singular street. I look around us to see if this neighborhood has a name, but I see nothing not even a street sign. It must be a private community. Kai lifts the lid to a matching ornate keypad built into the podium next to the gate and presses a few choice numbers then pound and the gate opens up silently, letting us in.

We ride by the line of luxurious mansions on either side of us until we arrive at the end, a col-de-sac circled by four mini mansions. As we pull into the driveway of the second mansion on the right the sensor lights in the front of the house turn on. I look at Kai, as he kills the engine and he looks at me.

"Come on," he says, nodding toward the mansion.

I follow him to the door where he pulls out a pair of keys and unlocks the door. I try not to let my mind wander where it is going, excitement bubbling in me, as he turns the knob and allows me in first. Champagne brick exterior, ornate French glass double doors, big arch silhouette square windows, and a manicured lawn with vibrant rose bushes. I categorize it all inside my head. I step inside and am immediately greeted by a large expansive grey marble foyer.

I pull my shoes off against the wall afraid to scuff up the marble floor and walk further inside letting my curiosity lead me.

"This was my house when I was with the clan," Kai says and I stop turning to him.

"You didn't live with the clan?" I ask, surprised by that information.

Kai shakes his head silently.

"I couldn't do it. All that I had seen, I couldn't live in a place where it was a constant reminder of all the choices I had made and all that I was forced to do. Come."

He holds out his hand and I take it, letting him lead me through the house. Passing out of the foyer I notice a black spiral wrought iron staircase hidden away behind a doorway leading upstairs. A strange choice of placing a staircase, but remembering how Kai was living his life in secret back then it made a lot of sense. I find myself amongst the maze inside a kitchen with stainless steel appliances, a long island with a bottle of Big Red sitting at the corner with two wine glasses, white marble countertops over steel cabinets, and a long LED lined wine cellar built into the wall.

"You lived here by yourself?" I ask.

With his back turned, I feel Kai smile. Again, Kai silently pulls me through an archway out the back of the kitchen and up another hidden spiral wrought iron staircase. He leads me across a hallway landing and over the banister I look down into a living room open and vibrant with warm red modern furniture and orange oversized bean bags. Orange swirling cloud like designs snake up the ivory walls onto the ceiling. My and Kai's staple: candles decorate the black coffee table set in between the chairs and couch. DVD's, blue rays, and books line the inside of two built-in wall bookcases on either side of the flat screen mounted up on the wall.

A wall then blocks my vision as we pass and come up to a door stopping and Kai looks back at me with a small smile that doesn't quite reach his eyes. He places his hand on the doorknob and turns throwing the door open revealing the - twin's nursery. My mouth drops as I look around the room. Two watercolor painted yin and yang symbols hang over the twin's cribs, one in white and the other in a black-brown against opposite walls. Overhead against a backdrop of navy blue and spattered stars is a large painted eclipse on the ceiling. Two ivory cherry blossom silhouettes frame an amethyst velvet love seat against the back wall over a large navy blue rug rolled out over a bleach wooden floor.

"What do you think?" Kai asks behind me.

My eyes land on the changing table and wooden dresser with little yin and yang knobs in the far corner to my right.

I cover my mouth with a hand in complete surprise and turn to Kai.

"I love it. When did you have time to do all of this?" I ask breathlessly.

"I already had it in the works when we got married, I just had to add another crib." He smiles, truly smiles. The smile suddenly dropping from his face, he looks down at his feet and back up at me.

"Listen, Ashiya -"

"Hold on, before you say anything," I interrupt. "Back at the manor I wasn't trying to blame you. I was trying to let you know you have to take responsibility for yourself. We're bringing a family into this world. You're so busy protecting me that you're neglecting yourself. You can't do that when you want to look into the eyes of your children one day."

Kai looks at me and says, "And yours *every day.*"

I smile.

"You're right. I'm sorry. I've been so busy trying to protect you from all of this that I forgot to share this part of myself with you, so that you would understand."

I nod, already understanding.

"Follow me." He nods and turns out the door, beckoning me to follow him. I follow him around a small bend down the hall where it ends with a closed door on our right circling to a gated staircase leading down to another level. My guess down to the living room.

Kai turns to the door on our right and says, "And this is our room," opening the door.

Purple brocade foil wallpaper decorates the walls matching the blue wallpaper in the connecting bathroom, as rounded mosaic mirrors in the ceiling reflect over the contemporary style red platform bed in the middle of the room. Sexy and romantic, I let my hand roam over the long black dresser to my right. It comes to me what Marcus meant when he said, "I take care of my family." I never questioned how Kai was able to pay for anything when we dated, because he always lived within his means. Now, I know. With a mafia like Marcus' and a manor able to house all of those vampires, Marcus evidently set Kai up with a fund where he would never have to want for anything. And if Kai was going to use the money for anything he was going to spend it on his family. I smile and turn to Kai, walking back up to him.

I stop, running my hands down the jacket he's *still* wearing.

"I believe I told you, you were getting lucky tonight," I say sultrily, lifting my eyes to his.

I push up on my toes hovering over his lips teasingly, as Kai swoops down impatiently sweeping me into a bruising kiss. I pull at the collar of his jacket ripping it in half from his torso and Kai pulls back.

"That was my favorite jacket," he jokes.

"Then we're even." I smile against his lips and pull Kai back into the kiss.

All gentle I run my nails down Kai's strong biceps, as his hands caress and kneed into my sides possessively, lovingly. Every inch of his skin is mine to worship, as I take and meet his every thrust. His favorite place my neck he kisses, as he takes his sweet time with me, wanting me to feel him, every inch of his love for me. His hand runs over stomach. I pull him up to me, riding with him to our waves of pleasure. I take his fingers and intertwine them with mine taking them around his back and pull him closer into me. Savoring every stroke, I feel our friction begin to build to its peak and with our final climax, I thrust my K9's into his shoulder.

"Tha- that was -" Panting next to me I listen to Kai trip over his words, but all I can see when I turn and look at him is a *very* satisfied smile. I chuckle at his loss for words. He turns over to me with a euphoric smile and tucks a lock of my hair over my shoulder. I smile and pull up to him, snuggling into his warmth. Though it's quiet and light from our love making, there is still tension hanging over our heads.

"Marcus still has a hold on me," Kai says into the quiet. "I've spent the last four months trying to run away from this life that the moment I'm in the presence of my clan I'm pulled back in."

I push up on my elbow and look down at Kai. All serious.

"You were family, Kai. It's okay to miss family," I say.

A heartbroken chuckle breaks from his lips, tears welling up in his bleeding steel grey eyes.

"Ashiya, I'm not supposed to miss *this*. The fight, the commitment of a mission, the steel trap of shutting down every emotion I have just to stay focus. I'm not supposed to *miss* what it was like to be a vampire in that clan."

His use of the word 'that' shows his desire to separate himself emotionally from his clan. I reach a hand down and touch his cheek, running my thumb over the bone soothingly.

"I don't know the first thing about this life and you miss it. What are we to do about that?" I ask softly.

He meets my eyes and shakes his head, unable to say the words I can hear in my head.

I push down into the bed and press my face against his.

"Remember when I said your clan didn't give you that type of distinction, but you have it now? You have it in me?" Kai turns his head to me staring in my eyes. "This time let's do things differently," I press his hand against my stomach. At that, I feel a fluttering in my lower abdomen and it takes Kai and I both by surprise. We look at each other and I say, "I guess that's a yes," and as if agreeing, I feel another fluttering. Chuckling, Kai presses his forehead against mine.

CHAPTER 22:
Reign

An unknown force wakes me and I turn over to find Kai gone from bed. I feel his aura near and his melancholic thoughts wrap around my heart. Slipping out of bed, naked as the day I was born I follow his aura out of our bedroom and find him down the hall leaning against the doorway of the twin's room. I walk over to him and wrap my arms around his waist, comforting him from behind. He unfolds his arms from his chest and runs his hands over mine.

"You okay?" I ask, pressing my lips against the back of his neck.

"Yeah," he says.

I walk around him and wrap him back in my arms. He looks down at me and glances back around the room.

"I want to say thank you for being so supportive, understanding, and ultimately patient with me." His eyes land back on me and he smiles. "You are my foundation."

"Always baby." I smile up at him. "Wait, you aren't trying to say goodbye are you?"

"No. No. I *am* coming back to you." He rubs his hands down my arms, as if to convince me he's still here. He's not going anywhere. "I just want you to know that. You got me through some of my darkest nights. In a life that felt like death, you were and *are* my beautiful afterlife."

Tears unwillingly pool in my eyes.

"Don't make me cry." I huff. "*Thank you.*"

"You're welcome baby." Kai pulls me into a hug and I gratefully take it.

"Let's go back to bed," Kai whispers in my ear, stealing a kiss from my lips, as we pull apart and walk back to our room.

The next morning has Kai and I standing in the BMW's driver's side doorway together, intensely sober. Kai stares down at the keys in his hand, as if contemplating if he should go or not.

"I wish it wasn't us leaving to do this, but coming back home," he says, looking up at me.

"Just think we'll be back here before you know it," I say encouragingly.

"As if I would have it any other way," he states with a smile.

"Come on. We better go. A Princess and Prince is never late," I joke, as I walk around to the other side of the car.

"Yeah. Yeah," Kai snarks, as he climbs into the driver's side.

We arrive at the manor with 10 minutes to spare.

"Hungry, Princess?" Z walks passed me into the room eating a bagel with vegan strawberry cream cheese.

"No, thank you. I already ate." I wink at Kai, as he looks back at me.

"Too much information," Z says. "Kai, we're meeting in the conference room," before walking out of the room.

"I'll be back," Kai says, placing a comforting hand on my arm.

I give him a small smile in answer, before he turns and follows Z. Marcus then walks into the room passing me to follow behind Z and Kai, when he stops turning to me at the doorway.

"Are you coming, Ashiya?"

I frown. "I'm not fighting."

"But we could use your mind," he says. "Help us strategize."

"There could be a million outcomes," I say, nervous at the prospect.

"We just need one," Marcus states, having complete faith in me.

I swallow my nerves and follow behind Marcus into the conference room.

Vampires upon vampires of Marcus' clan surround a round mahogany table with Chief, Z, and Tiberius standing over a map in the middle of the room. The conference room is surprisingly like nothing I would have imagined. Smart and businesslike auditorium hall style seats with connecting desks surround the table in a semicircle to give everyone a high vantage over the planning. Overhead from an asymmetrical false ceiling hangs a projector. Against the back wall hangs a projection screen with an image of the map on the table, as Chief's big hands move over it in animation. As Marcus and I enter everyone turns and looks, but their eyes are not on Marcus but on me wondering as of why I am here. My eyes immediately find Kai's and he looks just as surprised at my being here.

"I figured we could use the Princess' perspective," Marcus says, as I follow him down the few steps to the round table in the center of the room.

Those near me bow in acknowledgement, as I take my place beside Marcus, Kai on my other side.

"Let's get started," Marcus orders in a way I've never heard him before. It's dark, commanding just like his spirit. Immediately, his clan turns and takes their seats behind a desk each. Chief, Kai, Z, Tiberius, and I are the only ones that stay at the bottom. I believe based on chain of command.

I look down on the map across the table showing the property schematics of a mansion.

"What do we have so far?" I ask Chief, leaning over the map.

"It's day time, so we want to hit them when they'll least expect it," Chief starts, "taking them from each end of the house. Spreading out the heard, then thinning it for Kai to work his way through to Ryo." Chief points out from different ends of the map.

The scenario plays out in my head not looking good. Too much space and too much time in cause for casualties.

"No. If it's me he's after, they know this is what you'll do. They're going to be waiting for you. They'll be expecting you to come to them, not the other way around. You need someone to get in on the inside, draw them to a post and cut them off. Z's fire would be potent enough to keep them in, but we need a Shatan to tap into the powers of Blaizinium to enhance the fire. A powder would be best. Kwan-Min should have enough on supply. You need to go in team by team, a constant wave of power hitting them taking out his clan. Ryo will want to be observer and participator, so Kai, Marcus you're going to need to get him away from his clan. Get him alone and take him out, while the rest take care of the others. Believe that if Marcus can get his hands on Blaizinium based hoods so can Ryo. We've got to expect the unexpected."

I look up from the map to the whole room staring at me in respect.

"Damn, Princess." Chief huffs in awe. "Who knew you were a strategist?"

"No. Just a lot of Criminal Minds and imagination," I answer modestly.

"And that's why I requested your presence," Marcus says to me. "That imagination of yours is what's going to save this clan." He turns to those in the room. "Are we all in accord with this plan?"

"Sir!" they yell in agreement.

"Alright," he turns back to the map, "let's go over this in detail."

Over an hour of breaking down the plan, positions, assigning teams and leaders, and making calls, we were ready.

Z walks out of the conference room into the living room, where I hang up my phone from talking to Cassius. Niani was awake.

"I told Niani we needed someone like you in this world. That plan was solid," Z compliments, as he walks up to me.

"I heard. Thank you," I say. "Niani's awake."

"Good," Kai says, also walking into the room followed by Chief and a group of vampires.

"Is she okay?" Z asks.

"Cass says, he hasn't noticed anything yet. The doctor came in and checked on her, and her vitals are fine. Also, the sun appears to have no effect on her," I answer.

"Well that's great, right?" Chief asks, picking up on our silence.

"Yeah," I assure him. "It's just, we were worried if we made the wrong call about her being immune and not giving her Kai's blood, when we had the chance."

"Well, you did. I wouldn't write it off as a bad thing. Knowing you and her with this curse I wouldn't put it passed her to be immune," Chief says encouragingly, placing a comforting hand on my shoulder.

"Alright, let's get moving," Marcus says, walking into the room with the rest of the clan and Tiberius in tow.

Kai turns to me and I look around the room at the men that have become the closest thing to brothers. Chief, Z, and Tiberius' eyes all fix on me. Chief is the first one to come forward and give me a big hug that carefully lifts me off my feet. He groans reluctantly, as he sets me down and steps back.

"See you when I get back," Chief promises with a small smile.

I smile and nod. "See you when you get back."

Next, Z steps up and silently hugs me. He doesn't let go for a long while. Everything he wants to say is in his hug. Finally, he lets go unable to look me in my eyes. He can't if he's going to have to steel himself for battle and return. Last, but not least Tiberius walks up to me.

"Since it's likely I won't return," he starts.

I frown. "Don't say that."

"Just let me finish," he says and I quiet. "I want you to know that working with you has been one of my greatest adventures. You may not know it, but you changed me. You accepted me and fought for me and I will never forget that. You gave me a chance to be a father figure and I love you."

The last chip in my armor breaks and the tears form, but they dare not overflow.

"I love you, too," I say and draw forward pulling Tiberius into a hug.

We pull apart and Tiberius bows low before sweeping out of the room following behind Marcus' clan to get ready. Immediately, Kai pulls me into his arms as the tears threaten to fall. I can't afford to cry not when I have to face Kai. I pull away and look up into Kai's eyes.

"I want you to go about your day as regular as possible. Go visit Niani. Anything. I want your mind as far away from this as possible. Act as if I'm on a business trip and I'm on my way home to you. I'm going to leave you with Mahina. I would leave you with one of my brothers, but this is something we have to see through.

"I understand," I assure him.

"As soon as this is done with I'm coming home straight to you."

We pull a part and Kai looks down at my rounding stomach and grins up at me.

"Gives us a moment," he quirks.

"I'm not here," I say, turning my head as if I'm not there, as Kai kneels down before my stomach.

He gently places his hands over his twins caressing softly across the fabric and says, "Daddy's got to go be a hero now. You take care of your mommy. She's going to go take you to see Aunt Niani. I love you and I'll be back home soon."

His eyes closed, he places his forehead against my stomach savoring the moment before forcing himself to stand up. When his eyes land on me his eyes are the brightest silver, the stars in his pupils shining.

"I love you," I say.

"I love you, too," Kai returns, before swooping in and kissing me fiercely. I return it with equal intensity feeling his desperate need to return back to us. This whole wordless conversation of wills and need begins to feel like a promise and not a battle against the odds. He pulls away reluctantly and looks down at me, cupping my face in his hands.

"You come back to us," I say forcefully.

"Say it again," Kai requests.

"Come back to us," I repeat.

"Always," Kai promises, staring into my eyes before forcing himself to walk out of the room.

I turn to Marcus still in the room behind me and say, "Bring him back to me."

"On my life, Princess." He bows and he too walks out of the room leaving me with Mahina.

I walk up to the receptionist desk with Mahina beside me in her Blaizinium hoodie and I see the same receptionist at the desk from last night on Niani's floor and she smiles.

"Here to see Niani?" she asks rhetorically.

I answer her with my own smile and make my way on to Niani's room.

The guard is gone when I reach the door. Expecting him to have gone on break or something leaving Cassius to watch Niani, I leave Mahina outside the door and walk in. Closing the door behind me, I round the corner to find Niani's bed empty, the room empty. I frown, my eyes finding black scorched marks on the wall. Then a sharp, metallic, almost mellow scent fills my nose. *Blood.* Faerie blood. My ears pick up shallow breathing. I follow the sound around the bed to find Cassius on the ground his white button shirt slashed to ribbons and bloody.

His barely open pain filled eyes stare into mine in alarm. "Run Ashiya," he rasps.

I back up away from him quickly, self-preservation taking over. Sensing someone behind me I turn around quickly to attack, spinning a dagger into my hand, only to receive a palm full of dark grey powder blown in my face. I only get a good stab in, when I lose control of my limbs and collapse into a pair of arms. The last thing I see is the blonde female Shatan from Kwan-Min's store letting some men into the room and the officer guarding Niani's room dead in the en suite bathroom shower, as the person collects me in their arms.

"Be careful with her," I hear her say and feel something ice cold drop down my back before everything goes black.

Weightless. Nothing under me and nothing around me. Only darkness. When I'm suddenly unceremoniously dropped in something roughly, jars me awake. I can only associate it with being a chair as my fingers find grooves in the beaten metal of the arm rests. I try to pull my arms up only to find my arms cuffed down to the metal. Shackles. The smell of metal, ash, sweat, and tension tell me enough where I am.

A flash of blues. *Kai.*

"Wake up!" a male voice suddenly yells in front of my face and instead of opening my eyes instantly in alarm like he wants, I open my eyes and hold Ryo's blue eyes with a glare.

He laughs in my face delighted and says, "She's not scared!" looking over his shoulder at someone and I follow his line of sight to Kai chained to a wall across the room from me. His hair lying in sweat matted layers against his face, his face healing from recent assault.

"No!" Kai screams, pulling madly at the chains, as he sees me.

My eyes fall onto the floating sword pointing at my stomach before me and I look up at Kai meeting his eyes, fear startling my heart and he stops pulling at the chains, rasping over and over again, "I'm sorry. I'm sorry."

"You should be sorry!" Ryo yells back at him tauntingly.

'It's okay,' I mouth to Kai, trying to be strong for the both of us.

I look around the large chamber, when suddenly Mahina's body falls from the ceiling hitting the floor with a bloody and broken splat. I look at Mahina's body in horror joining the carnage of dead and injured bodies littering the stone room and I have a front row seat to the event. Body matter and blood smeared across walls and rivers of it flow freely over the stone steps onto the ground. I want to close my eyes at the lost, but the man jerks my face back to him grabbing my jaw so hard I'm afraid with one flick of his wrist he could break it. He makes me look into his big doe eyes and behind him I hear Kai yell, "Ryo!"

"Hold on," he says, holding up a finger to Kai, as he continues to stare into my eyes. "You are something. A human falling in love with a vampire. That is so fairytale," he shudders sarcastically and he rubs my belly, lewdly. I jerk away from his touch feeling sick with violation and he laughs in my face again, dropping my jaw and turns walking over to Kai.

Wiggling my aching jaw, I catch sight of Marcus laying a few feet away from me on his stomach unconscious on a stair his face covered in blood. I see a figure out of my peripheral vision and look over discovering Niani in her hospital gown hunched over unconscious in a corner chained to the brick wall with shackles hanging from her wrists. My eyes meet Kai's again and he shakes his head knowing I want to break out of this chair and kill Ryo myself, as Ryo approaches him.

"What? You're trying to find a way to get me away from your *wife*? Well, it's futile," he taunts Kai. "With one gesture I will have him kill her regardless of if I'm there or not, starting with your children."

Kai closes his eyes against his anger and Ryo steps closer into his face saying, "You know this is all your fault. You and Marcus. You thought turning her was going to bring restoration?" Ryo spits on the ground in disgust. "People like you and Marcus are the reason for our descent! Making deals with the faeries and we're the ones left with the raw end of the stick! We can't even eat because you let them make the rules! Traitors. You know if you had of just left the poor girl alone, I probably wouldn't have come after her. She's a decent writer I give you that. She has our world pretty spot on. But you thought the procreation of more of *you* was a betterment for our race?! If I ever thought I wanted to kill you then. I want to kill you now," Ryo spits with hate and Kai opens his eyes.

Kai's venomous look doesn't phase Ryo. Instead, Ryo cranes in close to Kai's ear and whispers, "You're going to die." He nods his head, before backing away from Kai.

Ryo walks to the middle of the room and nods his head to the man behind my chair holding the sword to my stomach and he flicks his wrist out, a sword floating over to Ryo. Ryo looks at me as he unsheathes the sword and tells me to watch. He turns to Kai and slashes him across the torso. I scream out, as Kai's cry of pain reaches my ears. And he keeps going until Kai's front is shreds of flesh and my throat is raw. Finally, he stops panting and Kai's front starts healing. Ryo turns to me and smirks. "Ready for the show?"

I whimper a stop, as he walks over to Kai and pulls the chains from the wall letting Kai fall to the ground in a bloody heap. I look at the sword in Ryo's hand carrying the same residue the Shatan blew into my face. Kai was paralyzed. I pull at my cuffs needing to get to Kai, as Ryo steps up to him and kicks him over.

"Kai! Remember, you have it in me! You have it in me!"

Ryo laughs at my feeble attempt to rouse Kai, as he raises the sword high above his head ready to stab Kai. He brings it down hard, when Kai suddenly grabs the blade between his hands stopping it just before it can connect with his chest. Then in a flash he's gone, the sword hitting the stone floor with a stab. Ryo looks around the room for Kai, but it's nowhere for him to be seen and nowhere to hide, when a chain suddenly wraps around Ryo's neck and he's slung into a wall, crumbling stone. Kai's eyes are blown in a white-hot rage, as he yanks sending Ryo crashing into another wall. He pulls Ryo back to him like a yo-yo, when the sword Ryo had appears in his hand and he rips it through Ryo's middle.

I feel my binds give a little bit, when I hear stirring and I look over into the corner at Niani waking up. She picks her head up, her eyes searching the room, when her eyes find mine and I'm shocked by the citrine orange eyes looking back. Ryo knocks Kai's arms off of him and pushes him away with both hands. Kai slides across the floor catching himself and he's gone again, as Ryo pulls the sword from his middle. The chain smokes around Ryo's neck made of Blaizinium and in a blinding rage Ryo rips it from his throat not caring that it's burning his hand.

Kai appears behind Ryo kicking him with a double side fly kick in the back sending him reeling and the sword sliding across the floor from his hand. Not giving him a chance to move, Kai is on him punching, blocking, dodging, and kicking through every move Ryo makes.

I look over at Niani, as I pull at my cuffs giving little by little and she looks up at the vampire behind me. Ryo grabs Kai flipping him over and Kai lands gracefully on his feet. But the damage is already done, as a dagger sticks out embedded in Kai's chest and he falters to his knees. Ryo turns and looks at me giving the vampire the signal and Kai looks at him to me and screams, "Nooo!"

At that moment, my cuffs break and the vampire behind me directs the sword away from my stomach with a wave of his hand and I don't question it as I look up at Ryo. Feeling that familiar cold chill against the bottom of my back I take no chances. I stand and Kai looks down seeing the sword on his left. Ryo charges at me and I pull the cold piece from my back, lining it up with my blown mercury and mint green eyes and fire, a Blaizinium bullet flying from the chamber, as Kai rushes up on Ryo from behind and sweeps the sword clear across Ryo's neck.

Ryo's head rolls across the floor, a bullet between his eyes, as his body burns with an orange metallic fire a few feet away.

I whirl around on the vampire behind me holding the Blaizinium Desert Eagle up and Niani's voice next to me pulls me from him, "He's not going to do anything."

I look over to Niani stepping up to me, power swirling in her orange eyes making them look like orange crystals. Taking her word for it, I turn around to Kai lying on the floor on his back breathing painfully. He pulls the dagger out of his chest with a yell ricocheting off the walls and

I'm by his side in a second. He looks up at me and nothing stops the tears from falling from my eyes. He weakly presses a hand to my stomach and says, "I'll be alright. It didn't puncture a lung," he jokes.

A sob mixed with a laugh escapes my lips and I bend down pressing my forehead to his.

EPILOGUE

A year and two months later...

Kai and I walk down the red carpet together, as flashing lights and the screams of raving fans rain down on our heads. A coordinator comes up to us and directs us to a young female journalist for our first interview.

"Hi, Rachel Nickson with BBC News," the journalist begins confidently.

"Hi!" we reply, smiling warmly.

"Thank you for giving me this opportunity to be the first to interview you and for *finally* introducing you to the world," she says, my eyes sliding to the camera over her shoulder.

"My pleasure," I say.

"First things first," she begins. "How do you feel tonight with this being your first movie and premiere?" she asks, directing the microphone near my face.

"Reign was my first venture in to Vampire novels. It's my baby and to see it turn in to a feature film is like watching it grow up. I'm very proud of her," I answer, giggling at the quirky comparison.

"Speaking of babies, how are your twins Aria and Soul?" She puts the microphone between Kai and I, obviously excited by the topic of our twins.

"They're beautiful. Right now, they are at home with their Godparents," Kai answers.

"Great. Three more questions and I'll let you go. How do you feel right now with all of this?" she directs the question to Kai, gesturing to the surrounding excitement.

"I'm proud right now. All of this is due to everyone and Ashiya's hard work and I'm ready to celebrate this night with my wife."

Kai looks down at me with a proud smile and I return it.

"Awww! I love it!" she exclaims. "Now, Ashiya. We know this is the premiere, but can we look forward to *Coup* coming to the screen and will you be writing more movies outside of this one?"

I turn back to her and say, "I think so. I enjoyed writing *Reign* in script form. It was a new venture for me. So, I think I will add Screenwriter to my occupation. But as far as *Coup* coming to the big screen, the production company and I haven't discussed it, yet. We're looking to see how *Reign* does first."

"I'm sure you won't have anything to worry about, but good to hear we could be seeing more work from you in the future," she nods excitedly, turning back to Kai. "Now Kai, your music to the movie is all over the internet and everyone is begging to know if you yourself will come out with anything. Can we expect a music video from you anytime soon?"

"Like my wife I'm more of a writer, but we have a few ideas in the works," Kai replies mysteriously into the microphone.

"Alright, I hope to hear something soon! Thank you, both! Enjoy the movie and the rest of your night," she smiles, ending the interview.

"Thank you and you too," Kai and I say simultaneously, as we move on to the next interview.

Attendees make their way to their seats, as the lights blink off and on signaling the start of the movie soon.

"I'll be right back. I'm going to the restroom," Kai whispers to me in my ear.

I turn to him with a smile and nod.

"Hurry back," I say playfully.

Kai smiles back at me, as he gets up and excuses himself through the row.

Turning back to the big screen, I watch as the curtains roll anchoring the screen.

A flash of cream and black.

Someone takes Kai's seat next to me and I pull a dagger from my hip instantly placing it against the person's main artery in their thigh.

"Try anything and I will kill you," I threaten him.

"I'm sorry to surprise you, Queen," a young male voice reaches my ears.

Queen? No one calls me that. This young man's scent is ice fresh and new, something I've never smelled before. He's a new vampire, still a baby. Feeling no ill will coming from him, I remove the dagger from his thigh.

"What can I do for you?" I ask softly, finally looking over at him.

He looks younger than I thought, sixteen even, but his deep voice makes him sound older. Tan skin, fine cheek bones, blue-brown eyes, and curly dark hair. Bi-racial, just like my kids.

"I'm sorry to have to bother you with this, but you and Kai are needed. I was traveling with Marcus, when we were attacked. That's why he had to turn me. Marcus has been murdered."

My heart drops. My first thought is of Z.

"He gave me this to give to you," the young man says.

He places a folded piece of paper in my offered hand and I open it to an address.

"Trust no one, Queen. Meet the clan at the Geisha House after your festivities. Please, enjoy the rest of your night."

The young man gets up and leaves quickly, passing Kai on the way out of the aisle. Kai reclaims his seat beside me and looks at me, as the lights dim.

"What's wrong?" he asks concerned.

"Marcus has been murdered," I answer.

I can feel Kai's heart stutter in surprise and sorrow. Through their connection with me their relationship had gotten a lot better over the last year and now he was gone. Kai frowns, as I pass him the piece of paper and he opens it. The last thing we knew Marcus was off the coast of New Zealand looking into something about the curse. Could that be why someone would want to murder him? Because he was getting too close?

"I know this place," Kai says, looking up at me. "It used to be a hotel. Now it's a hold for Hypers. A sort of safe house."

I look down at the address in Kai's hand and the writer in me can't help but wonder what a safe house would have to do with Marcus' death. Maybe it had nothing to do with the safe house at all.

"The boy said to meet the clan at the Geisha House after the movie," I inform Kai.

Kai stares down at the paper and wonders the same thing as I. How can a movie take precedence over something as important as Marcus' death and finding out who did it? But Kai nods his head anyway, folding the paper back up, scrunching it up in a fist. He looks up at the screen, as the movie begins. I too turn looking at the screen. But then as the opening scene begins I realize just like a movie even when you think it's over and the credits roll, the story never ends.

CPSIA information can be obtained
at www.ICGtesting.com
Printed in the USA
BVHW031736251118
533955BV00001B/35/P